Hammers and Homicide

Hammers and Homicide

A HOMETOWN HARDWARE MYSTERY

Paula Charles

CROOKED
LANE

NEW YORK

Published in the United States by Crooked Lane Books, an imprint of The Quick Brown Fox & Company LLC.

Crooked Lane Books and its logo are trademarks of The Quick Brown Fox & Company LLC.

Library of Congress Catalog-in-Publication data available upon request.

ISBN (hardcover): 978-1-63910-599-1
ISBN (ebook): 978-1-63910-600-4

Cover illustration by Jeri Rae

Printed in the United States.

www.crookedlanebooks.com

Crooked Lane Books
34 West 27th St., 10th Floor
New York, NY 10001

First Edition: January 2024

10 9 8 7 6 5 4 3 2 1

To my grandparents—Rolin and Leoma Simmons,
for letting me spend hours in their hardware store, dusting paint cans and counting nails

Chapter One

Kicking aside a jumble of tomato cages and terra-cotta pots, I searched for a pair of gardening gloves heavy enough to tangle with the invasive milk thistle threatening to take over my herb garden. The pegboard attached to the wall above the workbench in my gardening shed didn't have a single thing hanging from it. Heaven forbid I hang my tools back up as intended. No, instead I preferred to irritate myself as much as possible by having to move piles of rubbish around every time I needed something.

Heaving aside a stack of black germination trays, I finally spotted my heavy-duty leather gloves peeking out from under a bag of garden mulch. I pulled them on, grabbed a sharp shovel, and marched back to the herb garden.

The thistle sprouted from the ground, smack dab in the middle of a large rosemary bush. I studied it from every angle, but the only way to get to the root involved crawling under the rosemary bush. Better get to it.

Victorious, I came up for air ten minutes later with the offending thistle clutched in my fist. Sure, my arms sported a few scratches, and there was a new hole in my blouse, but losing a shirt as a casualty of the thistle war seemed worth it.

I tossed my nemesis into an old, rusty wheelbarrow to deal with later, pulled off the gloves, and brushed dirt from the knees of my jeans. When I straightened, a shadow crossed my face and caused a small yelp of fright to escape from between my lips. For a second, I would've sworn Bob Carpenter, my husband of thirty years, had been standing in front of me. I shook my head. Either a cloud had crossed the sun, causing a trick of the light, or I was really, truly losing my ever-loving mind.

Just in case Bob had really been there, I gave him a tongue-lashing. "Dang it, Bob, you startled me. Stop doing that."

I could almost hear him chastising me for tackling the thistle and making myself late for work. Bob always ran on the theory that if you weren't fifteen minutes early, you were late. For me, I tended to slide in right on time. Our opposing senses of urgency, or nonurgency on my part, had created a bit of irritation throughout our lives together.

"I know, I know. I'm hurrying."

In my mind, my handsome husband leaned against the porch, his foot tapping and an indulgent smile lighting his face. I rubbed at a bit of dirt drying into mud on my cheekbone and promised him nobody would be firing me today.

"No such luck." I chuckled, then glared at the thistle. "This's all your fault."

The thistle sat there, a prickly mess, and glared right back at me.

Throwing a quick wave over my shoulder, just in case my husband was more than a figment of my imagination, I headed off to work, replaying in my head the events of the night that changed my life forever.

The evening, a little over three years ago, had been just like any other. I'd served a meal of what amounted to hamburger meat fried and mixed in with a box of macaroni and cheese, which we'd eaten on the couch in front of the television while we yelled wrong *Jeopardy* answers at the screen. After a couple of episodes of our favorite murder mystery, Bob and I went to bed at our normal time, but I woke up the next morning and he didn't. The coroner ruled his death a massive heart attack.

I'd missed Bob like crazy and didn't want to live without him. Plus, the guilt was killing me. Why would my slender, active husband die from a heart attack? It had to be my penchant for serving the easiest meals I could come up with. Until Bob's death, I hadn't given a second thought to the amount of sodium and cholesterol in the boxed meals and pop-can biscuits I fed my family our entire married life. Convinced I'd as good as murdered the love of my life, I could barely breathe.

A few weeks after the funeral, the house didn't feel empty anymore. I opened the door after work one day and swore Bob was home. His personal aroma of coffee and sawdust trailed through the house.

Since then, I'd been searching everywhere for him, but no ghostly apparition appeared. Some nights, I wasn't above crying and begging him to come back. So far, nothing—only a lingering scent of him. I kept hoping one of these days I'd draw back the sunroom curtains and find Bob sitting in a shaft of sunlight. Most people would be scared to death at the thought, but the only thing surprising to me was why he hadn't bothered to show up yet. My best childhood friend had been a ghost, after all. Or at least I think she was. Of course, I could've just had an overactive imagination. That's what everyone told me, but I'm still not sure that was the case.

My older brothers had teased me without end about my imaginary friend. I'd thought it was plain mean how they pretended they couldn't see her standing right beside me, but it didn't seem to bother Karen, so I ignored them. The boys were always too busy to play with me, and Karen and I had a lot of fun together. She was my best friend, even though I didn't understand why she didn't talk and never came to school. When my family and I moved to Pine Bluff the next year, I never saw Karen again, though I can still see her plain as day in my mind's eye.

I shrugged. Either I was a little cuckoo as a child, or I'd lost the ability to see ghosts, as they say kids do as they grow older. Fast-forward fifty some odd years and here I was, talking out loud to Bob as if he were still alive, and doing everything I could to get that lost ability back.

No wonder my grown kids thought I was as crazy as a bedbug.

Chapter Two

At a fast walk, it took thirteen minutes to get to my store, Carpenter's Corner Hardware and Building Supply, in downtown Pine Bluff, Oregon. I knew because I'd timed myself more than once. With Bob gone, I was the sole proprietor and had zero plans to fire myself for being late today. The August morning was already sweltering, so I fanned my face with my hand and slowed my pace, wishing I'd opted for a pair of shorts this morning instead of jeans.

Turning the corner from Alpine onto Main Street, I glanced at Rocking M Coffee Shop, longing for my usual weekday latte. Cars lined the drive-thru windows on both sides of the little hut. *Shoot.* I waffled back and forth about stopping anyway, but duty won out and I kept moving, praising myself for making getting to work a priority. I'd have to make do with the sludge I brewed at the hardware store.

A block away from my store, the sound of a heated argument penetrated my single-minded desire for a cup of joe. I stopped and listened. The yelling seemed to come from Elk River Realty.

It was out of place in peaceful Pine Bluff. I cocked my head, trying to hear better. The high pitch of an angry woman, followed by the deeper rumble of a man's voice. The shouting stopped as I stood there gawking, so I shrugged and picked up my pace. None of my darned business anyway.

Carpenter's Corner was in a gray stone building on the north end of Main Street. We'd had our hardware store in the building for only a year when it'd come up for sale. We'd jumped at the opportunity to buy instead of paying rent. The stone was typical of the oldest buildings in Pine Bluff, having come from a quarry outside of town. I dug the key out of my pocket, unlocked the front door, and wedged a wood block under the door to keep it open. I flipped the plastic sign in the front window from "Closed" to "Open," stashed my purse under the front counter, and headed for the coffeepot. Even a bad cup of coffee had to be better than no coffee at all. With the coffee started, I opened the safe and took out the money for the day's till, put it in the cash register, and closed the drawer with a satisfying ding.

"Alright, ready for business," I said to no one in particular before realizing it was quieter than normal in the store. Too quiet. Steve should have been in by now. I checked the time to make sure I wasn't crazy. Sure enough, he was late. It wasn't like him. *Should I be worried?*

Steve Harrison was Carpenter's Corner's only employee. After Bob died, I'd needed help around the store and was tickled when Steve applied for the position. Bonus points he'd come with a construction background. He'd worked for a contractor in Walla Walla who gave him a glowing recommendation. The guy knew his stuff and gave brilliant advice to the customers. Until today, he'd never been even a minute late for work, but I didn't set the best example. If the boss tended to run late, why should I expect my employee to arrive on time? I'd better change my ways.

I'll give him a mulligan today since he's never been late before, I thought.

When the coffee finished dripping, I poured a steaming mug full, anticipating the moment the caffeine would hit my brain. Two packets of sugar and three mini cups of French vanilla creamer later, it resembled a creamy caramel and looked good enough to drink.

"Yuck." I shivered when the coffee hit my tongue. How in the world could something taste so bitter and so grossly sweet at the same time? I dumped it down the drain. "Disgusting."

With no coffee to drink, no employee to chat with, and no customers yet, there was plenty of time to water the flowers out front. I grabbed the blue watering can I kept under the front counter and popped into the bathroom to fill it with water. Carpenter's Corner shared a bathroom with the shop next door, Lipstick and Lace. It was accessed through a short hallway running between both shops. The bathroom was small—room enough for a toilet and sink with a small cabinet—but I'd made it a showpiece with porcelain tile floors made to look like whitewashed hardwood. White beadboard extended up the wall behind the gleaming cherry wood vanity, to chair-rail height, and a simple silver-framed mirror hung above the vessel sink. The walls were a soothing sage green, and the silver chandelier dripped with faux crystals, adding a bit of sass and glamour to the room.

I filled the watering can, dumped in a packet of liquid fertilizer, then gave it a quick swirl to mix the fertilizer in.

"How are you lovelies this morning?" I asked the lipstick-red geraniums spilling over the tops of twin wine barrels flanking the store's entrance.

All up and down Pine Bluff's Main Street, similar planters stood in front of each business. The planters had been my idea. I'd proposed them at a chamber of commerce meeting and was pleased when the other business owners jumped onboard. I loved the charm the flowers added to our little town. Even more surprising was how we'd managed to keep them alive all summer.

"Good morning, Daw-Na," a loud, snarky voice rang in my ear.

Startled, I jerked around and bumped into Darlene Lovelace. The movement caused water and fertilizer to splash out of my watering can and land on the front of the black silk blouse the thirty-something woman wore. It ran down her top and puddled at her feet.

"Oh gosh. I'm sorry. You surprised me."

"You better be sorry. You've ruined my favorite blouse." Darlene tapped herself on the chest with a long, manicured fingernail.

I mentally rolled my eyes. *Here we go.* "It's only water." Mostly. "Are you going to tell me you don't wash that thing?"

She scoffed. "No, of course I don't. Dry clean only, but I wouldn't expect you to know anything about how to care for nice fabric." She gave me a condescending pat on the shoulder. "You can, however, expect to see the bill."

I rolled my eyes. "You can take it off your rent."

"You can bet I will."

I have no doubt.

Darlene owned the pricey boutique next door, Lipstick and Lace, but since I owned the building, she rented the space from me. She stocked makeup and clothes for people a whole lot flashier than I would ever be. Today, despite the forecast, Darlene wore a sable fur vest over her low-cut blouse; black leggings; sparkly, teal-colored spiked heels; and enough turquoise jewelry to deck out two rodeo queens. Her shiny, jet-black hair stood tall, teased as high as a two-layer cake. Neither wind nor rain would disturb her rat's nest.

Does she use lacquer to keep that hairdo in place?

Apparently, Darlene was wondering about my hair at the same time I was contemplating hers. She looked me up and down, a frown line creasing her forehead. "When are you going to let Carly color your hair? The gray is making you look old, my dear. The look isn't professional for a businesswoman."

"It's my head and my hair, thank you very much. I happen to like my natural color. It's the real, authentic me. Don't look at me if you don't like it," I bit back, annoyed that I felt the need to explain myself. I shook my thick, pearly white hair. Not for one minute did I regret the decision to stop dying it. I loved my natural color and thought it made my chocolate-brown eyes stand out.

"To each their own. I will never let myself go like you do."

I wanted to wipe the smug look right off Darlene's long, horsey face but decided an early morning brawl on Main Street wasn't the best way to start the day. Lucky for her.

"Not to change the topic, but guess who I went out with last night?" Darlene's tone turned sticky sweet as she batted her fake eyelashes at me.

How could she be so oblivious to the fact I wanted to slap her silly?

"If I were to venture a guess, I'd say the real estate developer who's new to town. What's his name again? Warren Highcastle?" As far as I knew, he was the only available man in a hundred-mile radius she hadn't already had a go at. No wonder she was in such fine form this morning.

"Don't look at me with that judgy face of yours."

I wasn't sure what other face to look at her with.

"I haven't been on a date all summer, and Warren is one interesting specimen." Darlene twirled a strand of dark hair around her fingers. "I know he came into Carpenter's Corner yesterday. Spill what you know about him."

I shrugged. "Not much. We all know he's in town to buy the old opera house and turn it into a swanky hotel. He came in to ask about local contractors, so at least he's not planning to sub the work out to Portland companies, though I don't know who he thinks he's going to rent all those high-priced rooms to in Pine Bluff."

"Oh, I'm planning on spending time in them. With Warren, of course." Darlene twirled her hair faster and thrust out a hip. "Did you notice how he dresses? Those Wranglers with such a nice crisp crease and his expensive tweed jacket? Puts the hayseeds around here to shame." She fanned her face.

I sighed. "Too bad we couldn't get the restoration project off the ground before he swooped in to take it out from under us. The building should be restored to the grand old opera house it was in its heyday." It'd been an enormous blow to the Women's Service Club when we found out the owners had accepted an offer from Warren to purchase the Emery Theater.

"Warren will do far better things for this town than your little committee ever could." Darlene patted my arm like I was a stupid old thing.

The phone inside the hardware store rang, so I hightailed it back inside and away from my least favorite person in Pine Bluff. Saved by the bell.

The phone call was a customer placing an order for fencing materials. It made a great start to the day's sales. I'd recently seen a dip in revenue since a new big-box home improvement store opened last month in nearby Greenwood. Losing customers to them wasn't in my plans, and I needed to figure out a way to keep Pine Bluff residents shopping at Carpenter's Corner despite my slightly higher prices. It was something I needed to figure out sooner rather than later. Plus, if I ever wanted to retire—and I did—I needed to keep socking away money in my retirement fund.

"Mornin', Dawna. Coffee on?" Ernie Ford's overall-clad frame blocked the sun as he stood in the doorway.

Ernie had been Bob's closest friend and owned Ernie's Garage and Gas kitty-corner across the street from my hardware store. He was a giant of a man who always smelled slightly of mechanic's grease, like he'd slapped a bit behind his ears and rubbed a dab through his hair as part of his morning routine.

"You know it is. How's Evonne? I haven't talked to her much this week." I tucked a pencil behind my ear and leaned on the counter. Ernie's wife, Evonne, was my dearest friend.

"Mean as a bag of rattlesnakes, like always." He heehawed at his joke. "You know how it is. The citizens of our fine town always keep my wife on her toes. When she's not at the office, she keeps herself busy with the grandkids and her garden."

Evonne had worked as the Pine Bluff city manager through two different mayors, each holding the position for two terms. My best friend knew more about the happenings of our little town than anyone else could ever dream of knowing.

"Well, tell her we need to get together. It's been too long." Even though I could see Evonne's office from my store window if I craned my neck at the right angle, it'd been a week since I'd laid eyes on her.

"Evonne thinks she's dragging me to the park tonight for the concert. We'll see. You going?"

A local band, Blue Mountain Thunder, would cover Johnny Cash songs for the last concert in the park for the summer season. I'd been looking forward to it all summer.

"Heck yeah, I am. April's going with me. We're bringing fried chicken and potato salad for a picnic. Why don't the two of you join us? I'll save you a spot."

"You're not cooking the chicken, are ya?" A teasing grin split Ernie's broad face.

"No, Mr. Smarty Pants. The deli at Mill Street Market is doing the cooking." I glared at him over the top of my glasses.

Ernie never let it drop. Several years back, Bob and I had invited the Fords over for a roast chicken dinner and a rousing game of Rook. Between the card game and a few rum and cokes, it took me an hour to notice the chicken wasn't cooking. Turned out you had to turn the oven on to roast a chicken. Who knew? I dumped the bird in the trash and took everyone out for pizza instead. The entire town knew I was no Betty Crocker, but that dinner had been a disaster, even for me. Ernie still liked to give me a good ribbing about it whenever he got the chance.

"There they are."

Ernie's buddies, Bill Wilder and Rick Montgomery, came in through the warehouse at the back of the store. You'd think Carpenter's Corner was a diner instead of a hardware store, as often as the three men dropped in for coffee. They were all old friends of Bob's and had been meeting here for a cup of coffee in the mornings for years. None of those fancy lattes for these guys. They all kept coffee mugs here, and I'd put a small table and chairs near the coffee cart to keep the men out from under my feet.

"Was the back door unlocked?" I reached under the counter and pulled a set of keys out of my purse, frowning at them.

Bill hooked a thumb toward the warehouse. "Yeah, like it always is. Why?"

"I don't remember unlocking it this morning. Guess I must have." I shrugged and dropped the keys back into my purse. "Steve usually unlocks that door, but he's not here yet."

The guys poured the sludge they called coffee into their mugs, plopped into the chairs around the table, and chattered like a flock of hens. So much for the quiet morning. I grabbed a bottle of water and leaned back against the counter to listen to the gossip. They discussed the weather, whose truck Ernie was working on in the garage, which fishing holes had dried up in the August heat, which ones they were still pulling trout out of, the concert in the park, and Warren Highcastle. Every conversation these days eventually turned to the real estate developer and the old Emery Theater.

"Highcastle asked me to do the renovation." Bill crossed his arms and tilted his chair back.

Bob and Bill had been partners in CW Construction. When Bob died, Bill bought me out and became the sole owner. He'd renamed the company Wilder Construction and had a solid reputation for building beautiful custom homes and restoring vintage buildings.

"Kim and I invited him out for dinner to talk about the project. The guy's a pompous donkey. It's going to be a big job, but I have plenty of work to keep my crew busy without taking it. I will not work for Highcastle."

"What did he do to make you think he's a pompous donkey?" I asked.

Bill dropped the front legs of his chair back to the floor with a thud. "The guy's arrogant. High and mighty. Thinks his poop doesn't stink."

"Huh. He was in yesterday asking about local subcontractors. Seemed alright to me."

"Sure, but you never see the bad in people. Be careful with your dealings with him, Dawna. I don't think he'd think twice about screwing you over."

"Yeah, I will. Not sure how many supplies he's planning to buy here anyway, with the new big-box hardware and lumberyard in Greenwood. I can't compete with their prices. And if he goes with a contractor from out of the area, I'm sure it'll leave me out of the running." I gave Bill a pointed look.

He shook his head. "It won't be me. You can count on it."

Darn it. If Bill had taken the job, it would have seen my store through this coming winter with ease. Even with better prices twenty miles down the road, Bill still bought all his lumber and building supplies from Carpenter's Corner. I appreciated his loyalty and crossed my fingers he was right about having enough work to keep his crew, and my store, busy.

"Doesn't sound like we're gonna solve any more world problems today." Rick scraped his chair back from the table and stood. He stretched with a growl and spread his arms wide. "I better get after it. See y'all later."

Bill had dish duty today, so he gathered the coffee mugs and took them into the bathroom to rinse out. He tossed out used stir sticks and wiped off the table before leaving for the day. In the beginning, I'd cleaned up after them every morning until I got fed up one day and lost my temper. A couple of foot stomps and one come-to-Jesus meeting later, the guys got it through their thick skulls I wasn't their maid and started picking up after themselves.

Alone in the store again, I dialed Steve's number. It didn't even ring before going straight to voicemail. This was so not like him. I hoped nothing was wrong, but a steady stream of people started to flow through the store, so I didn't have a lot of time to dwell on it. One man needed help to decide which size screws to use in order to hang a screen door. A woman wanted a gallon of paint mixed. A few customers were content to browse on their own.

During a lull in business, I glanced at the clock. Ten already? Time sure flew when you were having fun. Steve better have a darn good explanation for not showing this morning.

A newer model baby-blue VW Beetle rumbled to a stop in front of the store. The car door slammed, and April, my youngest daughter, bounced into the store, her short raspberry-red hair a tousled mess. Dressed for the late summer heat, she wore a faded black T-shirt with the iconic triangle and rainbow of the band Pink Floyd on the front, with half of a feather tattoo peeking out below her left sleeve. Paint-splattered denim cutoff shorts showed off her freckled, muscular legs, and a pair of ankle-high black work boots completed the outfit.

I only had eyes for the coffee she held in her hands.

"Is that for me?" I think I purred as I reached for the iced hazelnut latte with the Rocking M logo on the side of the plastic cup.

"Hello to you too, Mama." April's voice tinkled with laughter as she handed me the coveted coffee. April had moved back to Pine Bluff after getting fed up with the fast lifestyle of San Francisco. After high school graduation, she couldn't get out of here fast enough. Now, she said she was tired of the corporate world, city life, and city men. I was suspicious her brother and sister had decided she was the best candidate to keep an eye on their nutcase of a mother, but after sixteen years of her absence, I didn't care what the reason was. I was happy to have her back.

I took a long sip of my coffee and closed my eyes, savoring the first mouthful. "Mmm. So good. Thank you for this. I didn't have time to stop by the coffee shop this morning and desperately needed it." The caffeine hit my deprived brain and I smiled. "Hello, dear daughter."

April eyed me with suspicion over the straw in her own iced coffee. "Everything okay, Mom? Why were you late?"

I waved her off. "Everything's fine. A thistle was trying to take over my herb garden, so I dug it up when I should've been leaving for work. Not a big deal. The only problem I'm having, now that I have coffee, is Steve skipping out on his shift today."

April came behind the counter and climbed onto one of the two tall swivel stools stationed behind the cash register. "Did you try to call him?"

"Yep, twice. No answer. I'm sure he'll show up sooner or later." I shrugged and pushed my round glasses back into place. They were forever slipping down the bridge of my nose. I looked around to make sure no customers lingered nearby before leaning toward April. "Crazy Darlene told me she went out with Warren Highcastle last night. I feel like I should warn him next time I see him. That woman gets her claws in every man who wanders into town."

"True story. Which leads me to the reason I stopped by. Warren left a voicemail asking if I'd be interested in helping design and decorate his new hotel. I'm a little hesitant because I've only worked on houses so far, and I hate the idea of the Emery Theater being turned into a hotel. Do you think I can do it?"

I sighed. "I know you can. You've got a lot of talent. We're all a little upset about losing our opera house, but the fact is, nobody local stepped up to buy the building and keep it going. The Women's Service Club didn't get enough money raised in time, so here we are. Things change, whether we like it or not. It'd be a fantastic project for you. Lucrative. Somebody's going to get the job. Why not you? Think on it anyway. You know I'll help with what I can." It was nice to know my daughter valued my opinion. I remembered what Bill had said this morning, and raised a warning finger. "However, Bill thinks the guy's a shyster. Wouldn't hurt to talk to Warren, but pay attention to any red flags, and make sure he pays you what you're worth if you decide to take the job."

When April moved back to Pine Bluff last year, she'd taken over my design and furniture restoration business so I could focus full-time on the hardware store. I didn't have the energy to do both anymore. Something had to give. April had worked with me restoring furniture when she was a teenager. Even back then she had a better eye for style and color than I ever did. My old clients were tickled pink with the work she'd been doing for them since she'd come home.

She nodded. "I trust Bill's opinion. Maybe I'll give him a call before I talk with Warren." April slurped the last of her coffee, tossed the cup into the garbage can underneath the checkout counter, and pulled her car keys out of the pocket of her shorts. "Well, I'd better get going. The Kiplings' house isn't going to finish itself. I'm putting a last coat of sealer on the kitchen cabinets today, and it'll pretty much be done. Oh, I need a few more stir sticks."

"You know where they're at. Take as many as you need. Before you go, though, watch the register for a minute while I use the bathroom." I swung off the stool and headed to the bathroom.

An icy shiver ran up my spine as I reached for the hallway door. Something felt off. Creepy. I pulled the door open and stumbled, catching myself against the doorframe. A metallic scent filled the small space. My heart slammed against my chest as I tried to make sense of what I was seeing. Warren Highcastle's alligator-skin cowboy boots stuck out of the open bathroom doorway, and an old, worn framing hammer, the prongs covered in blood, lay on the floor beside him.

Chapter Three

I slammed the hallway door shut and took a step back, my breath coming in jerky spasms, as if I'd run a marathon. My first reaction was to flee. The man appeared to be dead, but what if he wasn't? What if I could save his life?

I forced myself to open the door.

Warren's head was wedged between the wall and the toilet. His open eyes stared straight up, and his mouth hung open. Had he seen his attacker?

I crouched beside him and reached to check for a pulse. Before my fingers made contact with his skin, I snatched my hand back. *Pull it together, Dawna. Dead men don't bite.* I exhaled a long breath and pressed my fingers to his neck. Nothing. The pompous donkey was dead as a doornail.

"April, call J. T." My voice came out a screech as I yelled for my daughter. "Tell him to hurry. And don't come back here."

It took all of two seconds for April to ignore my orders. She slid around the corner, rammed into my back, and knocked me face-first onto the dead man's chest. I scrambled to my feet and shimmied from head to toe, like a dog shaking off water.

"Whoa. What's going on? Is he dead?" April's green eyes were wide as her voice rose to a sharp pitch.

"Yes. Get out of here and call the police."

April fumbled for the cell phone in her back pocket, scurrying out of the hallway like a squirrel being chased by a cat.

I pressed a shaky hand to my racing heart and leaned against the doorframe to keep the room from spinning. There'd be plenty of time to fall apart after the crisis passed. With the dizziness under control, I studied the dead man's face. "Who did this to you? And why here, in my bathroom?"

Paralyzed by the sight of the body on the floor and my own racing thoughts, I stood transfixed until a thump on the opposite door leading into Lipstick and Lace jump-started my heart. I reached over and slid the dead bolt into place. The last thing I needed was one of Darlene's customers coming in to use the bathroom right now.

"There's nothing I can do for you," I told the dead man. "Don't worry, though. The police will be here before you know it." I stepped back into Carpenter's Corner and closed the hallway door, snapped the lock on my side, and left Warren's corpse alone on the floor.

The instant I stepped away from the door, Steve flew out of the warehouse. He wasn't watching where he was going and knocked into me.

"Oh, I'm sorry, Mrs. Carpenter—I didn't see you there." Steve attempted to button his shirt with trembling fingers and tuck it into his jeans while he continued to apologize without making eye contact with me. "I'm sorry I'm late. I promise I'll make it up to you. Gotta use the bathroom, and then I'll be ready to get to work." He reached for the hallway door.

I stepped between him and the door and held my hands out to stop him. "No, you can't go in there. There's been an accident. April's calling the police."

"The police? I'm sure I can fix whatever's wrong with the bathroom. The police aren't plumbers." He shook his shaggy dishwater-blond hair out of his eyes.

"It's not a plumbing issue. There's been a death. Believe me, you don't want to see it."

Steve stopped fidgeting with his buttons and looked around the store in confusion. He took a step back, an expression of horror on his face. "What're you talking about? Someone got killed? In the hardware store? Who died?"

April interrupted. "I got a hold of J. T. They're on their way."

April strode to the front of the store, pushed the door closed, and flipped the "Open" sign over. A customer had wandered in during the initial chaos and was studying the paintbrush supply. April let him know the store was closed temporarily for an emergency, handed him a paintbrush on the house, and ushered him out of the store. At least one of us was thinking and taking care of business. I hadn't even noticed anyone was shopping. *Good grief. Get it together, Dawna.*

It took exactly three minutes for Jeremy "J. T." Dallas, Pine Bluff's police chief, to pull up to the curb in front of Carpenter's Corner, lights flashing and siren blaring on his police car. I yanked the front door open and beckoned for him to hurry. People were already ducking out of businesses up and down Main

Street, curious to see what the commotion was about. Police lights and sirens aren't an everyday occurrence in our little town.

"What's going on?" A man jogged across the street to join the crowd forming.

People gathered around, a few even pressing their noses against the front window of my store. J. T. ignored their questions and hurried inside. Not wanting to be rude, I waved to my neighbors before pulling the door closed behind the police chief and locking it.

"Dawna." J. T. dipped his head in greeting, then acknowledged April and Steve in the same manner. Dressed in the standard navy-blue uniform, he wore a gun in a black leather holster on his side and a police radio clipped to the pocket of his shirt. Instead of the usual police-issue heavy boots, Chief Dallas wore a pair of dusty brown leather cowboy boots. With his lanky frame, glossy dark hair, and icy-mountain-lake-blue eyes, J. T. looked like he'd be as comfortable riding a horse in a Marlboro commercial as he was writing parking tickets in Pine Bluff.

"April said you found a dead body? Show me."

"Back in the bathroom. Follow me," I replied. "April stopped by, so I took advantage of her being here and went to use the restroom before she left. Never in a million years did I expect to find . . . well, see for yourself." I stepped aside to let the police chief into the narrow hallway.

Chief Dallas squatted beside the body and checked for a pulse, then shook his head, confirming Warren was dead.

"Do you know who this man is?" J. T. asked.

I glanced at the corpse and swallowed hard. My voice shook as I spoke. "Yeah, it's Warren Highcastle, the real estate developer who was buying the Emery Theater. I met him yesterday."

April touched my arm. "Mama, you've had a shock this morning. You need to sit. Come on."

J. T. agreed. "April's right. Go find someplace to sit. We're going to do everything we can to find out who killed Mr. Highcastle, and why. Take a minute to get yourself together, then I'm going to have to ask both of you some questions. Steve too."

April narrowed her eyes and growled. "Now, wait a minute. Are you trying to say my mom's a suspect? We're *all* suspects?" She puffed up her small body like a snake ready to strike, a red flush climbing her face.

"Don't get snarly, April." I stepped between the two of them. "I found the body, after all. Of course he needs to ask us questions. Let the man do his job."

I wanted to laugh out loud but held it inside. April had always been a scrapper, ready to fight for what she believed in, and prepared to protect her family at all costs. The girl was no shrinking violet, and I was proud to be her mother. I'd raised a strong, independent woman.

April deflated, the fight leaving her. "I know, but you've been through enough. Can't it wait?"

"For heaven's sake, I'm not an invalid. Settle down." I turned to J. T., my voice stronger. "I'm fine to answer questions whenever you're ready."

A pounding on the Lipstick and Lace side of the hallway door made us all jump.

"Hey. Dawna. Why is the door locked? I gotta go. Open up. What's going on in there?" Darlene's shouts penetrated the locked door. The doorknob jiggled as she tried to get into the bathroom.

"Hold on. This door goes into the shop next door?" J. T. scowled at the closed door. "Was it locked all morning?"

"We share the bathroom between Darlene's shop and the hardware store, so yes, there's a door from each store into this hallway. I lock it at night and unlock it each morning so Darlene and her customers can use the bathroom. After I found the body, I relocked it so nobody would come in and compromise the crime scene before you got here."

The pounding started again. "I hear you in there, Dawna. Hurry. I need to use the bathroom while I don't have any customers," Darlene pleaded.

"Miss Lovelace? We can't let you use the restroom right now. Please go lock your front door, but don't leave. I'll need to talk to you in a bit," J. T. shouted through the door.

"Chief Dallas, is that you? What's going on? Why do I need to close my store?"

"Go lock your door, Darlene. That's an order. I'll be over to explain everything in a few minutes."

One more loud slap reverberated against the door before Darlene's footsteps stomped away.

Chapter Four

"Now I think I need to sit." I wrapped my arms tight around my torso, to stop the shakes that had me feeling like a phone on vibrate. My knees threatened to betray me and dump me on the floor, so I pulled out a chair at the guy's coffee klatch table and dropped into it. "My insides feel like Jell-O all of a sudden."

April snorted. "About time. I've been trying to get you to sit for the last fifteen minutes." She started a fresh pot of coffee.

Ignoring my daughter, I closed my eyes and took a couple of deep breaths, trying to calm my vibrating nerves. I counted to ten and took another deep breath. My heartbeat returned to normal, but my mind continued to race. What had Warren done to get himself killed? Bill thought the guy was a jerk, but he'd been pleasant enough when he was in the hardware store yesterday. None of us wanted him to buy the Emery, but someone being upset enough over it to have killed him didn't make sense. What else could it have been? A jealous husband? A snubbed business partner? I sighed. I didn't know enough about the man to even speculate. Motives for murder were usually love, money, or revenge, weren't they? At least in all the murder mysteries I read, it was the case. I'd spent my life avoiding ghosts, but I found myself thinking it would've been nice if Warren's spirit had stuck around long enough to tell us who'd killed him. Then again, that wasn't really a door I wanted to open. Or even knew how to.

J. T. slid back a chair at the table as April plunked a steaming mug of cheap, bitter black coffee in front of each of us. Caffeine was the last thing my nervous system needed right now. My shaky stomach threatened to revolt, so I pulled the mug close without taking a sip and wrapped my hands around it, craving the warm comfort holding it provided. J. T. reached for the sugar jar in the middle of the table. He spooned three heaping teaspoons into his coffee and gave the sludge a quick stir.

"Holy fright. Have a little coffee with your sugar." The words fell out of my mouth before I could pull them back.

"What? This stuff is terrible. Adding loads of sugar is the only way I can swallow this coffee." He added another spoonful for good measure. Even with all the added sugar, when he took the first sip, his lip twisted up and he winced. The chief set his coffee cup back on the table and pulled a small red notebook out of his shirt pocket, flipping it open. "All right, Dawna, let's start at the beginning. You said you were in the bathroom earlier this morning, correct? Before you found the body?"

I nodded, then reconstructed the events of the day. I told him about filling the watering can and chatting with Darlene out front before the store got busy. He asked for the names of the customers who'd been in the hardware store since I opened, so I rattled off the people I remembered being in.

"These folks are our friends and neighbors, for crying out loud. I can't imagine any of them could've had a thing to do with Warren's murder." I twisted my wedding ring around my finger over and over as I talked over the events of the morning.

"Mom, settle down." April gripped the edge of the wooden table with both hands, trying to hold it still. "You're making the whole table bounce."

"I'm not doing anything."

Both April and J. T. stared at me with eyebrows raised. I glanced at my legs. They were jittering so hard it seemed like a minor earthquake shook the table as they bounced. I pressed my hands to my thighs until the shakes were under control.

"One more question, Dawna." The police chief sounded apologetic. "What type of security do you have in the store? Is there a camera I can review footage from?"

I shook my head. "No camera. Bob and I talked about it at one point but didn't think we needed to invest in a security system. We've never had any problems. Sure, a few small items go missing now and then, but I figure if someone steals a battery or a handful of nails, they must need them pretty bad." I shrugged. "A camera sure would've come in handy today."

J. T. blew out a breath, rubbed the back of his neck, and tapped his pen against the notebook. "Times have changed since you opened the store. People aren't as trustworthy as they were thirty years ago. I suggest you look into getting a security system installed."

Great. One more major expense to worry about.

"What time did you get here this morning?" the chief asked April.

"Ten o'clock on the nose." She grinned as if she'd gotten a *Jeopardy* question correct.

"True," I verified. "I looked at my watch right before she pulled up."

April answered questions about where she'd been earlier in the morning and shared her version of events taking place at Carpenter's Corner until the police arrived. Satisfied with our answers, J. T. asked to talk with Steve next.

I pushed my glasses back up my nose and shook my head. "No need. Steve wasn't even here yet when I found Warren's body. Which reminds me, I need to find out why he was so late this morning."

As soon as the words left my mouth, I regretted them. *Shoot. Did I accidentally throw Steve under the bus? Where's he gotten off to again anyway?* I scanned the store, but my salesclerk was nowhere in sight.

"Interesting," J. T. jotted another note. "Even so, I still need to speak to him."

"Steve," I called out.

"Right here, Mrs. Carpenter." Steve emerged from the warehouse. "I couldn't remember if I'd locked my car or not. Since the store isn't open, I thought it'd be all right to check." He clasped his hands together and rocked back and forth on the balls of his feet with nervous energy.

With the toe of his boot, J. T. pulled out the empty chair and motioned for Steve to take a seat.

"Dawna tells me you were late for work this morning. What time did you get in?"

"Uh, a few minutes after ten, I think." Steve glanced at me, his head sinking into his shoulders. "I'm really sorry, Mrs. Carpenter. My alarm didn't go off, so I overslept. I need this job. Please don't fire me," he pleaded, his fingers beating a staccato on the tabletop.

"Oh, good night! I'm not going to fire you over being late one time. If I can't handle the store for a few hours by myself, I might as well pack it all in." Why was Steve acting so nervous? Something was off with him today.

The police chief cleared his throat and checked his watch. "Let's get this done, shall we? Now, Steve, who can verify you were at home this morning?"

"Uh, nobody. My roommate is out of town. I was home alone," he muttered. His gaze roamed the room, looking everywhere except at the three people watching him.

What is he hiding?

J. T. grunted. "Alright. You parked in the back of the store today? Did you see anything out of place when you pulled in this morning? Anybody leaving, maybe?"

"No, nothing." Steve shook his shaggy head.

The police chief stared at him for a beat, but when Steve offered nothing else, he pushed back from the table and stood. "No more questions for now, though I may need to talk to each of you again later." He flipped his notebook closed and shoved it into his shirt pocket. "Looks like the coroner has arrived. This could take time—even a few days—to process the crime scene. I'll let you know when you can reopen the store, but in the meantime, we need to have full access to the building, and you all need to stay out."

"I need to count my cash register and make a run to the bank. Can I at least stay until I get that done?" It hadn't occurred to me my store was now a crime scene, and I'd be missing out on a few days' worth of sales during peak season.

J. T. rubbed his chin, then sighed. "Sure, I guess it'll be okay. Do what you need to do at your front counter. Don't touch anything you don't have to, and nobody else can stay with you. Probably wouldn't hurt for you to stick around until the coroner removes the body, anyway, in case we need any further information from you."

The phrase "the body" sent electrical currents zinging from the top of my head to the ends of my toes. My mama used to say when that particular sensation settled over a person, a spirit was passing through. I spun around to check if Warren's ghost had shown up after all. Nothing. I breathed a sigh of relief.

"Are you doing okay, Dawna?" J. T. stared at me with concern. "Finding a dead body can shake a person up pretty bad."

I looked him straight in the eye and lied through my teeth. "I'm fine. Had the jitters there for a second, but I'm good now. Really."

Steve was halfway to the back door when I remembered to ask him for his set of keys to the store.

"The police need them so they can come and go as they please. You'll get them back later."

He pulled two keys off his chain and handed them over. "You'll let me know when I can come back to work?"

"Of course. I'll keep you in the loop whenever I find out more."

Steve nodded, then turned to leave through the warehouse doorway. J. T. grabbed him by the arm and spun him back around.

"I need you to exit the building through the front. We haven't searched the warehouse yet, and I don't want anyone to compromise the scene."

Steve jerked back, his gaze shifting between the police chief and the warehouse. "But I'm parked out there. I need to go out through the back door."

"Pretty sure you won't melt if you walk around the building instead," I told him. *Good grief, what is with this guy today?*

"Mom, call me when you leave here, okay?"

April looked over her shoulder at me as Chief Dallas herded her and Steve out of the hardware store. I gave her a thumbs-up.

I opened the cash register and removed the cash drawer, then pulled the battered old green ledger out of my desk and settled in to get the day's deposit ready. With only two hours' worth of sales, it was going to be a tiny one, barely worth the effort. I flipped open the ledger and stared at it, my mind blank.

A knock on the window beside my head startled me, and I let out a sharp shriek. The mailman stood on the sidewalk, his nose flat against the plate glass window. I was jumpy—wound tight and ready to recoil at the slightest noise. I pressed a hand to my racing heart. *At this rate, I'm going to have a heart attack and join Bob before the day's over.*

Unlocking the door, I stepped outside.

"Hey, Jesse. Got mail for me?"

He handed over a stack of envelopes, then unclipped an ink pen from his mailbag.

"You've got a certified one here today. Sign right there." He pointed to a signature line on a green form attached to the letter.

I signed, then pawed through my mail. It contained a couple of bills and a handful of advertisements. Back inside, I tossed the junk mail in the trash and sliced open the top of the certified envelope with a stainless-steel letter opener I kept on my desk. I pulled out the letter, unfolded it, and read.

No. This was wrong. This letter was intended for someone else. Whoever had filled out the notice of default on a promissory note had made a huge mistake. Carpenter's Corner Hardware and Building Supply was listed where the name of the actual business who'd defaulted on their loan should have been. I'd never taken out a loan with Elkins National Bank in my life. Whoever the poor fools were, they had one hundred and eighty days to come up with nearly twenty-five thousand dollars. Glad it wasn't me. I shoved the letter aside to deal with later.

Chapter Five

The bank deposit was prepared and ready in record time, so I turned my attention to finishing the week's ledger entries. Or tried to turn my attention to it. The numbers in the debit and credit columns ran together instead of registering in my foggy brain. Outside, cars rolled past; a horn blew from somewhere down the street, and people chattered as they walked by the front window while going about their day. It was surreal to think the county coroner was analyzing a man's death a few feet from where I sat. It wasn't shaping up to be a typical day in our sleepy little town of Pine Bluff.

I tapped the pencil against the ledger, thinking about Warren's death instead of the numbers in front of me. Who could've done such a horrible thing? I mean, sure, maybe he wasn't the nicest guy, but nobody deserves to go out with a hammer lodged in the back of their head. Hopefully, he'd died fast and hadn't suffered.

Chief Dallas had left a few minutes before to question Darlene at Lipstick and Lace next door. She'd been dating the man. Was she a suspect? What if Warren had canceled their date for tonight? Told her he didn't want to see her anymore? Could it have made her mad enough to bonk him over the head with a hammer? I shrugged. Maybe.

The murder was bad enough on its own, but I worried it would change the peace and quiet of our small mountain town. Pine Bluff had always been a great place to raise a family. Safe. Bad things didn't happen here. Maybe I was naive, but I couldn't imagine anyone from our community committing murder. Sure, I knew every town had its little secrets—every person, for that matter. Heaven knows I had my own, but murder? I drummed the yellow pencil against the ledger and stared, unseeing, out the window.

Once he was back from chatting with Darlene, J. T. leaned against my front counter, scratching notes in his little spiral notebook. From my vantage point, I watched Darlene step outside and lock her shop door. Tears and mascara in equal measure streamed down the distraught woman's face in rivers. She dropped her keys into her purse and walked away, a flattened version of the woman who'd been harassing me this morning. She didn't appear to have the demeanor of a person who'd recently killed a man.

"How'd it go?" I asked J. T. "Did you find out if Warren had been in Lipstick and Lace today?"

The chief of police nodded without looking up from his notebook. "Yeah, Darlene was busy when he came in, and by the time she had a free minute, he'd already left, or so she thought."

"Do you think she killed him? Is she a suspect?"

With my questions, J. T. looked up and pinned his penetrating blue eyes on me. "No more than you are."

I frowned. Now what in the world did he mean by that?

When the coroner called for J. T. to join him, he finally dropped his hard stare and walked away. I sat still for a second until I was sure the chief's attention was focused elsewhere, then reached out and snuck into my lap the little red notebook he'd left lying on the counter. I flipped it open. Inside, he'd made a list of the customers who'd been in Darlene's shop this morning. One name stood out to me: Kristi Fisher. It was well known in town that Kristi was working as Warren's real estate agent, and I'd definitely heard an argument happening at Elk River Reality this morning. Was it Warren and Kristi yelling at each other? Were there problems with the Emery Theater transaction? I pulled out my phone and snapped a quick picture of the list, then slid the notebook back where I'd found it. I glanced toward the hallway where J. T. and the coroner stood in deep conversation. Both of them had their backs turned to me, so my sneakiness had gone undetected.

With the crime scene assessment finished, a team of paramedics rolled the gurney, topped with a sheet-clad body, right by me and through the open front door. I couldn't tear my gaze away until they'd finished loading Warren's body into the waiting ambulance and slammed the doors closed.

"Well, we've finished our initial investigation." J. T. swiped his notebook off the counter and deposited it into his shirt pocket. "Didn't find much. With any luck, we'll come up with a lead or two from what evidence we were able to gather, and make an arrest. The store is still a crime scene, and we'll keep the

building closed until we're sure there's no more evidence to col-
lect. I'll keep you updated and let you know when you're clear to
open back up for business."

"You said you didn't find much, which leads me to believe
you found something. Am I correct?" I raised my eyebrows, curious to hear what the police had unearthed.

"It's an open investigation, so I shouldn't be telling you, but it
is your store. Don't let this information get out, you hear?"

I nodded my agreement.

"We found a partial footprint with a bit of blood on it in
some sawdust back in the lumberyard. One of my officers also
found a pillow and a red wool blanket tucked behind a stack of
garden hoses in your warehouse. They seemed out of place. Do
you know anything about them, by any chance?"

"Um, no. A blanket and pillow? Are you sure? We don't sell
blankets and pillows." I shoved my glasses back up my nose.

"These aren't new. Maybe your guy, Steve, slips away for an
afternoon nap?"

I shook my head. "No. Never."

"Not to harp on it, but this is one more reason you should
invest in a camera and an alarm system."

Disgusted with the thought of spending more money than I
had budgeted for, I flung my arms wide. "For crying out loud.
This is Pine Bluff we're talking about. Not once in thirty years
have I even worried about shoplifters. Now this."

"I know," J. T. answered to placate me. "Like I said earlier, times change. While Carpenter's Corner is closed for the
next couple of days, take some time to look at various security

systems, and find one that will work for you. Don't make me get April involved."

I counted Jerry and Patty Dallas among my closest friends. They lived in Florida now, but while our kids were growing up, we'd spent many long summer days together on the Dallas family's ranch on Simmons Ridge. J. T. was like one of my own kids.

"Don't you dare threaten me, young man." I rolled up a piece of paper and swatted at him over the counter.

"You know I'll tattle on you in a heartbeat. I'd suggest you heed my advice and get it done." J. T. flashed a crooked smile and walked out into the sunshine.

Chancing one more peek at the murder scene, I gritted my teeth and turned around. Yellow crime scene tape roped off the door leading into the hallway, making my store feel unfamiliar and surreal. I spun back around, picked up the bank bag, grabbed my purse from under the counter, and hustled outside.

Chapter Six

I pulled the door to Carpenter's Corner shut behind myself and twisted the key in the lock, pulling hard on the handle to make sure it was secure. Those motions were the only security system I'd ever needed up until today. Leave one light on, close the door, lock it, give it a final pull to check, and done. Not anymore.

"Good night! How much is a security system going to run me?" I blew out a hard breath. With any luck, I'd be able to find one at a halfway reasonable price. It wasn't an expense I'd budgeted for, and with winter around the corner, well . . . *I sure hope I'll be able to keep Steve on full-time.*

With the police cars and ambulance gone, the town had settled into the everyday quiet routine of Pine Bluff. Before hurrying off to the bank, I took a minute to soak it in. My building was at the end of a block, with Lipstick and Lace being the last shop on the corner. A cross street separated our building from the Emery Theater—the old stone opera house that had brought Warren to town in the first place. The Emery was the tallest building in town and filled one full city block. Steeped in history, construction on the theater had been completed in 1922.

In the early days, Pine Bluff was the end of the trail for the Blue Mountain Stage Line. Passengers disembarked in town, choosing either to stay or to make their way by mule or foot into the rugged mountains surrounding our valley. When the railroad pushed through, the local sawmills were able to ship the region's plentiful lumber all over the Northwest. More mill workers and their families arrived. Pine Bluff grew and flourished.

Richard Steinman, the owner of the most prosperous sawmill in the area, decided the town needed some culture, so he hired local stonemasons and commissioned them to build a European-style theater; thus, the Emery Theater was born. Inside, it featured ornate columns framing the stage, plush red velvet seating, a pressed-tin ceiling, and a magnificent crystal chandelier Steinman had shipped in from New York.

For sixty years, people from all over the area had flocked to the Emery for live music and plays. To keep up with progress, the theater had morphed and changed over the years. A big screen was added in the early 1930s for the talking picture craze, and the theater continued to thrive. With the era of television sets in every home, and then, later, home movie systems, there wasn't enough business, and the grand lady fell into disrepair. The beautiful opera house had closed its doors more than a decade ago.

Six months back, the Women's Service Club had voted to raise funds to buy the Emery Theater and restore the building to its former glory. I was fully on board with the idea and had volunteered for the committee. The theater had been sitting empty for years now, so we thought we had all the time in the world to come up with a solid plan. For the first event, we decided on a cookbook fundraiser and collected recipes from everyone in town who would give us one; then we sold the books from a booth at the weekly farmer's market. All of our not-so-well-laid plans came to a screeching halt when Warren came to town flashing around his shiny plans to buy the old opera house out from under our indignant noses and convert it into a fancy hotel.

I raised my hand to block the sun and contemplated the Emery. Highcastle's purchase hadn't been finalized, as far as I knew. What would happen now? Maybe our Women's Service Club would get another shot at it. I dropped the keys to Carpenter's Corner into the depths of my carry-on-size purse and dug out my cell phone.

"Mom," April answered on the first ring. "It's about time. I've been worried sick. Are the police still there? Any updates? How are you feeling? Are you okay?"

My head spun with her rapid-fire questions.

"Sheesh, girl, take a breath. I told you earlier I was doing fine, and nothing has changed. Yes, they're done for now, so I'm headed to the bank. Do you have time to meet me at the Stage Stop Café in a few minutes? It's been a long day, and I'm in dire need of a slice of butterscotch pie." My stomach rolled and rumbled. Not sure if it was hunger or nerves, but I planned to feed it to find out.

By the time I made the bank deposit, answered a few morbid questions about the murder, and headed for the diner, it was almost two in the afternoon. The heat of the day had settled in with a vengeance, leaving the air muggy and heavy. I glanced at the dark, ominous sky. Another of our mountain thunder and lightning storms was threatening to move in. Fire danger was high. I hoped today's storm brought a good amount of rain with it so it wouldn't start any new forest fires.

The normal cheerful buzz in the diner stopped abruptly when I stepped inside, and all heads swiveled like owls' to look at me. *Awkward.*

"Shh. She's here. Stop talking about her." Making a joke out of it, I held a finger to my lips and bugged out my eyes.

As intended, my joke broke the tension, and everyone started talking at once.

"Dawna, are you okay?"

"Oh, sweetie, I've been worried about you since I heard the awful news."

"That poor man."

"Can you believe a murder happened here in Pine Bluff?"

"Who did it? Have the police made an arrest?"

"Are we all in danger?"

I held my hands up in surrender. "Yes, it's terrible, but I'm fine. Really. The police don't know much of anything yet. As soon as they make an arrest, I'm sure we'll all hear about it. The only thing I know right now is I need a big old slice of butterscotch pie." I slid into the red vinyl booth across from where April sat waiting for me.

The Stage Stop Café was an old-fashioned-style diner. Vinyl booths with white Formica tables lined the front windows, with a few matching round tables placed wherever they could be squeezed in. Two teenagers sat on twirly barstools in front of the stainless-steel counter, sipping chocolate milkshakes and munching fries. A few booths were filled with gray-haired, wizened men arguing over the state of the world while sipping cups of black coffee. A handful of other locals munched on late lunches.

A waitress brought over two large, blue plastic cups of ice water with slices of lemon wedged on the rims. She wiped off the already clean table and winked at me. "Glad to see you've got your normal sassy pants on today. I've got a big slice of butterscotch pie coming right up." She scribbled on a ticket book before turning her attention to April. "What can I get you this afternoon, sweetheart?"

"A double order of fries with lots of fry sauce, please, and a glass of sweet tea."

"Add a mug of coffee for me, please, DeAnn. I need my afternoon caffeine fix. With cream." I squeezed the lemon wedge into my water, dropped it into the cup, and took a sip.

"You got it."

Sitting back against the cushion, I let out an enormous sigh and closed my eyes. "I still can't believe someone killed Warren in my bathroom. It's gotta be a bad dream I'll wake from soon."

My eyes flew open when my daughter reached across the table and pinched my arm.

"Nope. You're wide awake."

I scowled at her and rubbed the pinch away.

"You know, the thing I've been wondering about all day is the hammer. Was it from the hardware store? Did the murderer take it off the display to kill Warren with?" April wrinkled her nose and shuddered.

"No, no, no," I reassured her. "I saw the hammer. It didn't come from the store—at least not any time recently. It's old and worn, with rust on the claws. Well, I think it was rust. Could've been blood, I guess." I shivered, mimicking my daughter's body language. "Anyway, no, it wasn't a new hammer from the store, thank goodness. J. T. thinks they should be able to get finger-prints off it and make an arrest fairly quickly. I sure hope so."

DeAnn arrived with our orders, setting the fries in front of April and handing the plate of pie to me. She pulled a paper-wrapped straw out of her black apron pocket and laid it on the table next to April's glass of sweet tea. "Anything else you need, ladies?"

"Nope, can't think of a thing." April dipped a French fry into the creamy orange fry sauce and popped it into her mouth. "Hot, hot, hot." She fanned her open mouth to cool it off a bit before swallowing.

I picked up my fork and nibbled at the pie. On my way to the café, I'd thought I was starving, but all the talk about murder had killed my appetite. The image of Warren's dead body kept playing on repeat in my mind. My inner gaze-detection radar tingled, and I tore my eyes away from the pie and sat straighter. Was the whole café still looking at me? My shoulders sagged in relief. It was only April, staring at me from across the table.

"What're you staring at? Eat your fries and leave me alone. Geesh."

"I'm making sure you're not lying to me about how well you're dealing with this whole thing. And I'll look at you all I want, lady. You're not the boss of me," April teased.

"Like it or not, you're my daughter, so I'll always be the boss of you." I chuckled and set my fork back onto the table. "You know, there wasn't much blood, and no gore at all, but I guess it's still bothering me more than I let on. At first, I thought there was red paint spilled on the floor. It took a minute for my brain to register it was blood, not paint. Honestly, finding a dead body wasn't as bad as I've always imagined it would be. More weird than scary."

April nodded her agreement. "I get what you're saying. I thought it was paint at first too."

"Hey, maybe you should stay at the house tonight. With a killer on the loose, I don't like the thought of you being alone. It might be a good idea to pack a bag and come to stay, at least until the police catch the culprit."

"Good grief, Mom. I'm a grown woman, for criminy sakes, or have you forgotten? I lived in San Francisco all by myself for years. Pretty sure I can handle staying by myself in scary Pine Bluff." April grimaced and blew an irritated breath out of the side of her mouth. She stared at me a beat before adding, "Or is it more about you not wanting to be alone tonight?"

I shrugged, not wanting to admit she'd hit the nail on the head. "Of course not. I'm fine, and if you are too, it's not a big deal." *I'll just sleep with all the lights on.*

"No, you're right. I guess I don't want to be alone tonight either." April changed her tune. "How about I make us a batch of pancakes tomorrow morning?" She dipped a fry in the sauce and shoved it into her mouth while waiting for a response.

"Sounds good." Relieved neither one of us would be alone tonight, I reached across the table, snagged a fry off April's plate, and ate it quickly, then grabbed my fork and tucked into my pie. Buttery, creamy sweetness exploded in my mouth, taking me right back to my aunt's kitchen. "Yum. Boy, does this ever hit the spot. It tastes exactly like Aunt Alta used to make it." I closed my eyes for a second, savoring the sensation.

"Guess who called me this afternoon?" April pulled me out of my pie-induced bliss.

"How do I know? Hugh Jackman?"

"Don't I wish. No, not quite that exciting." April laughed. "Megan Hill. She's coaching the high school girls' soccer team this fall and needs an assistant coach. She wanted to know if I'm interested."

"Are you? Coaching might be fun for you. Do you think you'll do it?"

April chewed on another fry and nodded. "Yeah, I think I might. We made an appointment to talk about it in more detail on Monday. She'll be in her office at the high school, getting her planning done for the first week of school."

April started playing city league soccer the summer she was nine. Feisty and tough, she was excellent on defense and a great wingman for the strongest kickers on the team. She was named captain of the team her senior year of high school, then later played on an adult league in San Francisco for a few years.

"It seems like a great opportunity, coaching on my high school turf. You know I've never stopped loving the game. I'm glad Megan thought of me." Her green eyes sparkled with excitement.

"I think it's a fabulous idea." I beamed at my daughter, already looking forward to cheering her team on at the games.

I would need a new purple and white knit hat, scarf, and gloves to show off the school colors. So would April. I'd commission Evonne to knit us each a set. And lap blankets. You always needed lap blankets for fall sports in the mountains.

"Speaking of blankets," I said, "I have some news."

April swiveled her head in confusion. "Wait, what? Nobody was talking about blankets."

"Oh, yeah. I guess I was, but apparently not out loud." I laughed and leaned across the table so I wouldn't be overheard. Small towns have big ears. I whispered to my daughter. "I'm not supposed to tell you this, but the police found a pillow and a blanket in the warehouse."

"A pillow and blanket? What in the holy heck?"

I shrugged. "I don't know, but it's strange, right? J. T. said they were wadded up and hidden behind the stack of garden hoses. I don't have the foggiest idea why they'd be back there."

April ran a hand through her pixie-cut red hair. "Do you think Steve's been sneaking off to take a nap in the warehouse?"

"J. T. asked the same question, but no, I can't imagine he was. He's never disappeared during his shift. He even tells me every time he's going to use the restroom, and he's never a minute late for his shift or coming back from lunch. Until today, anyway." I shook my head. "It's weird, but maybe the pillow and blanket have nothing to do with the murder. Still, I don't have a clue why they were there. They were probably in a stroller, and some little kid shoved them back there. The parents are most likely pulling out their hair, trying to figure out what happened to them."

"I'm guessing it's probably something that simple," April agreed.

Keeping my voice low, I told her about snooping in J. T.'s notebook and snapping a picture of the list of people who'd been in Lipstick and Lace this morning. "Kristi Fisher was on the list. She was working as Warren's real estate agent, and when I was walking to work this morning, there was yelling coming from

Elk River Realty. I'm going to drop by and have a chat with Kristi. See what I can find out."

"Mom. Stay out of it. J. T. is more than capable of doing his job," April warned. She pointed a crisp French fry at me. "Why would you think you need to get mixed up in this murder investigation any more than you already are?"

"Because Warren was killed in my store, and J. T. indicated I might be a suspect. Isn't that reason enough? Besides, I'm sure J. T. would be grateful for any help he can get. There're only two other officers on the Pine Bluff force, and they're both young. I can't imagine either of them has any experience investigating a murder." I didn't know that for a fact, but saying it out loud helped me justify what I planned to do.

"Oh, and you do?" April snorted.

"Maybe not, but I've sure read my share of murder mysteries. Carpenter's Corner is closed for a few days at least, and I know how to poke around. I'm going to ask a few questions, for curiosity's sake. How hard can it be?"

"Then you also know poking around in a murder investigation can be dangerous to your health. A person can wind up dead from asking the wrong people too many questions. If you're going to do this, you need to be super careful. Curious and careless tend to go hand in hand. I don't want you to get hurt and have to report back to my siblings how I let you do something so stupid."

"Aha! You did move back to Pine Bluff to keep an eye on me. I knew it." I crossed my arms on the table and glared at her.

My obstinate daughter rolled her eyes at me and glared right back.

"Fine. I promise to be careful. If you're so worried about it, help me out. All good sleuths have a trusty sidekick." I sipped my coffee and raised my eyebrows, waiting for a reply.

April studied me for a minute, then lifted her glass of sweet tea, reached across the table, and clinked it against my coffee mug. "Okay, but at the first hint of danger, we dip out. Deal?"

"Deal." I winked. *Gotcha.*

April's eyes twinkled as she leaned in close. "Okay, now what about Kristi? She was a couple of years behind me in high school. I didn't know her super well, but she's always seemed like the all-American girl—blond, blue-eyed, and bubbly. What I mostly remember is how Kristi was always nice to everyone, whether or not they were in the popular crowd. From what I've seen since I've been back home, she's still the same. I seriously doubt Kristi had anything to do with Warren's death."

"Yeah, I have to agree, but after all the yelling I heard this morning, I think it's worth talking to her anyway. I'm going to pop in there now and see what I can find out." I opened my wallet and tossed a twenty-dollar bill on the table, to cover our snacks. There'd be enough left over for a nice tip for DeAnn. I slid out of the booth and looked at my daughter. "Well? Are you coming?"

April flicked her gaze back and forth between her half-eaten order of fries and my intent stare. Wadding the paper napkin in her lap, she threw it on top of the plate of fries with a huff. "Oh fine, but you owe me another order of fries."

Chapter Seven

The brass bell above the door at Elk River Realty jingled, announcing our presence to the receptionist sitting behind a large maple desk.

"Hi, Marti. Boy, does it ever feel good in here. This heat is ridiculous. I'm sure ready for the cool fall weather to hit. It can't come soon enough." I smiled and, without being too obvious, glanced around for Kristi.

The realty office was welcoming, with walls the color of a sun-kissed wheat field. Rich honey-brown, wide-planked oak floors ran the length of the room, and colorful photographs of local landscapes graced the walls. Arctic air blew from a ceiling-mounted unit. *Geesh. Are they keeping penguins alive in here?*

"Well, hello there." Marti Campbell tore her gaze away from the computer screen on her desk. "Is there something I can help you two with? Are you finally ready to sell that big, beautiful house of yours?"

Marti had been trying to get me to list my house ever since Bob died. Without asking, she'd put me on an email list and sent me daily notifications of smaller houses around town that were for sale. Usually, the email contained a note imploring me to downsize and stressing how my house was too much upkeep for a single, older woman such as myself. *Not today, lady, not today.*

"Oh no. They're going to have to carry me out of there in my coffin." I gritted my teeth. "April and I dropped in hoping to talk with Kristi for a minute or two. Is she in this afternoon?"

I looked around again. Darn. The office behind the reception desk was dark and quiet.

"You missed her. Kristi left a few minutes ago. Was she expecting you this afternoon? I'm sorry if she forgot. It's been a tough day, to say the least." Marti ran a finger down the page of an appointment book on her desk. "I don't see either of your names here."

"No, I didn't have an appointment. It's okay. We'll catch her another time." I bit my lower lip, wanting to ask Marti a few questions, but not knowing how to start.

April had no such qualms. "You mentioned it's been a tough day. You and Kristi must have heard about Warren's death, then?"

Marti nodded. "Chief Dallas came by about an hour ago and filled us in. My poor girl. It really shook her up, not to mention the way that awful man yelled at her this morning." She crossed her arms and narrowed her eyes. "If you ask me, it couldn't have happened to a more deserving man. You can't treat people the way he did and get away with it." She gestured to the two small brown leather chairs placed in front of her desk. "Go ahead and have a seat. You might as well stay for a minute and cool off, since you're here."

Marti had been the receptionist at Elk River Realty from the day it opened. She was the first person anyone coming in to buy or sell a home dealt with. Her desk faced Main Street; not much went on in Pine Bluff undetected by Marti's eagle eye. She loved to lean in slyly and relay the town gossip to anyone who would take a minute to listen. Kristi was Marti's niece, her youngest sister's daughter. It'd been Marti who encouraged Kristi to give real estate a try when the girl was at loose ends after high school. Marti didn't have any kids of her own, but she was a mama bear when it came to her niece—fierce and loyal.

"Who yelled at her? Warren?" April asked, throwing me an inconspicuous wink.

You go, girl. I mentally patted myself on the back for having the foresight to get my fearless daughter involved in my unofficial investigation.

"One and the same. That terrible man barged in here this morning right after I unlocked the door, and he stormed into Kristi's office without even a howdy-do to me. He slammed her door shut, but good grief, he yelled so loud I'm sure half the town heard." Marti's voice, thick from years of chain-smoking, was as deep and low as a foghorn. The stale scent of menthol cigarettes on her breath made my nose twitch.

I nodded in sympathy. "I'll admit, I did hear raised voices coming from the realty office when I was on my way to work this morning. Any idea what Warren was so mad about?"

"Well, I'm not one to gossip," Marti began, leaning in, "and I don't know all the details, but he was yelling about needing to get the deal on the Emery Theater closed as soon as possible. Highcastle wanted Kristi to sign some documents. I heard him say if she didn't do it, he'd find someone who would. Not sure which documents he was referring to, and with Kristi so upset after he left, I didn't ask right away. A few minutes later, she went out to go on a drive and clear her head. By the time she got back, Chief Dallas was here. After he told us about the murder, Kristi was beside herself and needed to go home and lie down. I still haven't had a chance to find out what all the ruckus was about this morning." Marti sighed, settling back in her office chair and crossing her arms over her belly. "I'm glad it's Friday and my poor girl can take time to unwind. She needs to be with those sweet boys of hers and forget this ugliness ever happened."

"Sounds like a good idea. We'll let you get back to work. If you talk to Kristi, give her my best." I turned to April. "Ready to go?"

I fished my purse out from under the chair I'd been sitting in. Before pushing the front door open, I turned back to Marti. "By the way, you seem to have lost an earring." I pinched my right ear to illustrate my point.

Marti rubbed her earlobe, her mouth falling open in surprise. "Oh no!" She fingered the dangly silver earring still attached to her left ear, then caressed the long matching necklace she wore. The earring was beautiful. It featured a turquoise stud with a silver concho dangling from the stud. "Shoot. This is one of my favorite sets. I wonder where in the world I could have lost it." She shuffled a stack of manila files around on her desk, searching for the missing jewelry.

Marti taught square dancing every Wednesday evening at the Sage Creek Grange Hall but dressed the part of a square dance instructor every day. Today she was decked out in a mid-calf denim dress with suede fringe on the yolk, sleeves, and around the bottom of the skirt. She wore tall brown and teal cowboy boots with intricate embroidery and decorative brass studs in a chevron pattern. The turquoise and sterling silver jewelry set topped off the Western outfit and glinted against her tanned skin. Thrice weekly tanning sessions left her skin a deep golden brown, but as wrinkled as an old leather saddle.

"I hate it when an earring gets lost. April and I can help you look for it, if you'd like." And it would give me a reason to poke around the realty office. Maybe Kristi left the documents in question on her desk. A glimpse at them might shed some light on what she and Warren were arguing about.

"Oh no. Thank you, but not to worry. I'm sure it'll show up somewhere. Who knows, maybe I only put one earring on this morning. They say the mind is the first thing to go, you know." Marti laughed brightly and shooed April and me out of the realty office while she reached for the ringing phone on her desk.

Dang it.

Outside, the thunderstorm that had been threatening for the last hour let loose. A bright sheet of lightning flashed a brilliant silver across the gunmetal sky. A deafening crack of thunder boomed seconds behind the lightning before the sky split open, pouring out buckets of rain. Big fat raindrops bounced like little rubber balls when they hit the concrete. In seconds, the gutters flowed as fast as a raging river. It wouldn't have surprised me to see a trout or two splash by. April and I looked at each other and burst out laughing while we made a run for the nearest overhang. We ducked under the burgundy awning in front of the local bookstore, Literally, to wait it out, already soaked to the skin from the ten seconds it took to make it to shelter. I eyeballed a copy of Agatha Christie's *And Then There Were None* in the front window, but restrained myself from going in. The unread stack of books at home was already out of control. One of these days it would probably topple over and kill me, but what a way to go.

"The rain feels so good," April yelled over the crashing thunder. "If I wasn't afraid of getting struck by a bolt of lightning, I'd stand right smack dab in the middle of it."

I broke into a refrain of "Raindrops Keep Fallin' on My Head." A lady scurrying by with a magazine held over her head and dragging a toddler by the wrist gave me a dirty look. "Guess she didn't appreciate my spectacular singing voice." It felt good to laugh after the heaviness of the day.

April and I huddled under the awning and chatted about our visit to Elk River Realty. Not that we'd learned much, but I found it a little odd how Kristi had gone for a drive all by herself to clear her head at the exact time Warren was being knocked over the head with a hammer. Fishy, Mrs. Fisher. April agreed. Of course, J. T. would have found the same information when he talked to Kristi and Marti, so we hadn't managed to uncover anything new. I'd have to keep digging.

Mountain storms passed fast, and this one was no exception. Less than fifteen minutes later, the last raindrop splashed to the ground, and the storm clouds continued their journey west. Steam from the wet road rose in tendrils under the scorching afternoon sun.

"Now the excitement's over, I'm headed to the grocery store to get the chicken for tonight. I made the potato salad last night, so we're all set there." I pushed off the wall and started walking.

Even though I was a terrible cook, and everybody knew it, I still had a few signature dishes up my sleeve. Both my sisters and I made potato salad exactly the way Mama'd taught us. It was delicious and a staple at all family picnics. The salad was one of the few things I cooked that I'd never managed to screw up. So far.

April broke into a jog to catch up with me. "'Kay. I'll pick you up about seven. The park's going to fill fast tonight, and I want to make sure we get there early enough to get a good view of the stage. Maybe six thirty would be better. What do you think?"

"Yep, let's do six thirty. It'll give us enough time to eat before the music starts. See you then." I saluted my daughter and hurried up Grand Street to the grocery store. There was plenty of time to pick up the groceries and get a couple of chapters in my book read before the concert tonight.

Chapter Eight

Mill Street Market was a busy place on this late summer afternoon. The only grocery store in town, it was a small mom-and-pop store where a person could get most anything they needed without having to drive twenty miles to a bigger chain store. There was even a meat counter where the owners' stocked meats from local ranches; a fantastic produce section; and a deli serving everything from fried chicken to lasagna.

I grabbed a handheld shopping basket and navigated through the other shoppers, headed for the deli counter. Four people stood at the counter in front of me, so I took my place in line. The tantalizing smell of fried chicken made my stomach rumble. I really should've eaten more than a slice of pie for lunch. I craned my neck to see around the rear end of the woman standing in front of the glass display case. Jo Jo potato wedges called my name, and cream cheese-filled jalapeño poppers left my mouth watering. When it was my turn, I ordered twelve pieces of fried chicken, a half-pound of potato wedges, and six poppers. The poppers would be my afternoon snack as soon as I got home.

Maybe before. One of these days, I was going to have to stop eating so much junk. Today was not that day.

I took my goodies and started for the checkout counter, but a watermelon in someone's shopping cart made me pause. Was it even a true picnic without sweet red watermelon juice dripping off your chin? I changed course and headed over to the produce section instead.

A giant stack of Hermiston melons were piled on a display stand. No other melon came close to the sweet goodness of a Hermiston, in my humble opinion. But how could you tell which one was the sweetest? I gave one melon a good solid thwack.

"Hey, be gentle. What'd that watermelon ever do to you?"

I turned to find Bill standing beside me, perusing the watermelon stack.

I grinned. "The smack was for what it was thinking about doing." I winked at my friend. "Isn't thumping them how you're supposed to tell if they're good or not?"

Bill grinned back, made a fist, and knocked on a few melons, as if he were trying to wake them. I laughed and thwacked a few more with an open palm.

"Uh . . . there's a little too much fun going on over here." Roy Dejean, the produce manager for Mill Street Market, flashed a smile over his shoulder as he reeled up the spray hose he'd been using to mist the green leaf lettuce. Tall and slender, with light-brown hair beginning to thin on top, Roy wore a green apron over a pressed, white button-down shirt and black slacks. His outfit was finished with black oxford work shoes that seemed to be the standard foot attire for grocery store employees everywhere. His military-short haircut and clean-shaven face gave the impression of a solid and dependable man. He was someone who could be counted on to step up when assistance was needed.

"Do you need help picking one out? I could give you a quick lesson on how to find the sweetest melon in the bunch, if you'd like," Roy offered.

"Sure, I'd love help."

Bill shrugged but stuck around for the lesson.

"First, study the pile for a minute. Find a dark-green melon, but not one too shiny."

I studied the green globes, then moved around the display to stand by the melon I liked best. Bill did the same, choosing a watermelon on the opposite side of the stack from the one I'd picked out.

"Good, now pick it up. It should feel fairly heavy for its size. The weight indicates the melon is full of water and will be juicy."

Bill and I hefted the watermelons into our arms.

"Now turn it over. Do you see a yellow spot? The darker yellow, the better. That's called the field spot. It tells you the watermelon ripened in the field, on the vine. A white spot, or no spot at all, means they picked the melon before it was ripe, and it's probably not going to be as sweet as it should be."

I flipped my melon over, revealing a creamy yellow field spot. "Perfect." I felt like I'd won a contest. "Thank you, Roy. That was fantastic. You should really think about holding mini classes here at the grocery store, to teach people how to pick the best fruit. I'd come for sure."

"I'll give it some thought. Enjoy your melons," he called over his shoulder as he disappeared through the black vinyl swinging doors leading into the cold storage area of the store.

"Cool. If he's right, Kim'll be tickled when I bring home such a good melon. She'll think she finally has me trained." Bill loaded the watermelon he'd picked into his shopping cart, then crossed his arms across his broad chest, tucked his hands into his armpits, and planted his feet in a wide stance. He resembled a bulldog, hackles raised and ready to protect his property. "Tell me what in the holy tarnation happened at the hardware store today."

"Ah. You've heard about the murder, have you?"

"Yep. Stopped by Ernie's Garage when I finished at the job site today. It's all they were talking about. Said a masked man came in and shot Highcastle right in front of you. Is that right?"

"What? No. Good grief."

News traveled fast in Pine Bluff. It got passed from one person to another, like a game of telephone, until the story was barely recognizable from the reality of what had actually occurred. At least they still had the name of the dead guy right. I wouldn't have been a bit surprised to hear it was me who had met my Maker.

I gave Bill a rundown of the actual events. "The whole thing's crazy and kind of a blur in my mind right now." Tears welled in my eyes before I could stop them, but I darned well wasn't going to cry like a baby in front of Bill. I sniffed hard and rubbed at the end of my nose. "Allergies getting to me." I tried to explain away my watery eyes.

"Even though I couldn't stand the guy, it's a terrible shame someone killed him here in our little town. It makes you wonder who did it and makes you look at everyone a little sideways." Bill shook his head, trying to wrap his mind around the facts I'd relayed to him.

"True story, but I'm bound and determined to put it out of my mind for the rest of the day. I'm really looking forward to unwinding and listening to some good music in the park tonight." I glanced at the watermelon I'd picked out and pushed my glasses back up my nose, with a frown. "Oh, dang it. I forgot I'm walking. This thing's a bit heavy to be carrying two blocks. Would you mind giving me a lift home?"

"No problem. The wife texted me a shopping list, so let me grab a few more things, and I'll meet you at the truck."

"Sounds good. Thanks."

All the talk about murder reminded me Roy was on the list of people who'd been in Lipstick and Lace this morning. I pulled out my phone to double-check and noticed I'd missed two calls. Both were from the same number, and not one I recognized. If someone wanted to talk to me, they could leave a voicemail. I deleted the missed calls and opened my gallery to take a look at the picture I'd snapped of the list in J. T.'s notebook. Yep. Like I'd thought, Roy had been in Darlene's boutique today. I wished I'd thought to ask him about it. So much for not thinking about the murder anymore today.

I milled around the produce section, hoping to get the chance to talk to him again. As luck would have it, the produce manager came back through the swinging doors while I was squeezing the avocados. Before I had a chance to decide how to approach him, a man breezed by, not stopping until his nose was a hair from Roy's. The guy was breathing fast and talking in a closed-mouth, tight whisper. His right arm was in a plaster cast from his shoulder to his wrist, with a blue sling and a neck collar holding his wrist to chest level. I kept my head down and shuffled closer so

I could better hear what was being said. I hadn't gotten a good look at the man's face yet, but I was pretty certain I'd never seen him around Pine Bluff before.

"Did you do it? Did you get the job done?" The guy was half an inch from Roy's face, their noses almost bumping. "Tell me. I need to know how much trouble we're in. You better not have told anybody." Agitated, the stranger moved his feet nonstop in a series of nervous dance steps as he leaned in close to Roy. He swept off his ball cap with his free hand, revealing tousled, dark, wavy hair.

"Not here," Roy growled. He scanned the store, his eyes skimming right over the top of my head as if I were invisible. Roy motioned for the man to follow him, and the pair disappeared through the swinging doors.

Holy fright. What was that about? Did it have anything to do with Warren's murder? I glanced around, but nobody else in the produce section of the store seemed to have paid any attention to the exchange. It obviously wasn't a good time to talk to Roy. I hurried to the checkout stand.

Bill was already waiting for me in the parking lot. He swung the passenger side door of his truck wide open and got busy clearing a space for me to sit. An aluminum clipboard, a yellow hard hat, a neon high-visibility vest, and a few small hand tools got tossed from the front seat into the back seat of his gray, extended cab Chevy work truck. "Sorry about the mess," Bill commented with a chuckle. "This thing isn't only a truck; it's my mobile office too. Probably have more tools in here than I have at the job site."

"You never know when you might need to fix something."

Once he'd made room for me, I rolled my watermelon onto the floorboard, reached around and took hold of the grab bar, and pulled my five-foot-two frame into the cab of the truck.

With my house only two blocks from Mill Street Market, it seemed like I was getting out of the truck almost as soon as I'd climbed in.

"Thanks for giving me and my watermelon a lift. Are you and Kim coming back into town for the concert later? Blue Mountain Thunder is playing tonight." I reached into the truck and lifted my groceries and melon off the floor.

"Nah, too many people for my liking. By Friday night, I want to enjoy a beer in my own backyard. Going to fire up the barbecue and grill those rib-eye steaks I bought. Some corn on the cob from Kim's garden too." He rubbed his belly in anticipation. "Might even mow the lawn after we eat. Get an early start on the weekend's yard work. You guys have fun, though. Stay safe, and don't hesitate to call if you need anything. See ya soon." Bill raised his hand in a backward goodbye as he drove away.

Turning to head into the house, I paused. Forty years and I was still proud to call this big brick house home. A cobblestone path led to the wide concrete wraparound porch, the perfect place to enjoy the breeze on a warm summer night. White, fluted columns supported the sloping porch roof and kept the rain off, making it possible to sit outside during three seasons of the year. The porch ended where the round tower room began. It wasn't a true tower, but instead a rounded room off the living room, but it made the outside of the house look like something out of a fairy tale. When the kids were young, they'd called our house Carpenter's Castle. I'd have to ask them if they still referred to it the same way.

Hammers and Homicide

My house took up a large corner lot, with a dense hedge of lilac bushes creating a nice buffer and providing privacy from the street on the east side of the house. The flowers smelled incredible when they bloomed in the spring. An ancient elm tree stood guard in the front yard. Its branches stretched wide, throwing deep, luscious shade on the front of the house all summer long.

Above the porch roof, a dormer with a single, multipaned window looked out from the upstairs apartment. The view from the upstairs window was spectacular in all seasons. It faced west and was high enough that you could watch the sunset behind the Blue Mountains.

The first blacksmith in Pine Bluff built the house, and it was one of the oldest houses in town. At one point, a large barn and a carriage house stood on the property. The barn was long gone by the time Bob and I purchased the place, but the carriage house still stood. We'd converted it into a small, one-bedroom cottage I rented out to an elderly lady named Bertha Smith. Smitty for short.

At one point, I'd looked into what it would take to have the brick house added to the National Register of Historic Places. It turned out to be a lot more work than I wanted to deal with, and when I found out about all the stringent codes I'd have to adhere to, I decided it wasn't worth it to have the prestigious brass plaque on the wall.

I closed my eyes and inhaled the sweet scent of the orange nasturtiums cascading from the wooden planter boxes under the windows. Home. I shifted the watermelon in my arms and headed into the house, hoping today was the day my deceased husband would show up.

Chapter Nine

"Bob? Are you here?" I set my groceries on the kitchen counter. "I could really use your company right now."

Of course, he didn't answer, so I got busy cutting the watermelon into chunks and imagined him strolling into the kitchen for a chat. In my imagination, Bob wore jeans and a soft, camel-colored wool sweater, too warm for the August heat. It'd been his favorite outfit and what I always imagined him wearing, no matter the weather. His striking blue eyes twinkled under pewter-gray hair. Suddenly, his signature scent of sawdust and coffee floated through the air, and a tingling sensation brushed my cheek. My hand jerked to my face in surprise, caressing the tingly spot. What was that? Was Bob's spirit in the room with me? I decided to pretend he was, and launched into a rundown of my day.

"Today's been unusual, to say the least. I spent a lot of time with J. T. this morning." I rinsed off the knife and filled a bowl with wedges of the sweet watermelon. "Before you ask, no I didn't go and get myself arrested. How could you even think that?"

I covered the leftover half of the melon with plastic wrap and put it in the refrigerator, then took a small purple Fiestaware plate out of the cupboard and poured my jalapeño poppers onto it. Sliding onto the bench seat at the breakfast table, I bit into a popper.

In my mind, I heard Bob launch into a tirade about my eating habits and my sky-high cholesterol levels. With my mouth full, I stopped chewing and looked at the half-eaten, deep-fried, battered jalapeño, stuffed with cream cheese, in my hand. The guilt I felt over Bob's death hadn't translated to a change in my own eating habits one bit. In fact, with no one to cook for, they'd only gotten worse. It was easier to make a pit stop for a burger than try to cook for myself. My diet consisted of iconic American food—burgers and fries and cherry pies—with an occasional green salad thrown in for good measure. The way I ate, I should've been the size of the Goodyear Blimp. Sure, I carried a few extra pounds and could be described as a bit chubby, but at sixty-two, I still burned off more calories than I consumed.

Instead of pushing the poppers aside, I crammed another one into my mouth and ignored my husband's imagined rant about my blocked arteries and premature death. Didn't I know the kids and grandkids still needed me to stick around for a while longer? I kept chewing but got less and less enjoyment out of my fried food with every word my guilty conscience tossed my way. Spending too much time alone in my head these days was never a good thing. It was the main reason why I usually ate in front of the television set.

I swatted at the air around me. "Get out of my head, Bob. How can I miss you if you won't go away?"

Of course, I didn't mean it. But then again, when I'd imagined Bob's ghost keeping me company, it never occurred to me he'd harangue me about my eating habits. The scent of sawdust that had been swirling through the kitchen all but disappeared.

"No, I'm sorry. You know I don't want you to go away. You're right. I'll put more thought into what I eat. Please stay. I really want to talk with you about what happened today."

Geesh. If my kids could see me now, they'd have me committed to the loony bin before I had time to blink. I glanced over my shoulder guiltily, glad nobody could hear me talking to myself. Satisfied I was alone, I took a deep breath and plunged ahead, telling my nonexistent husband every detail of the day's events.

"So that's why I spent a lot of time with J. T. today." I headed over to the sink to finish cleaning up the mess I'd made cutting the watermelon. "Of course, J. T. needs help to solve the case, so between that and the fact the murder took place in Carpenter's Corner, I guess I'm involved."

The plate and water glass I'd left on the table shimmied and shook, rattling together and causing me to jump while the hair on the back of my neck stood on end. Was that Bob's way of telling me his hackles were up at this conversation? I knew if he were here, he'd be lecturing me about how I didn't have any business getting involved. He'd be wanting to protect me like I was some kind of fragile doll.

"Listen here, mister," I told the empty room, "I'm perfectly capable of making decisions for myself. You've been gone for three years, and besides the fact that I was a tangled mess with missing you, I've done a pretty good job of running our business and taking care of myself. I don't need you rushing in to protect me like I'm some simpering female without a lick of sense."

I imagined Bob setting his jaw, arms crossed while he glared at me.

I tried to slam the cupboard door, but the soft-close feature wouldn't give me the satisfaction. "J. T. didn't ask me to help, for crying out loud."

I hated to admit it was my own curiosity that had me sticking my nose into the murder case, and not any hint of a request for help from the police chief, but imaginary Bob wasn't about to let it drop. I felt his displeasure swirling through the air.

"Yes, I know I don't have any experience as a detective, and I know getting involved with a murder investigation is dangerous." I put the knife I'd been using to cut the watermelon in the dishwasher. "But the fact remains the man was killed inside our store, and the whole thing feels personal to me. I need to do all I can to protect my business and make sure Pine Bluff is still the safe little town it's always been. I don't know why you can't understand why I feel compelled to do this."

I knew if Bob were really standing in the kitchen with me, he'd tell me I was being emotional and not thinking straight; that he was worried about me and that I needed to leave the investigation up to the police. Nothing gets my hackles up faster than someone telling me I can't do something. Even though I was only imagining the conversation, it only made me more determined than ever to get myself firmly involved in solving the mystery of who murdered Warren. I could set my jaw and plant my feet with the best of them.

At the same time, I could understand Bob's point. It's not like I'm unreasonable. "I'll be careful. I promise. You need to trust me."

I pictured Bob running his hands over his face and wishing out loud for a couple of fingers of bourbon to sip on right now.

Chapter Ten

Steam Engine Park was already full of people when April and I dug our picnic supplies out of the back seat of her car and slammed the doors shut. I carried a yellow, reusable market bag filled with paper plates, napkins, and plastic silverware. A green bag of sour cream–and–onion potato chips stuck out of the top of the bag. April pulled a blue and white cooler behind her, and we both had lawn chairs strapped across our shoulders and banging into the back of our legs as we walked across the park.

"Looks like practically everybody in town is here tonight," April observed.

The lawn in front of the bandstand was littered with people eager to enjoy a night of live music. Some sat on lawn chairs while others sprawled across blankets spread on the thick green grass. Kids ran back and forth between the playground equipment and their parents, giggling and squealing with their friends.

A slight hint of smoke wafted by in the breeze, mingling with the smell of a hundred picnic dinners. "You smell smoke?" I asked my daughter. "I hope the storm this afternoon didn't start a fire. Lord knows it's dry enough. We've been lucky so far this year."

"I think it's somebody's grill getting started."

Some years the forest fires were so bad, the entire valley filled with smoke as thick as London fog. You could barely see your hand in front of your face, and breathing was next to impossible. During those times, the air quality got dangerous, and the news reporters suggested people should stay indoors with the windows and doors closed. What the reporters in the city didn't understand was country life still had to go on. Livestock needed to be fed, and hay still had to be brought in out of the fields. In a rural area where so many counted on the land for their livelihoods, few people had the option of staying inside. With any luck, this year's fire season would be an anticlimactic one.

"Looks like a perfect spot over there." I pointed to the right of the bandstand where there was still an empty patch of grass. "Close enough to the stage, but I'll be able to see the crowd at the same time. It'll be perfect."

"Why do you need to see the crowd? We're here to listen to the band, not people watch."

"I'm going to people watch. See if I can suss out any new suspects."

April scowled, pulling at her black cotton T-shirt and fanning it around to circulate the air trapped under her shirt. "Seriously? Can't we sit and enjoy the concert tonight, Nancy Drew?" She huffed but followed me to the spot I'd picked.

When you've lived in the same town for fifty-three years, like I have, it's hard to walk across a packed park quickly. Tonight was even more brutal than usual since the rumor mill was in full swing. Most people had heard something about the murder and knew I was the one who'd found Warren's body. People grabbed my hand as I tried to hurry by. Everyone clamored to hear a tidbit or two about the most excitement, albeit tragic, Pine Bluff had experienced in a long time. Now, I was a talker, but by the time April and I finally made it to the spot where I wanted to sit, even I was tired of flapping my jaws.

We pulled our lawn chairs out of the carry bags and got them set up as the sun dipped behind the trees. Rays of orange sunlight spread through the branches in a final, glorious display. I took a minute to breathe and admire the sunset before opening the cooler and unpacking our picnic.

"Holy cow, Mom. How much fried chicken did you buy? Are you planning on feeding the entire town?" April gaped at the three plastic containers of chicken I'd pulled out of the cooler.

"It's only a twelve-piece. It's not too much. Ernie and Evonne might join us, and I want to have enough food to share if they haven't eaten. Leftovers are never a bad thing either."

"I think you've got every base covered." April laughed, shaking her head in amusement. "We definitely won't go hungry."

I dropped to my knees and continued to rummage around in the cooler. I grabbed the market bag and dumped it upside down on the picnic blanket. A heap of paper plates and napkins lay on the ground. A shaker of salt rolled under my chair.

"Well, for crying in the buttermilk!" I smacked my thighs with the palm of my hands in frustration. "Good thing I brought so much chicken, because it looks like I forgot the blasted potato salad."

"You've got to be kidding me." April jumped out of her chair to take a look for herself.

"Go ahead and paw through the cooler. You won't find it."

April was already worried I was starting to get forgetful, and this was going to seal the deal. A couple of weeks ago, I'd gone grocery shopping and hadn't realized I didn't have my purse with me until I was standing at the checkout counter. I called April, who was working only a block away, so she ran over and rescued me. Then a few days ago, I'd left my phone at home, and she couldn't get a hold of me. I wasn't buying it, since Carpenter's Corner had had a landline with the same phone number for forty years. If April couldn't remember the number, maybe she was the one getting forgetful. Besides, everyone forgot things from time to time, and I'd been distracted lately, what with trying to figure out if Bob was hanging around the house and all. Of course, I couldn't tell April I was doing my best to get her dad's ghost to visit, or she'd be one hundred percent convinced I'd lost every one of my marbles. I wasn't so sure myself. I sat back on my haunches while my daughter dug through the cooler like she'd find the potato salad hiding under a plastic fork.

"You're right. It's not here. No worries—the chicken, watermelon, and chips are plenty. We can have potato salad for a midnight snack later tonight." April shrugged. "My mouth has only been watering all day thinking about your delicious salad. Oh well," she teased, "not the end of the world. I've had bigger disappointments—just can't remember when."

I smacked her lightly on the arm. "Thanks. It's not like I feel bad enough without you pouring lemon juice into the wound. I sure hope I didn't leave it sitting out on the counter in this heat. Good night!"

"Good night, dear," April replied, channeling her father and teasing me about my weird habit of using the term *good night* as an exclamation.

I didn't mind being the butt of my family's jokes as long as they teased me with good intentions. One evening years ago, when the kids were all still home, I'd been going on and on about something the city council had proposed that I didn't agree with. I finished my rant with my trademark, "Good night!" Bob calmly replied, "Good night, dear." The kids rolled on the floor, laughing until they cried. Ever since, whenever I let loose with my favorite exclamation, whoever was in earshot replied with Bob's "Good night, dear" response. It never ceased to tickle my funny bone and lighten the moment.

Forgetting all about the missing potato salad, we filled our plates with the food that had managed to make it to the picnic. I rescued the salt shaker from under my chair, gave a liberal sprinkle to the chicken breast on my plate, and sat to eat, with only a slight thought about shoving more unhealthy fried food down my gullet. Watermelon is a fruit, after all. At least I was eating something healthy.

Eager to tell April about what I'd witnessed in the produce section at Mill Street Market that afternoon, I scooted my chair closer to hers. With all the talking and laughter around us, I wasn't too worried about being overheard, but I kept my voice low anyway while I filled her in.

When I finished telling my story, April drew her eyebrows together and frowned. "How in the world did they not notice you standing there? Are you sure they didn't? You promised me you would be careful, remember?" She crunched on a potato chip and glared at me.

I took a bite of my chicken, licking my fingers before I answered. "Interestingly enough, since I let my hair go gray, younger people tend to overlook me. It's like I'm invisible, hiding right in plain sight. Trust me, those men did not pay any attention to me."

Most of the time it made me mad when young people looked right past me, assuming I didn't have a relevant thought in my head because I had gray hair. Today was the first time that particular irritation had come in handy. Being a card-carrying member of AARP had its benefits.

"I don't believe for a second they didn't see you." April shook her head in denial while licking potato chip salt off her fingers. "You're kind of hard to ignore."

I shot her a wry, one-sided smile. "Unfortunately, it's true." I shrugged, changing the subject back to the murder. "You know, Roy was in Lipstick and Lace this morning. His name is on the list from J. T.'s notebook. The entire exchange between him and the other guy was suspicious. They were up to something, and I'm betting it was murder."

April clasped her hands together and pressed them against her forehead. "But why would Roy kill Warren?" She slid her gaze my way and looked at me through the triangle of her fingers. "What possible motivation could a grocery store clerk have for killing a real estate developer who is brand new in town? Unless they knew each other from somewhere else, I suppose, but Roy has lived in Pine Bluff his entire life, as far as I know."

"Doesn't make much sense to me either, but we need to add him to our list of suspects." I dug a bottle of sweet tea out of the cooler, wiping the condensation off with a paper napkin. "Want one?" I asked, holding the bottle out to my daughter.

"Sure, though I think I could use something a little stronger. Do you have the Long Island version in that magic cooler of yours?" April teased. She opened the bottle of tea and took a long, cool swallow. "All right, I need a recap." She twisted the cap back on her tea and settled it in the cup holder on the arm of her chair.

"You found Warren's body a little after ten this morning. The police tell you they found a bloody footprint and, weirdly, a rogue blanket and pillow in Carpenter's Corner warehouse. It looks like the murder weapon was an old framing hammer. The hammer could have come from anywhere. We know Kristi got into an argument with Warren earlier in the morning. We also know she was in Darlene's shop at some point, and was supposedly on a drive all by herself most of the morning, leaving her without an alibi."

April paused, tapping a finger against her chin. "Then there's the whole sketchy episode with Roy and an unknown man. So far, those are the suspects on your radar, correct? Kristi, Roy, and mystery man." She held up three fingers.

I squinted into the setting sun. "You're mostly correct, except you left a couple of people off the list." I held up five fingers to contradict April's count of three. "There are five viable suspects as far as I'm concerned."

"Five? Who're the other two?" April asked, her voice squeaky with surprise.

Eyeing my daughter over the top of my round glasses, I let out a deep breath. "I hate to say it, but one of them is Steve. He was so late this morning. Showing up right after I discovered the body is suspicious at best, don't you think? Then he disappeared again for a while when you and I were talking with J. T. He said he was out back, checking to see if he'd locked his car, remember? Didn't sit right with me. I could almost smell the lie." I pushed my glasses back up the bridge of my nose. "Something's fishy about that guy."

April nodded her agreement. "Yeah, now that I think about it, you're right. He was acting super strange, even for Steve. I mean, he was still buttoning his shirt when he finally came in, all in a big rush and out of breath, like he'd been running." She paused, looking thoughtful. "Yep. Add Steve to the list. Who else are you suspicious of?"

"Not sure if *suspicious* is the right word. Distrustful, maybe," I answered. "Darlene." Of course, I didn't trust the flamboyant and prickly woman on the best of days. She had a way of getting under my skin.

"Darlene? Why?" April leaned over and plucked a loose napkin off the ground, then dug around in my purse until she found an ink pen. She wrote "Suspects" at the top of the napkin, with an underline that tore right through the thin paper. Underneath the line, she scribbled down the names of the first four people.

"Well, she told me she'd started dating Warren, and she was already bound and determined to keep him. She thought he was here to rescue her from this Podunk town, as she put it."

"Which is exactly why she wouldn't have killed him. Dead men don't rescue damsels in distress."

"Hang on—hear me out. What if Warren broke it off with her? She admitted he was in Lipstick and Lace this morning. Did he tell her it was over? Or what if Darlene found out he was married or had a girlfriend somewhere else? Could it have made her mad enough to whack him over the head with a hammer?" I threw my hands in the air and shook my head. "I don't know. It's another theory I've been kicking around. I'm probably crazy, and there's nothing to it."

"We all know you're a little nuts," April teased, "but you might be on to something. I don't know Darlene well enough to know if she has it in her to kill, but the woman is definitely a piece of work." She added Darlene as number five on the suspect list.

*　*　*

Forty-five minutes and three slices of watermelon later, Ernie and Evonne found their way through the crowd and set up their lawn chairs next to April's and mine. The first strains of "Ring of Fire" thumped out of the speakers. The next thing I knew, I was singing along. I glanced at April, who swayed to the music, with her eyes closed and her pixie face pointed at the evening sky. All the years she'd lived in San Francisco, I'd worried constantly about her. It was a gigantic relief to have her back home and watch the tension of city life melt away from her slight shoulders. I was perfectly aware she was a grown woman and more capable than most, and I knew my worry was unfounded, but a mother never stopped being concerned about her kids, no matter how old they got.

"Mom, I can feel you staring at me. Knock it off. Pay attention to the music." April scolded me with a slight smile.

"I can't help it. You're too darn cute, April Bean." I used her childhood nickname, knowing it would irritate her even more.

As a newborn, she had been a tiny little thing. The first time Bob held her, he'd remarked how she was such a little bean. The nickname morphed into April Bean, and she obliged by staying bean-sized her entire life. We joked she was small but feisty, so she must have come from a can of spicy chili beans.

"I'm so glad you're home." I leaned over and gave my daughter a kiss on the cheek. Being the graceful person I am, I leaned a hair too far and ended up tipping butt over teakettle until I sprawled in the grass with my chair on my upturned rump like a one-person tent.

From my personal cave, I heard my daughter and friends jump to their feet. Someone pried the chair off my derriere, and I pawed around in the grass until my fingers found my glasses. Unbroken, thank goodness. Not a single soul asked if I'd hurt myself. They couldn't because they were all laughing so hard they couldn't get the words out. I rolled onto my back and held an arm straight in the air.

"If you all could control yourselves, I'd appreciate a helping hand."

The trio howled even louder. Ernie doubled over and slapped his thighs in merriment. I glared. It looked like I was going to have to find myself some new best friends. Not sure what I'd do about the traitor of a daughter. I rolled back over, pushed my abused body to my hands and knees, then slowly stood and took an assessment. Every piece and part seemed to be working correctly.

"You should have seen yourself, Mom." April wiped her eyes, talking between giggles. "It all happened in slow motion. You looked like a turtle, all balled up under your chair."

The laughter had died down somewhat, but with April's comment, Ernie and Evonne guffawed again. Nothing hurt except my pride, and the laughter was contagious. Before I knew it, I was hee-hawing right along with them.

"Glad I could provide tonight's comic relief."

We stifled our laughter when the last strains of the song ended, and the lead singer of Blue Mountain Thunder introduced the band.

"Hello, Pine Bluff!" Dressed all in black to emulate Johnny Cash, he enthusiastically greeted the town as cheers rang through the air. "Now, I understand there's been a tragedy today, and we truly appreciate all y'all coming out despite the bad news. Your police chief has asked to say a few words before we get going in full force. Chief Dallas? Come on up."

J. T. crossed the stage, looking like he could be one of the band members. Tonight, he was decked out in black snakeskin cowboy boots, dark blue jeans, a hand-tooled leather belt, and a white Western-style shirt with pearl snaps, sleeves rolled to his elbows. A gray Stetson hat perched on his dark hair. I glanced at April.

The girl's still googly-eyed over J. T., even though she'd never admit it. And I wasn't about to mention it, or April would be running fast in the opposite direction in a minute flat. As a teenager, April had nursed a huge crush on the charismatic high school football star. She thought she'd hidden it well, but we all knew.

Now that they were adults, I'd like nothing better than to see my daughter settle down with someone like J. T. The man was strong and reliable, tough on the outside but sweet as pie on the inside. He and his college sweetheart had divorced a handful of years ago, so I hoped the time was finally right for April and him to spark a romance. The fact that J. T. was a local boy was an added bonus. With April back, I wanted to keep her around. Even if her secret motive for moving back to Pine Bluff was to keep an eye on her lunatic of a mother, it was nice to have her home.

"Good evening," J. T. said. "By now, most of you have heard there was a murder in town this morning. The victim was Warren Highcastle. He's a real estate developer who was in town working on buying and renovating the Emery Theater."

A few shocked exclamations floated through the air from members of the community who hadn't heard about the murder.

"The victim's body was found in the bathroom Carpenter's Corner shares with Lipstick and Lace. While we're not releasing any other details at this time, I want to assure you we're working hard to determine who is responsible. We believe we'll be able to make an arrest soon. We're asking if anyone knows anything—if you've observed any strange behavior around town the last few days, please report it. We don't think you are in any danger, but please be diligent and pay attention to your surroundings. The Greenwood police force has generously agreed to loan us a few of their officers, so we have extra patrols on duty tonight. We will update the public as more information becomes available. Please, try to relax and enjoy the show tonight. Thank you." J. T. dipped his head in a nod at the audience. "Now, back to Blue Mountain Thunder. Aren't these guys the best? Enjoy!"

All was quiet as the police chief stepped off the stage. The townspeople looked around at one another, wondering if one of their own could've killed Warren. A feeling of unease filled the air, something Pine Bluff residents weren't used to. Several families called their kids back from the playground, making them sit on quilts at the feet of the adults instead of running and playing hide-and-seek in the dark with their friends like they usually did on concert nights.

Blue Mountain Thunder took back the stage, and the Johnny Cash songs flowed into the evening air. After a few minutes, people relaxed, singing along with the band once again.

Evonne reached over and squeezed my hand. My best friend wore her dark, salt-and-pepper hair short, like a jaunty cap. A pair of colorful and whimsical hand-painted reading glasses hung on a beaded chain around her neck, brushing against a blue-and-white-striped button-down cotton shirt she wore over a pair of faded denim-blue capri jeans. "I'm sorry you had to deal with that this morning."

After already telling my story to half the town, I appreciated Evonne's simple support and how she didn't seem to need to hear all the juicy details.

"I made a raspberry rhubarb pie today. Ernie has it there in the cooler." Evonne pointed to the red and white ice chest her husband had his feet propped on. "Tell me when you're ready for a slice."

"Uh . . . is now too soon?" I was already drooling at the thought of Evonne's luscious pie. "How about a piece now and another one a bit later?"

Evonne was famous in Pine Bluff for her delicious pies. Whenever any group hosted a bake sale, they hit her up for a dozen or more. Her pies were always the first to go, flying off the table as soon as they were set out. If anyone asked, I'd be hard-pressed to pick a favorite, but her raspberry rhubarb sat solidly somewhere in the top ten.

Evonne smacked her husband on the arm to get his attention. "Dig out the pie and a handful of paper plates, will you?" It wasn't a question, but instead a gentle command. "April, are you ready for a piece?"

"More than ready. In fact, I thought you'd never ask."

With a slice of tart, tangy pie in my hand, I scanned the crowd. Darlene sat in the middle of the crowd with a group of friends. Her dark head was thrown back, and her mouth was wide open, laughing at something one of her friends was saying.

"Darlene doesn't appear to be upset enough about Warren's death to need to stay home and nurse her wounds tonight." I leaned over to whisper in April's ear, careful to not upend my chair this time. With a subtle nod, I pointed out where Darlene was sitting. "Looks like the river of tears dammed up nicely. I wonder if it was all an act for the police's sake?"

"Could be. I remember she was a talented actress in high school. She played the leading role in a few of the drama club's plays." April wrote "drama club" next to Darlene's name on the list of suspects.

Darlene had been a few years ahead of April in school. The two didn't run in the same circles, but Pine Bluff was a small town. If nothing else, the students at least knew one another's names and faces.

I continued to scan the crowd. Kristi sat right in front of the stage with her husband, Travis, and their three kids. Her Aunt

Marti was with them as usual. The Fisher family had a blanket spread on the ground, with a red cooler open beside it. The boys munched on hoagie sandwiches. Kristi and Travis sat close together, hands entwined. Marti pulled the youngest boy off the ground and launched him into a country dance swing. They both grinned ear to ear as Marti's teal skirt swirled around them. The two other Fisher boys jumped up and down, eager for a turn to dance with their great-aunt. Nothing seemed amiss there.

Twisting around in my chair, I finally spied Roy standing by himself at the far edge of the crowd. His arms were crossed over his chest. He looked uncomfortable, on edge, like he was ready to fly away at any given second. Several times, he turned and looked at the parking lot behind him, like he was watching for someone. He reminded me of a wary rabbit. I squinted, trying to see better through the gathering dusk. Roy gave a final sweep of the park before stalking to his truck. He pulled out of the parking lot, a belt in the truck's engine squealing and gravel flying out from under his tires.

I wonder what he's up to. For a split second, I considered grabbing April's keys and following Roy, but the promise I'd made to Bob about being careful rang in my head. Plus, his taillights were long gone. I'd never catch him now. I'd have to be quicker next time.

Steve was nowhere to be seen, but it didn't surprise me one bit. It wasn't like he'd ever shown up for music in the park any other time. Frankly, it'd be weird if he were here tonight.

A warm wind rustled the leaves in the big oak trees as the sky darkened. Stars were beginning to twinkle in the midnight-blue sky. The golden smell of a late summer evening drifted by on the breeze, bringing the scent of ripe wheat and freshly mown hay. Good music blared from the stage, and I sat sandwiched between my youngest daughter and my best friend. If not for the dead man in my hardware store today, it would've been the perfect August night. I sighed. Murder put a huge damper on things, for sure.

"We have a special treat for you tonight," announced the Johnny Cash impersonator on the bandstand. "How many of you know your own police chief is a talented musician?" He waited for the cheer that erupted from the crowd to die down. "I've been after him to play with us forever, and tonight he's finally agreed to bless us with his presence. Let's hear it for J. T. Dallas!"

"Really?" April's eyebrows shot to the sky, and she sat straight as a board in her chair. "No wonder he's dressed so nice tonight."

"I think all those Dallas boys have some sort of musical talent. Back in the day, J. T.'s dad and a couple of cousins played guitar and banjo for all the town dances at the rodeo grounds. Ernie and Evonne here tore up the dance floor every Saturday night. We sure knew how to have a good time back then, didn't we?" I grinned at my friends.

"And we might could again." Ernie leaned forward and set his can of soda on the ground beside the cooler. He heaved his bulk out of the lawn chair and extended a hand to his bride. "My dear, may I have this dance?"

"You may." Evonne's face lit up with delight. She let Ernie pull her out of her chair. Once on her feet, she danced a quick jig. "Be back in a few." She winked before following her husband to the grassy dance area in front of the stage. Ernie grabbed her hand and sent her twirling even before the first notes of the song started to play.

When J. T. crossed the stage this time, he wore a guitar strapped across his chest. He stepped in front of the microphone and played a couple of test chords on the guitar before signaling to the band. With the first strains of "Ghost Riders in the Sky," J. T. leaned into the mic, crooning the lyrics in a deep, rich baritone.

April's eyes shone bright, like glittering stars, her gaze glued to his face. "Holy wow," she whispered breathlessly. "Why didn't I know he could sing like this?"

Applause exploded from the crowd. Whistles and catcalls filled the air when the last note of the song died away.

"Aw, come on now. You're all too kind." J. T. raised his hand and bowed his head as he left the stage. Unstrapping his guitar, he glanced around and noticed April and me sitting close to the end of the bandstand. He raised a hand in greeting as he made his way over to us, tugging the brim of his Stetson low to hide his eyes.

"J. T.! You were incredible. You really should play more often," I said when he approached.

"Well, thank you, but I'm really nothing more than a simple porch musician. Not sure why I let them talk me into playing tonight." He lowered his chin and flipped a guitar pick between his fingers.

It was cute and endearing to watch this strong, confident man act unsure and even embarrassed about his amazing talent. He could have been cocky and arrogant about it, but that wasn't J. T.'s style. I slid my gaze to April, hoping she noticed the same thing.

"Seriously, though, you're fantastic. Mom's right. You should play every chance you get," April chimed in.

"I'll tell you what. I'll do it again, but only if you agree to sing with me. We can do a duet of 'Jackson' next time," he challenged April with a wicked grin.

She cackled, choking on a swallow of sweet tea she'd taken a swig of. "Guess you won't be back on stage anytime soon then." April wiped tea off her chin. "My singing voice is as musical as a couple of cats fighting. In fact, during my freshman year of high school, the choir teacher didn't necessarily kick me out of class, but he strongly suggested I pick a different elective for the next semester. It was mortifying."

"True story. April's amazing singing ability is a trait that runs strong in our family. I got it from my mama and passed it down to both Patrick and April. The gene bypassed Becky, thankfully." I caught April's eye, and the two of us burst out laughing at our own musical shortcomings. "The moral of this story is, never accept an invitation to a Carpenter family sing-along."

"Duly noted."

The tinny sound of an old phone ringing interrupted our laughter. J. T. pulled a cell phone out of the back pocket of his jeans, looked at the screen, and excused himself. "I better take this. Good to see you two. Be careful on your way home, and lock your doors once you get there." He stepped back from the crowded park and into the full dark beneath the shadow of an enormous maple tree.

I leaned back in my chair as far as I could go, straining to hear if the phone call had anything to do with today's murder. *Dang it.* The band started playing again, so the music whisked away any hope of eavesdropping. Before I could straighten my chair back up, I fell backward, cracking my head on the ground. I lay there, stunned for a second. April didn't say a word. She just shook her head and pulled me up, chair and all. I rubbed the back of my noggin. It wasn't nearly as funny this time around. J. T. rushed by, gathered his guitar from beside the stage, and took off toward the parking lot. April and I both, for different reasons, watched him hurry off.

I rummaged around in my purse until I found my phone, pressed the button to wake the screen, and checked the time. "It's almost nine thirty. Do you think he'd get a call about the fingerprints this late? I guess I don't know if a murder investigation is a nine-to-five thing or if they work long hours when something like this happens."

"No idea. Maybe he's got a fence down, and the cows are out." April shrugged. "We could speculate all night, but it could be a million different things."

"True enough, I suppose." I looked over at my friend's empty chairs and frowned. "Where are Evonne and Ernie? Are they still dancing?"

April pointed to the group of people shimmying around in front of the stage. The stage lights spilled out of the bandstand, lighting the dancers like fireflies. "Yep. They're so cute. Still dancing like a couple of crazy kids."

Chapter Eleven

I stretched lazily and slowly opened my eyes. A cool breeze from the open window over my head mussed my bangs and caressed my cheek. The birds were putting on a symphony, twittering, chirping, and carrying on. They started well before the first crack of dawn, but it didn't bother me. Being woken by birdsong was a far cry better than being jolted out of sleep by the harsh ringing of an alarm clock. Those darn things should be outlawed. No wonder so many people had heart attacks early in the morning.

My brain was foggy, with tendrils of sleep hanging about. I reached for the dream prodding at the corner of my mind. Was it a dream? I distinctly remembered a fluffy white cat jumping from the floor onto my bed last night. Lilac.

By the time April and I made our way home after the concert last night, we were both starving, so we sat up late with bowls of potato salad and hashed over the events of the day one last time. It was nearly midnight before I fell into bed, exhausted. I was dozing off when the curious cat started nosing around my room. I rolled over, enjoying her antics until she jumped onto the bed with me. She'd pressed her little pink nose to mine, then hopped off the bed and wiggled through the open closet doorway, climbing onto the shelf and knocking a book off onto the floor. After peering and sniffing into every corner until she'd exhausted all the places where something interesting could be hiding, the little cat strolled out of the closet and padded on her little kitty feet across the hardwood floor. She jumped back onto the bed, gave herself a bath, and curled up for a nap. I snuggled under my cotton sheets and drifted off to sleep.

In the soft morning light, the realization settled in that Lilac couldn't have been in my bedroom last night. I didn't have a cat anymore. Lilac, a tiny, sweet cat who squeaked rather than meowed, died ten years ago. A cat hadn't lived in the house since. I sat bolt upright and looked at the floor in front of the closet. Sure enough, the paperback book the little cat knocked off the shelf in the middle of the night lay on the floor where it had fallen.

If I'm going to be haunted, I guess I don't mind a visit from my sweet Lilac, but if she's here, where in the world is Bob? I shook my head, sure my mind was playing tricks on me. I must've knocked that book off the shelf myself.

A look at the clock on my nightstand told me it was still only a little after six thirty. With Carpenter's Corner closed indefinitely, I didn't need to get up yet. Settling back into my pillows, I wiggled around to find the most comfortable spot, and closed my eyes. Catching a few more winks would do me a world of good. My eyes flew back open when the image of Warren on the bathroom floor rudely shoved into my mind. I thrust him away, but he wasn't having it. Sighing, I tossed the covers off, sat up, grabbed my glasses from the nightstand, and pushed my feet into the lambswool slippers waiting by the side of my bed.

The old house didn't have an attached master bathroom, so I shuffled down the hall to the family bathroom. When I passed Bob's old office, I stopped to watch the morning sunlight play across the wide-plank hardwood floors. Dust motes danced in the rays of light spilling through the tall windows.

"Good morning, sweetheart." I blew a kiss at the idea of my husband going about his normal morning routine.

Bob had always been an early riser. He'd spent the first hour of the day at his big walnut desk, sipping coffee and looking over the ledger from the previous day's sales at the hardware store. Before I went to bed each night, I still put the ledger on his desk, opened to the day's transactions, just in case he was still hanging about.

The bathroom was next to the spare bedroom that had once belonged to our oldest daughter, Becky. She was married now with a couple of kids of her own. A sweet boy and a feisty girl who made me smile by only thinking about the little rascals. They lived a day's drive away in a comfortable craftsman cottage in a pretty little town on the Oregon coast. Becky owned a small bookstore, and her husband, Dustin, was a commercial fisherman. I only saw them a handful of times a year. Not nearly enough, in my opinion.

This morning, the door to the spare room was shut tight. Instead of climbing the stairs to the attic room she'd shared with her big brother, Patrick, when they were teenagers, April had decided to sleep in Becky's old room. I slipped into the bathroom, careful not to bang around too much as I went about my morning routine. An April woken before she was ready was a grumpy April. Not something I wanted to deal with before I'd even sipped my first cup of coffee. It was best to let that bear sleep.

Ten minutes later, the coffee was brewing, and a blue jay was yelling at me from his perch on an empty birdfeeder.

"Okay, I'm coming. Settle down, you."

I pulled a bag of birdseed and a package of unsalted peanuts out from underneath the kitchen sink and headed outside to fill the birdfeeders and freshen the birdbath. I scattered a handful of peanuts around the base of the elm tree for Rocky, the red squirrel who lived in the big tree. The little guy was a hoot to watch. He scooped up peanuts and held them in his tiny paws while he nibbled. It amazed me how loud the little critter munched. One morning while I was sitting on the front porch swing, reading, Rocky scampered out of the tree and gobbled a peanut. When he finished, he cupped his tiny paws around a strawberry leaf in the flower bed and took a long drink of water that had pooled on the leaf from my early morning watering. It was the cutest thing I'd ever seen. I'd kicked myself for not having my phone handy to snap a picture.

By the time the squirrels and birds were fed, the coffee was done perking. I poured myself a cup and added a splash of vanilla creamer before grabbing a murder mystery off the top of my book stack and heading into the sunroom. The sunroom was in the round turret feature of the house. Three tall windows curved around the room and provided a view of both the front and side yards. The light in the room was perfect for reading at this time of day.

I was engrossed in my book when April shuffled through the arched entryway, hands cupped around a steaming mug of coffee and her laptop tucked under her arm. She settled onto the couch and covered her lap with a colorful handknit throw draped over the armrest. Opening her computer, she tapped at the keys, disturbing the peace of the morning.

I huffed and opened my mouth to ask her to take her computer to another room, but thought better of it. It was me who'd insisted April stay overnight, after all. So what if a little noise came along with the deal?

"Mornin', sunshine."

April grunted in lieu of a greeting.

I made a face at my daughter, who wasn't looking at me anyway, then turned my attention back to the book, trying to ignore the tapping keys. My concentration level was zero. Zilch. I slapped the book closed and sighed louder than I meant to.

"What?" April finally glanced up from her computer screen.

Not wanting to make her feel unwelcome, I made up a fib. "Oh, I was talking to myself. Here I am, reading a mystery about a man found near an ice fishing camp with a hatchet in his back, when I realized I was looking for clues in this story to help me figure out our own real-life mystery. It was silly, so I told myself to knock it off."

April laughed, then went right back to tapping away on her keyboard.

"What're you working on already this morning?"

"I woke up thinking about how we don't know enough about Warren. Where is he from? Why did he pick Pine Bluff, of all places, for his fancy hotel? I'm looking to see what I can find out about him." She buried her nose back in her computer screen.

My coffee had gone cold, but I sipped it anyway. "Good thinking, daughter. Get after it."

"I'm on it. Now leave me alone," April joked, throwing me a quick smile.

Hmm. I wonder where she gets her attitude from?

Curiosity propelled me out of my reading chair and onto the couch. I plopped down beside April. "Not going to leave you alone. I want to see what you find." I nudged her with my shoulder. "Well? What're you waiting for? Google away."

Deciding I needed another cup of coffee, I hoisted myself off the couch and trotted into the kitchen to pour myself one. I was adding creamer when a snort of laughter burst out of the sunroom. *What in the world?*

"What's so funny?"

Tears of mirth rolled down April's face. Her mouth was wide open in laughter, but no sound came out. She beckoned me over and pointed at the computer screen. "You've gone viral." She giggled out the words. "Someone turned you into a GIF."

"Viral? What're you talking about?" I'm not an idiot; I know what the term means, but me going viral made no sense whatsoever.

Putting my full mug of coffee on the side table, I sat on the couch and jerked April's computer screen around so I could see it better. Instantly I wished I hadn't looked. Ten seconds of watching myself, in high speed, as I tipped over in my lawn chair and ended up with the chair topping my broad backside like a maraschino cherry was plenty enough for me. The dang thing played on repeat.

"There's going to be devil to pay if I ever got my hands on the smart aleck who videoed my disgrace and turned me into a joke." I frowned and tried to sound outraged.

"Oh, come on, Mom. It's hysterical."

I tried to keep a straight face, but the longer I watched my own pain, the funnier it got. Not able to hold it back any longer, I laughed until I cried. April snorted and howled right along with me.

"All right. I've had enough. Turn it off now."

April let the darn thing play through two more loops before she clicked out of her Facebook page. "Fine. But I saved it to my computer so I can watch whenever I want."

Fantastic. I'd never much wanted my fifteen minutes of fame, and now my butt was in the air and out there for the whole world to see.

Heavy sigh.

April pulled her legs onto the couch to get more comfortable and got back to work. She typed *Highcastle Development* into the search bar, and hit "Enter." When the results populated the screen, she navigated to the company website. A picture of a smiling Warren standing in front of another historic stone building filled the screen.

"That's him." It surprised me how easy it was to find him.

The photo caption said the building had been a railroad station at one time. It closed for good when the railroad track was relocated. The building sat unused for quite a few years. Highcastle Development stepped in, saving it from ruin. Warren's company transformed the building into a multiuse space housing a high-end restaurant and two boutique shops on the ground floor. A large law firm occupied the second story. April clicked on the "About" tab. Highcastle Development was based out of Denver, Colorado.

April handed a notebook and pen to me. "Jot down the company's address and phone number, will you?"

"Sure, bossy cow."

Not finding anything else of importance on his company website, April opened a new window and searched for Warren by name. A couple of articles from a Denver-based blog popped up.

"Look at this."

"I hope it's not another video of me."

April chuckled and knocked me in the arm with her elbow. "No, but maybe another one will show up with your second fall of the night."

I stared at her, open-mouthed, then narrowed my eyes. "Did you make that video?"

"What? No. Let's say I wouldn't be above it, but no. I didn't have my camera out and couldn't have gotten it from that angle anyway." She directed my attention back to the screen. "Warren's tagged in all kinds of posts on this site."

April pulled up the website called A Mile Higher and scrolled through the articles tagged with Warren's name. It didn't take us long to realize the blog kept track of the well-heeled in Denver society. Picture after picture showed Warren dressed in sharp Western attire at one event after another. In the most recent photos, a pretty brunette was on his arm. Model thin and beautiful, at one black-tie dinner she wore a form-fitting little black dress and dripped with diamonds. The picture was captioned "Mr. and

Mrs. Warren Highcastle." A photo of her alone said, "Audrey Draper Highcastle."

"Well, we found our answer to the question about his marital status," I said.

April kept scrolling until the brunette was replaced by a stunning blonde: Colleen Cross Highcastle. The post was dated May 2016.

"Those are definitely two different women. Read the article to me, will you?" I asked.

It was an announcement of Warren and Colleen's divorce and was clearly told from Colleen's point of view. The couple had been married five years and had two small children. Colleen had been an actress on the brink of fame when the couple met in California, where Warren had been renovating a historic theater. He'd swept her off her feet, promising her a life of luxury. He'd come through with the luxury but had failed to mention there'd be other women to compete with. Apparently, the divorce was drawn out and ugly. When all was said and done, Colleen took the kids and went back to Hollywood. April finished reading and scrolled back to look more closely at the first article with Audrey hanging on Warren's arm.

"Check out the dates here. Looks like he married Audrey a whole two months after the divorce from Colleen was final. And you're right. He is—was—still married." April's lip curled in a sneer. "Apparently, that little fact didn't stop him from dating Darlene. What a creep."

"Nope, and it plays into my theory about Darlene finding out he was married and killing him over it." I pushed my glasses higher up my nose and shrugged. "It's sure a possibility anyway. I wonder if J. T. knows. Has Audrey been informed she's a widow yet?"

"I'm sure she knows. It's not like the information was hard to find," April replied.

"True enough."

April closed her laptop and stretched, yawning loudly. "I'm hungry. Time to make those pancakes I promised you. Do you have any huckleberries?"

My stomach growled as loud as a chainsaw at the thought of steaming pancakes. "Yep. Check the freezer. I froze a bunch last time we went picking. Good thing too. I guess they're pretty much done for the year. Evonne took her grandkids picking earlier in the week and said they barely got enough to cover the bottom of the bucket."

* * *

I was shoveling the last bite of a stack of pancakes in my mouth when the phone rang. I still owned an honest-to-God house phone, even though the thing rarely ever rang and scared me to death when it did. This time was no exception. It rang a second time. I jumped and stabbed myself in the lip with the fork, then whacked my shin on the table leg in my haste to shut the thing up. While I rubbed my sore leg, April answered the screaming telephone.

"Hello?" She listened to the caller for a minute before holding her hand over the mouthpiece. "It's Kim Wilder for you, though I can barely understand her. I think she's crying."

I forgot all about my bruised shin as I reached for the phone. "Kim? Is something wrong?"

"I tried to call your cell, but you didn't answer. I don't know what to do," Kim wailed.

"Do about what? You'll have to tell me what's going on." My cell phone was still somewhere in the depths of my purse after last night. Most likely the battery was dead since I hadn't plugged it in to charge overnight.

"Bill's been arrested. They said he murdered Warren Highcastle." Her voice shook, and I could hardly make out what she was saying through her tears.

"What? No, that can't be right. There's no possible way Bill had anything to do with the murder." I shook my head, not able to wrap my brain around what was coming out of Kim's mouth. "No. The police have it wrong."

"I told them the same thing, but they took him away anyway. I can't think right now, and I don't know what to do."

"Hang tight, sweetie. Give me a few minutes to throw some clothes on. April and I will be right there. We'll get this straightened out, I promise." I started for my bedroom before the phone cord brought me up short, reminding me it was still attached to the wall.

"Oh, my soul, it's all my fault. Please hurry." Kim was sobbing when I disconnected the call.

The morning's pancakes sat in my stomach like a stack of bricks. My voice sounded high and shaky in my ears when I told April what Kim had said. "They've arrested Bill. Get dressed as quick as you can."

Chapter Twelve

Gravel crunched under the tires as April pulled her car into the circular driveway outside of the Wilder's yellow, two-story farmhouse, where Kim paced back and forth across the long front porch. She rushed down the steps, yanking open the passenger door before we even came to a full stop.

"Thank goodness you got here so fast. I can't figure out what I need to do. I need your level head, Dawna." She flung her arms around me, holding on for dear life.

I hugged my friend back, then attempted to wiggle free so I could breathe. A hug was one thing; a death squeeze, quite another. I adjusted my shirt and rubbed the back of my neck, trying to get the feeling to return.

Even in her early fifties, Kim was a natural beauty. She reminded me of a sunflower: tall and slender, with bright blond hair and a smile that lit up the room. I envied her happy-go-lucky nature and always felt like a frumpy beige toadstool next to her. Today, her trademark smile was nowhere to be found. She had her honey-blond hair pulled back into a messy ponytail, and her eyes were red and puffy from crying. Dressed in an oversized baby-blue T-shirt and black yoga pants, she had bare feet.

Kim had been in Pine Bluff, staying with her cousins for a couple of weeks, during the summer she and Bill had met. He was ten years older than she was, but the two clicked from the beginning. They got married that fall and built their dream house on two acres at the edge of town before Kim gave birth to the requisite two children, one boy and one girl, to add to their perfect life. With both kids off in college, Kim tackled house projects and joined the local Master Gardener's chapter to help fill her spare time.

"Tell me exactly what happened this morning."

I led Kim back to her porch and urged her to sit in a wicker rocking chair before taking a seat for myself. April settled herself on a wooden bench at the far end of the porch.

Kim closed her eyes for a moment, then opened them and stared off into the distance. "Nothing unusual was going on this morning. I came out early to deadhead my flowers before the bees started buzzing around too thick. I like to get it done at dawn, before the sun comes up, so I avoid getting stung. Bill likes to make breakfast on the weekends, and he's a far better breakfast cook than I am anyway, so he was in the kitchen, making some sort of scramble for us. I finished deadheading and went into the house to pour myself a cup of coffee." She paused, tears glistening in her blue eyes. "I guess you don't need to know every last detail."

"No, go ahead. You never know what might be important. It helps to rehash everything. Keep going." My mind raced, going over the conversations around the coffee klatch table yesterday morning. *Did Bill say anything about wanting to kill Warren? He made it clear he didn't like the guy, but he wouldn't have killed him, would he?*

"Okay, so like I said, I went into the house. Bill said breakfast would be ready in two minutes. I washed my hands, poured a cup of coffee, and came back out here to wait. We like to eat breakfast on the porch in the summer. I don't know why, but it tastes better outside, you know what I mean?"

"I do. What happened next?"

"Well, I was watching a hummingbird drink from those gladiolas." Kim waved her arm at the tall, colorful blooms lining the front porch. "I heard a car pull into the driveway and looked to see who was coming. It was a police car. I started to panic, thinking something must be wrong with one of the kids. J. T. got out of the car and asked if Bill was home. One of the young police officers was with him."

While Kim talked, I'd taken her hand, trying to provide a bit of comfort, but she'd squeezed so hard I couldn't feel the tips of my fingers anymore. I pulled my hand back and discreetly tried to rub away the fingernail marks and get the blood flowing again.

"Bill came out with our breakfast plates right then. He was as surprised as I was to see the police, but being Bill, he asked if they'd like to join us for breakfast. He said he had plenty more in the kitchen." Kim swiped at the tears trickling down her cheeks. "J. T. said no, they were here on official business. He said there'd been a break in the murder case, and asked Bill to set the plates down. Once he did, J. T. said he was arresting Bill for the murder of Warren, and then he handcuffed him and read him his rights."

Kim gulped hard. Her face seemed to crumple in on itself as she sobbed harder.

I rubbed her arm and waited for her to gain a bit of control. "I'm missing something. Did J. T. say why? What was his reasoning for arresting Bill?"

"The hammer. He said Bill's fingerprints were all over the murder weapon."

I gaped at her. "Are they sure? I mean, I know Bill has a temper, but enough to kill someone? No way. I'm not buying it. Something's wrong with that story. And how do they know they're his fingerprints? He's never been arrested before, has he?" Could Bill have been framed?

"He was fingerprinted years ago when he first started coaching T-ball. It was Bill's hammer. Dawna, we have to prove he didn't do it." Kim stared at me expectantly.

We? It was one thing for me to feel the need to find out who killed Warren, but now Kim was insisting I needed to prove her husband wasn't the murderer. Holy fright. What in the world made her think I had a single clue how to go about solving a murder? April stared at me, bug-eyed, from the other end of the porch, obviously thinking the same thing.

"What are we going to do?" Kim asked again.

"Let me think a minute." I jumped up and paced back and forth, tapping my chin with a fingertip. "Did Bill say anything before they carted him out of here?"

Kim shook her head. "No, I think maybe he was in shock. I certainly was. When J. T. was putting him in the back seat of the police car, he looked at me and said he didn't do it, but nothing more."

"And I'm sure he didn't." I put an arm around my friend in an effort to comfort her. "We're going to sort this mess out. Bill will be home before you can blink an eye." I let out a long breath. *Man, I hope I'm right.*

"Bill can get all Foghorn Leghorn blustery, but he would never kill somebody," Kim said. "On the off chance he did, though, the whole thing is my fault." She wrapped her arms around herself and set her chair rocking at a frantic pace.

"Mom mentioned you'd said it was all your fault on the phone earlier." April had kept quiet the whole time, but she piped up now, her brows knit together in confusion. "What do you mean it's your fault?"

Kim lowered her face into the palms of her hands and let out a long sigh. "I never meant any harm. I would never have cheated on Bill."

"Spill it," I prodded, thinking about the information April had unearthed about Warren's womanizing. Had he been after Kim too? Lord knows love triangles were the oldest motive on the planet for murder.

Kim took a deep breath, pulling herself together before she plunged back into her story. "We asked Warren out to the house for dinner one night last week. He'd called Bill about doing the renovation work on the Emery Theater after the sale is final. A lot of times we have clients out for dinner before Bill decides whether he's going to take on their projects. Bill likes to get a feel for what the people are like, get to know them somewhat, you know? Anyway, Warren was here, and he was flirting with me, right in front of Bill." Kim shook her head as if the memory disgusted her. "It was strange but kind of flattering at the same time. I guess I flirted back more than I should have. Nothing serious. I laughed at his dumb jokes and kept his wineglass full. That kind of thing. He turned out to be the type of guest who outstays their welcome. We thought we'd never get rid of him. He finally left not long before midnight. The next morning, Bill left for work, and I went out to work in the garden, but before long, here came Warren again."

"Really?" April interrupted. "What did he come back for?"

"Me, apparently. He thought our little flirting was serious and wanted to 'take me up on the offer,' as he put it." Kim made air quotes with her fingers as she spoke. "What a creep. I told him I'm happily married and not interested in starting an affair with him, or anyone else."

I snorted. "'Happily married' wasn't an obstacle for Warren. April did some research and found out he was married himself. He has a wife in Denver, but it seems he was quite the womanizer." I looked to April for confirmation.

"Yep. True story. An ex-wife with two small kids in California, and a current wife in Colorado," April said.

"Why am I not surprised?" Kim grimaced.

"The guy also went out with Darlene on Thursday night," April added. "They were supposed to go out again last night, if he hadn't gotten himself killed."

I steered the conversation back to Kim. "How did Warren take it when you let him know you weren't interested?"

"Like you'd expect from a jerk. It made him mad. He called me a tramp and a tease. Told me he would have fired Bill if there'd been any other decent builders around. The funny thing is, Bill hadn't even accepted Warren as a client yet."

"You told Bill about all of this, right? Do you think he was mad enough to kill the guy over him threatening you?"

"I didn't tell him right away. It happened on Wednesday morning, and I didn't see any need to bother Bill with it. I'd handled the situation, and honestly, the theater would have been a great job to get us through the winter. But then I was out working in the garden most of the day, and I kept seeing the creep driving by in his silver, sporty-looking Cadillac. I know it was him. Nobody else in Pine Bluff drives such a fancy vehicle. He drove by real slow four or five times that afternoon, and a handful of times again on Thursday. I was getting a little spooked, so I told Bill everything when he got home from work Thursday evening."

"How'd he take it?" I asked.

"You know Bill. He was mad as a bull moose and raring to knock Warren into next week. I talked him down, or so I thought. Warren was killed the next morning." Kim clenched her fists in her lap and flicked her eyes between April and me. "You guys, I'm afraid Bill might have done it."

Chapter Thirteen

B ack in town, April dropped me off in front of the police
station with a promise to meet later. "There're a few estate
sales today I need to get to. The season's almost over, and I don't
want to miss out on any good antique pieces. I wish you could
go with me."

"Me too. Sounds like a whole lot more fun than what I'm
about to do. Maybe next weekend." I sighed and waved as my
daughter drove away.

*Okay. Pull your big-girl panties up and get your behind in
there.* Hands on hips, I struck the Wonder Woman pose to give
myself a shot of confidence before I marched into the Pine Bluff
Police Station like I knew what I was doing. My white sneakers
squeaked on the old tile floor, reminding me of walking through
the school cafeteria back in the day. An older police officer sat
behind a plexiglass window at a high counter separating the small
lobby from the back of the station. He talked on the telephone
while another line continued to ring. Sparing me a quick glance,
the man held up a finger to let me know he saw me and would

be with me in a minute. I leaned against the counter, waiting my turn.

Finished with the first call, the officer answered the ringing line and put the caller on hold before addressing me. "What can I help you with today?"

"I understand Bill Wilder was brought in this morning. I'm hoping to be able to see him."

"Are you family? You're not his lawyer." He tipped his head and studied me over the top of his glasses, eyebrows raised.

Del Williams had lived in Pine Bluff for as many years as I had. Probably more. When he retired from street duty, he'd taken over the front counter at the station instead of spending his free time with a fishing pole in his hand. Del knew full well Bill and I weren't related, and I certainly wasn't his lawyer.

"Come on, Del. You know Bill's a close friend of mine. Kim asked me to stop in and check on him. Please let me see him." I crossed my arms on the counter and leaned in, exasperated with the way the conversation was going.

"Nope. Can't do it. Mr. Wilder is still being processed. The only person allowed in is his lawyer." His tone was gruff and no-nonsense.

I didn't have a chance in perdition of getting past this sentinel. Del reminded me of an aged basset hound with jowly cheeks and droopy eyes. More bark than bite, he was bound and determined not to let any funny business get by on his watch. *Dang it. I should've brought him a T-bone to gnaw on.*

As I stood there contemplating my next move, the front door of the station swung open, and Chief Dallas strode in. He assessed the situation in a second flat and addressed the gatekeeper. "She's okay, Del. I'll handle it." J. T. motioned for me to follow him. "Come on, I'll take you back. Let's go into my office for a quick chat first, though, before I take you in to see Bill."

Del huffed and shook his head, muttering to himself. I caught something about young whippersnappers not following protocol. I grinned and followed J. T. into the inner sanctum.

J. T. led me through a maze of gray metal desks and battered beige filing cabinets until we came to the doorway of his office. He hustled me inside, pulled out a chair, and motioned me to sit, closing his office door behind us. Taking a seat in the swivel chair behind his desk, J. T. shuffled a stack of papers around, then finally propped his elbows on the desk and rubbed his eyes.

"I gotta be honest with you, Dawna—this is a tough one. You've known Bill for years. So have I. My entire life. Do you think the man's capable of murder?"

"No, I don't. Not for a second. He's blustery and has a temper, for sure, but Bill killing someone? No way. I'm positive you've arrested the wrong guy."

"I wish he'd use some of his bluster right now. Bill clammed up the minute I handcuffed him. I can't get him to say a word. We've all tried. From where I'm sitting, it doesn't look good, which is why I'm going against protocol and letting you in to see him today. Maybe you can get him to talk."

J. T. unlocked the door to the station's interview room and poked his head in to let Bill know he had a visitor. He held the door wide and stepped aside to let me enter the room. Bill sat on a hard, classroom-style plastic chair behind a long table. His arms were crossed over his chest, his face red like his blood was simmering and about to hit the boiling point.

"What're you doing here?" Bill bit out when I came into the room.

"Kim's worried sick. She asked me to stop by and check on you." I sat in the chair opposite him, leaned in, and crossed my arms on top of the table, meeting his glare with my own. Maybe if I glared hard enough, the stubborn old coot would start talking. "Now, dang it, tell me what you know. J. T. said you've shut down tighter than Fort Knox."

"I can't tell you anything 'cause the only thing I know is our esteemed police force thinks I killed Warren." Bill threw his hands in the air. "Now the guy had it coming, but I can tell you this: *I* didn't kill him. What's the use in talking to J. T. to try to explain myself? I've known the kid his whole blasted life. Coached him in Little League even, and now he's got the audacity to arrest me for murder? Are you kidding me? The whole thing's completely ridiculous." He slammed a fist on the table, causing me to jump like a scared bird.

I pulled myself back together, pushed up my glasses, and stared straight into his eyes. "Well? Did you? Kim said Warren hit on her and was basically stalking her after she told him to get lost."

"Did you really ask me if I killed a man?" Bill stared at me, his mouth slack. He shook his head in disbelief. "No, Dawna, I didn't kill Warren. Sure, I thought about poking the guy in the nose and running him out of town, but I didn't kill him."

"Okay. Good. Now I know you're mad, and I know you didn't do it, but there *is* the problem of the murder weapon. I know that J. T. doesn't think you're guilty either, but he didn't have any choice except to bring you in. I can tell you, he's really struggling with the whole thing."

"Well, goody for him. I'm struggling a bit myself."

I stood and filled a plastic cup with cold water from the dispenser in the corner of the room. I sat and slid the cup over to Bill. "Can you tell me anything about the hammer?"

He chugged the water before answering. "From what I've been told, my hammer was used to kill the guy. J. T. said my fingerprints are all over the thing. You know I was in Carpenter's Corner Friday morning so, sure, I coulda done it. Did I? No." He tilted the chair onto its back legs, a scowl on his face.

"Alright then, let's think about what might have happened. How did someone else get a hold of your hammer? Do you remember where you saw it last?" I prodded him.

Bill snorted. "It's a framing hammer, for criminy sakes. I have a half dozen of 'em. They're scattered all over the job site. How would I know where that particular hammer was?"

"Are you telling me you leave your tools scattered around willy-nilly at the end of the day? Up for grabs for anyone to steal? Come on, Bill. I know you better than that. You and Bob always cleaned the job site at the end of the workday. I can't imagine you've become a slob in the last few years."

"Well, no, of course I haven't. Yes, when we're finished for the day, the tools get gathered and put away. The crew takes their personal tools home with them, and the others get locked up in the tool trailer," he admitted sheepishly.

Now we're getting somewhere.

"I thought as much. Stop being so stubborn and think. Where was the hammer? If you sit here like a mule, you're doing nothing but looking guilty. Kim and the kids need you at home, not rotting in a prison cell somewhere because you were too mad to stand up for yourself." I pushed up my glasses again, leaned across the table, and focused my piercing eyes on him. At least I hoped they were piercing. "Now, where do you think you might have left that blasted hammer?"

Bill scrubbed his hands over his weathered face and the top of his head. "We've been working over at the Conklin place, building a new garage for them, since an oak tree smashed their old one last winter. The crew finished the framing Thursday, so we knocked off an hour early. There would've been a framing hammer in my tool belt. I always take my belt off and throw it in the front seat of my truck. You saw it for yourself yesterday."

I nodded, thinking back to hitching a ride home from the grocery store with Bill yesterday afternoon and the tools scattered all over his truck. "True enough, that's exactly where your tool belt was, but I didn't pay close enough attention to notice if it had a hammer hanging off it. Do you remember? Was the framing hammer still in your belt?"

He shrugged with a shake of his head. "I don't know. Should've been. We're waiting on those windows I ordered from you to come in, so we weren't on the job site Friday. I gave the crew the day off. After I left the hardware store, I went out to Olson's and helped Luke buck bales. We brought his last cutting of hay in off the field. We finished and not long after, I ran into you at the store. I didn't have any reason to use a hammer yesterday."

"Alright, so logically there should be one in your truck." I tapped my chin. "When you and the guys were in the hardware store for coffee yesterday morning, you parked out back like usual, correct? Was your truck locked?"

"Cripes no, my truck wasn't locked. I never lock it. It was already hot, so I rolled the windows down. Everything was wide open." Bill's face went slack, and the stubborn look slid away as realization dawned on him. "Yes, I parked out back. Someone grabbed the hammer from my truck and killed Hightower with it, didn't they?"

"Highcastle."

"Hightower. Highcastle. Whatever. Not the point." He scowled at me for correcting him.

"Fine, but see? I told you there'd be an explanation for all this madness if you'd talk it out. Things are starting to make sense now." I drummed my fingers on the table, concentrating on what my next step needed to be. "Okay, first I'm going to check your truck to see if there's a hammer on your tool belt. Did you happen to see anyone in the warehouse or lumberyard? Either on your way in or out of Carpenter's Corner yesterday?"

Bill thought for a minute, then snapped his fingers. "As a matter of fact, I did. The feller you've got working for you. Steve. He was in the parking lot. Well, his car was there anyhow. Thought it was strange when you mentioned he hadn't come into work yet. I was going to say something about it, but Rick started yammering on about some fool thing or another, and I forgot. The car was still there when I left, so I figured he must've shown up and I hadn't seen him. Didn't give it another thought."

I frowned. What he'd said didn't make much sense. "Steve didn't clock in until a while after you guys left. He said he'd overslept. I'm definitely going to ask him about it, and you need to tell the police what you've told me." I aimed my best don't-mess-with-me scowl his way before rising and banging on the door to be let out of the interview room.

"Well? Did he tell you anything? Did you get the stubborn old mule to talk at all?" J. T. asked as soon as the door shut behind me.

"Of course, I did. Turns out I'm the queen of interrogation." I bowed with a flourish. "Pretty sure he'll talk to you now."

"I certainly hope so. Thanks for your help."

"Anytime. Oh, before I forget. Did you know Warren was married?"

J. T. nodded. "Yes. We've been trying to reach his wife, but have only been able to talk with the Highcastle's household manager. Apparently, his wife is at the family's vacation property in the Caribbean. She has yet to return my calls."

"I guess my real question is whether or not Darlene knew he was married."

J. T. shrugged. "It's irrelevant at this point."

"Are you sure? What if Darlene got wind of the fact he was married and killed him over it? What if—"

"Dawna." J. T. shut me down mid-sentence. "If you haven't noticed, we've made an arrest. Now, I know you don't want to believe Bill's capable of murder. Honestly, neither do I, but the undisputed fact remains—his fingerprints are all over the murder weapon. It's as close to a smoking gun as we're going to get."

My mouth dropped open, and I stared at the police chief. "You can't be serious. You're not even going to look for any other suspects?" My voice went from a near whisper to the decibel of cow bellowing. I sounded like a crazy person but couldn't stop myself from shouting. "So that's it? You're going to lock him up and throw away the key?"

I stomped my foot and glared at J. T. He grabbed my arm and wrestled me into his office, kicking the door shut behind us.

"You need to settle down, unless you want to spend some time in a cell right next to your buddy."

Taking me by the shoulders, J. T. gently pushed me into a chair. I immediately stood back up and opened my mouth to protest, but he raised a hand and an eyebrow. I thought better of it and sank back into the chair.

"Here's the thing. Right now, every bit of evidence we have leads to Bill's doorstep. The man had motive. He had opportunity. The murder weapon belonged to him." He checked the items off on angry fingers. "If I can't prove Bill didn't do it, then I have to move forward as if he did. Those are the simple facts, like it or not."

"I one hundred percent do not like it." This time I stood and tried to look intimidating. It didn't work.

J. T. clenched his jaw and closed his eyes for a split second. "I hear you loud and clear, but it's not up to you."

I glared at him. "And what am I supposed to tell Kim when I give her an update on her husband?"

"I generally find it's best to go with the truth."

I marched out of the police station, huffing and muttering to myself. "If we can't count on the chief of police to find out who really swung that hammer, I'm going to have to do it myself." It was what both Kim and I were after anyway, and there was no way on the face of this earth I was going to let Bill rot away in a prison cell for the rest of his life.

Chapter Fourteen

B y the time I mad-marched all the way home to get my car, my anger had faded to the background, and determination stepped in to take its place. Sweat trickled down my back, and I'd have loved to take a nice, long, cool shower, but I didn't want to keep Kim waiting any longer. I pointed my chili pepper–red, sixteen-year-old Jeep out of town, cursing the fan that wasn't working right. Again. Then I cursed myself for not getting the Jeep into Ernie's Garage to get the dang thing fixed.

I pounded on the dashboard, even though the Fonzie touch had never worked for me in the past. And, no surprise, it didn't work today. I fiddled with the dial. The first setting on the fan wasn't strong enough for this heat. The second one didn't work at all, and the third one was so strong it about blasted me right out the window. Oh well, too much air-conditioning is better than no air-conditioning at all. Leave it to me to wait until August to get it fixed. Guess I wouldn't melt before I got out to Kim's place. Probably not, anyway. I rolled down the window to let some of the cold air out. Hot summer wind whipped through my hair while Alan Jackson's "Chattahoochee" blasted from the radio speakers.

At the Wilder place, I wheeled to a stop, gravel popping under my tires. Bill's work truck sat in front of the large green metal shop behind the house. Instead of heading straight for the house, I made a beeline for the truck. As I suspected, it was unlocked, so I opened the passenger side door and swung open the rear suicide door. What a hot mess. Hand tools were scattered everywhere, mixed in with candy bar wrappers and to-go coffee cups. Bill's brown leather carpenter's belt lay out of my reach on the back seat. I shook my head at the mess, then climbed partway in the truck and stretched my arm out to drag the tool belt across the seat.

"Dawna? What's going on?"

I shrieked, jerked upright, and smacked my head on the corner of the door as I slid off the seat. "Holy fright! You scared the wits out of me." I rubbed the knot rising on the back of my head. "Ow."

Kim stood behind me, hands on hips and giving me the stink-eye. "Sorry about your noggin, but what in the world are you doing in Bill's truck? I saw you pull in, but when you didn't come to the house, I came out here to see what you were doing." She tapped her foot. "So, indulge me. What are you doing?"

I held up my hands in surrender. "You're right. I should've come to the house first. Bill thought there should be a framing hammer in his tool belt. He remembers putting one in it Thursday when they finished working for the day, and hasn't used it since. Which means the hammer should still be in his truck, so I wanted to check as soon as possible."

Relaying to Kim everything Bill had told me, I turned and reached for the tool belt once again. I held it out for Kim to see. The hammer loop was empty.

"Do you think the killer took it out of his truck?" Kim asked. Tears spilled down her cheeks again. "This means he didn't do it, right? None of this is my fault? Bill will be coming home?"

I sucked in a sharp breath, gave my friend a quick hug, and stepped back to rub my sore head again to give myself a moment to think. Now wasn't the time to sugarcoat anything, but I didn't want Kim to lose hope either. "We shouldn't get too excited yet. The fact that his framing hammer is missing simply reinforces that it probably *was* the hammer used as the murder weapon. It doesn't mean anyone but Bill used it."

Kim's eyes were as big as the sunflower blossoms blooming in her garden. "You're right. With the hammer missing, Bill looks more guilty, not less. What was I thinking?"

"It's hard to think straight right now. We need to find out who took the hammer out of his truck and beaned Warren with it." I motioned to the jumbled disaster inside the truck. "Come on. Help me search to make sure it isn't buried somewhere else in this mess."

Kim swiped the tears from her eyes. "Let me see that head of yours first." She parted my hair then made a tsk-tsk noise with her tongue. "You have a knot the size of a cartoon goose egg. The good news is your head isn't bleeding, but I'm afraid you're going to have a nasty bruise."

I waved her away. "I'll put an ice pack on it when we're done. Let's get this finished and worry about my head later." The bump was definitely sore, and the beginning of a headache pushed at the back of my skull. Whether from the knot, the heat, or the stress of the last couple of days, it was hard to tell.

Kim trotted around to the driver's side of Bill's truck and jerked the doors open. Tools and garbage flew as she pulled out everything she could reach and tossed it onto the ground. I did the same on my side.

Once we emptied the truck, we surveyed the mess we'd made on the ground. Tools, bright-colored candy wrappers, white coffee cups, neon-yellow hard hats, scuffed work boots, and tan leather gloves were scattered before us. No red-handled framing hammer stuck out of the pile. No framing hammer at all.

"Well, there you have it." I placed my hands on my hips. "It's not here."

Kim nodded and sighed, gesturing at the muddle of things on the ground. "Look at all those candy bar wrappers. The man has a sweet tooth, but I had no idea he eats so much candy." She shook her head. "But you know what? When he gets out of this mess and comes back home, I'm not even going to say a word about it. Let him have his little secret. Come on—let's put all this stuff back, minus the garbage. I've got some freshly brewed tea at the house. And an ice pack."

* * *

An hour later, I drained my second glass of delicious, sweet peppermint iced tea and pushed myself out of the wicker rocking chair. Between the ice pack and the pain reliever I'd dug out of my purse, the headache had retreated. My noggin was still sore, but the goose egg was now the size of a marble. "I guess I'd better get going. I want to stop by Carpenter's Corner to make sure it's still standing." *And if I'm going to find out why Steve lied to me, I'd better get at it.* I didn't tell Kim about my suspicions concerning Steve, in case they didn't pan out. No sense in getting her hopes up.

Kim walked with me to my Jeep. "Thank you for going to see Bill and getting the stubborn man to talk to you. Neither one of us could ask for a better friend. Are you going to tell J. T. about the missing hammer? I still can't decide if it's a good thing or a bad thing."

I gave Kim a quick hug before climbing behind the steering wheel. "Agreed, but yeah, the police need to know. I'm surprised J. T. hasn't shown up here to look for it himself, now Bill's finally talking. I thought I'd barely beat him here, which is why I was in a hurry to look through Bill's truck." Except the police chief already had the "smoking gun" in his possession, so maybe he wasn't interested in looking for a hammer he figured wasn't there.

Kim cocked her head, a slight frown pulling at the corners of her mouth. "Hmm. Maybe they're still taking his statement. I don't know how long all of this stuff takes."

"You're most likely right. I'll call later to check on you and let you know if I find out anything else. Keep me posted if you hear any news from Bill, will you?"

Chapter Fifteen

The sun was high in the sky, scorching the earth with its August heat. My stomach growled, letting me know this morning's stack of pancakes were long gone. I glanced at my watch. Eleven forty-five. With everything that had happened, it felt like it should be at least three in the afternoon. Lifting my T-shirt away from my hot skin to let the air in for a second, I settled back in the driver's seat and rehashed the last two days as I drove slowly back to town. It all seemed surreal. I had to keep reminding myself a man had actually been killed inside my hardware store. Then one of my closest friends had been arrested and was cooling his heels in jail for the murder. I gnawed on my lip, contemplating the missing hammer and Kim's story about Warren stalking her. Was it possible Bill had snapped? I imagined him sneaking up behind Warren, raising the hammer and bringing it crashing down, smashing the man's skull. I shook my head to clear the image. Nope. No way. Not the Bill I knew.

Now, to top it off, I was suspicious my one and only employee might actually be the one who had committed the crime. What kind of motive could Steve possibly have? Had he and Warren known each other from somewhere other than Pine Bluff? Steve was relatively new to town, and he had come from a construction background. What if he'd worked on one of Warren's jobs in the past? It was a theory worth exploring.

I parked in the empty spot in front of Carpenter's Corner Hardware. Main Street was unusually quiet for a Saturday. *Ah.* It dawned on me that it was farmer's market day, and lunchtime to boot. Lunchtime at the farmer's market held in the park bustled with people flocking to the Chuck Wagon for their famous barbecue plate. The Chuck Wagon was Pine Bluff's version of a food truck. A local ranching family had taken an original chuck wagon used on their family's cattle ranch back in the early 1900s, and converted it into a food cart. They pulled it to town every Saturday from June through August, serving a full barbecue meal off the back door that lowered to form a table. The meal featured a barbecue beef sandwich made from their own grass-fed Angus beef cattle. Next, the plate was piled high with baked beans, corn on the cob, coleslaw, and a big slice of sweet cornbread. My mouth watered and my stomach rumbled, deciding for me. *I'll drop by the store for Steve's address and then go get a plate of barbecue.*

I unlocked the front door of my hardware store, pushed it open, and stood still for a minute before I stepped over the threshold. Never, before today, had I been apprehensive about entering my store. But then again, nobody had ever been killed on my bathroom floor before. I stood stock-still, listening for any small sound. Nothing. I tentatively placed one foot into the store. Stopped again. Looked toward the hallway and bathroom.

Nothing was out of place. I closed my eyes and let the feeling of the store wash over me. No strange noises. No weird feelings. It was my same old store, quiet and waiting for me. *Oh, thank God.* I released a deep breath I hadn't realized I'd been holding in, and opened my eyes. Still nothing. The police must have been back because even the crime scene tape that had been crisscrossed over the hall doorway yesterday was gone.

I closed the front door behind myself, stepped behind the checkout counter, and reached down to unlock the drawer to the small filing cabinet tucked under the counter. Lifting out the file labeled "Steve Harrison," I sifted through the contents, looking for the information form where he'd listed his physical address. Once I located it, I scribbled the address on a yellow sticky note and tucked it into my purse before locking the cabinet again.

A loud banging on the front window made me jump and let out an embarrassing shriek. Darlene stood outside, gesturing for me to come to the door.

"It's unlocked. Come in." As soon as the words were out of my mouth, I thought better of them. What if Darlene was the killer and planning to knock me off next? I didn't have any reason to rule her out yet.

Darlene flung the door open, her heavily mascaraed eyes wide and a colorful woolen purse dangling from her outstretched arm. "I rushed down as soon as I could. Is everything all right?"

"As far as I know. Why? Has something else happened?"

"My security company called. The alarm in my store is going off."

I cocked my head to listen. "I don't hear anything."

"The alarm is silent. When it goes off, it triggers another alarm at the security company, and they call me. I have to go in and shut it off or call the police. How long have you been here? You haven't seen or heard anything strange?"

"I've only been here about five minutes, but no, I haven't heard a thing." Except for an obnoxious woman banging on my window. "Does your alarm go off often?"

"No, it's never happened before. Well, except for when I've accidently triggered it myself. Will you go into Lipstick and Lace with me? I'm scared," she pleaded with a whine in her voice.

I sighed, thinking about the plate of barbecue waiting for me at the park. "Fine, but let's go in through the front instead of the hallway." The last thing I wanted was to see the spot where Warren had been killed.

I grabbed my purse and locked the door to Carpenter's Corner, and the two of us entered Darlene's shop. She popped open the cover on the alarm system to reveal a keypad and quickly tapped in a code. How she could push those small buttons with her long fingernails was beyond me. I peeked over her shoulder. The screen now stated "Alarm disabled" in red letters.

We crept through Lipstick and Lace, looking for anything out of place. Toward the back of the store, I noticed the door to our shared hallway and bathroom was open a crack.

I pointed at it. "Did you leave the door open? I could've sworn the police relocked it when they finished yesterday."

Darlene frowned and shook her head. "No, it has to be shut tight or it triggers the alarm. Which it apparently did. Before I left yesterday, I told them how important it was to keep it locked.

They assured me they would. Someone had to have opened it this morning."

Could the killer have been back? In the mystery books I read, it wasn't so unusual for the murderer to revisit the scene of the crime. But how would they have gotten inside? I put a hand on Darlene's arm to stop her from moving any closer to the open door, and pulled my cell phone out of my purse.

Chapter Sixteen

The Pine Bluff police chief answered on the first ring, and I spilled out the story without taking a breath. "How quick can you get here?"

"Already here." J. T. rapped on the front door to alert us before he entered the shop. He clicked off his phone and stuffed it into his shirt pocket.

Darlene let out a high-pitched giggle. "Talk about quick service."

"This building is a crime scene, remember? I have every right to be here, but the two of you aren't supposed to be anywhere on the premises." J. T. eyed us, hands on his hips. "You should've called me first before entering the building."

"Oh gosh, I'm sorry. It didn't cross my mind to call you. I stopped to get Steve's home address so I could go have a chat with him, and planned on being in and out of here lickety-split," I replied.

J. T. nodded grimly. "Steve's the reason I was already here when you called, actually. You don't need to stop by his house. He's out back."

"Why? Did he have something to do with the murder? Where is he?" I looked around for Steve as if he'd materialize from thin air.

"He was in his car out behind the store. In the lumberyard." J. T. took a deep breath and closed his eyes for a second. "Dawna, Steve's dead."

"*What?* What do you mean?" Instantly my knees went weak and my head spun. I stumbled to a chair by Darlene's dressing rooms and sank into it. My headache came rushing back in full force. "Are you sure? How did this happen?"

"He's been shot. Probably early this morning, if I were to venture a guess. The coroner is on the way. He'll be able to tell us more once they have a chance to look over the body."

"You've said those same words to me way too often lately. This whole thing is turning into a nightmare." I closed my eyes and wished with all my strength that Bob was standing beside me so I didn't have to face this madness alone.

Darlene fell into the chair beside me and echoed my words. "It does feel like a nightmare. With another murder, I'll never be able to reopen my boutique. I'm losing money every hour I have to stay closed. I thought since you'd arrested Bill, we'd get back to normal soon."

My heart beat a fast rhythm like frantic birdwings inside my chest. Darlene was right. This was so not going to be good for business. Maybe it was time, after all these years, to close the doors for good. With that thought, the guilt set in. *What kind of a person worries about their business when a man has lost his life? Two men, for that matter.*

J. T. nodded. "I understand you want to get back to normal, but it's going to have to wait. Now once you take a minute to process this latest development, I'm going to need to question both of you ladies again."

"You've said those words too many times as well. How did you find him? Were you looking for Steve specifically?" I blinked back the tears forming in the corners of my eyes.

"No, I wasn't looking for him. I was still questioning Bill when a call came into the station about some suspicious activity in the lumberyard at Carpenter's Corner. Officer Bowman and I came right over, but the only thing around was Steve's old Chevelle. When we approached the car, we saw right away something was wrong." He paused and pinched the bridge of his nose. "I'm sorry, Dawna. This must be hard for you to hear. Are you sure you want to know the details?"

I nodded, picking absently at an invisible thread on my jeans. "I need to know what happened. It's difficult to process. Steve and I weren't close or anything. He simply worked for me. I tried, but he wasn't someone who let anyone get close, unfortunately." I leaned back in the chair and pushed my glasses higher on my nose. "Who called the station? Did they hear the gunshot? Do you think he killed himself?"

J. T. shook his head. "No, there's not a gun in the car. It wasn't suicide. The phone call was anonymous. A woman. She went to the trouble of blocking her number before she dialed. Not sure we'll be able to find out who it was, but we'll try. Pine Bluff doesn't have all the fancy equipment that can track things like this."

A woman. Huh. I racked my mind for the women who'd made my list of suspects. The only ones coming to mind were Kristi and Darlene. Warren had wanted Kristi to file some fraudulent paperwork. According to her Aunt Marti, she'd refused. Had the real estate developer fired her for having scruples? If he did, she wouldn't be getting her significant commission off the sale. Would she have been mad enough to kill him over it? Supposedly she'd been out for a solo drive when the murder took place, but her name was squarely on the list of Lipstick and Lace customers from Friday morning. And where would Steve fit into all of this? His death couldn't be a coincidence. I'd better follow up with Kristi sooner than later.

Or maybe Darlene had made the call to the police station. I squinted at her out of the side of my eye. It wasn't out of the question to think she could've killed Steve, set off her store's alarm system, and then called the police. It'd be easy to double back and pretend she was there to turn the alarm off.

"Whoever did this to Steve has to be the same person who killed Warren. Two murders in as many days in Pine Bluff, and they're not related? No way. Bill sitting in jail when Steve was shot proves he's innocent." I was confident Bill would be released before the day was over.

J. T. rubbed his temples as if a headache nagged. "I don't know where you came up with your theory. At this point, it looks like these are two separate incidents. Steve's murder in no way changes anything about Bill's arrest. You're beating a dead horse."

Tears welled in my eyes and spilled down my cheeks. I swiped at my face before anyone noticed and straightened my shoulders instead of letting my body crumple like the brittle old napkin I was starting to feel like. Giving in to the emotions pressing against my chest wouldn't help anyone right now.

J. T. suggested we move to my hardware store to talk. Over there he could use the table to write his notes, and there were enough chairs for all three of us to sit. He directed us through the hallway, admonishing Darlene and I not to touch anything. As if we would.

Welp. So much for avoiding the place Warren was killed. I kept my gaze straight ahead as if I wore blinders and passed through the small hallway as fast as I possibly could.

J. T. stopped to inspect the Lipstick and Lace side of the door. He looked closely at the lock and doorjamb. "There isn't even a scratch here. Nobody broke in. Whoever opened it did it with a key."

Chapter Seventeen

"I'm going to put some coffee on. Anyone else need a cup?"

"Do you have tea instead? I'd love something to calm my nerves." One hand was entwined in her hair as Darlene unconsciously twisted and pulled at it. I slid a straw in front of her to keep her hands busy before she pulled it all out.

"I've got the perfect thing." I reached for a tea mug, plopped in a bag of lavender and chamomile tea, filled the mug with tap water, and put it in the microwave. My stomach growled again, reminding me of the missed lunch. I dug through my purse, coming up with three granola bars that had seen better days. I tossed them on the table as the microwave pinged, then I pulled out the steaming mug and slid it across the table to Darlene.

"There's sugar lumps." I pointed at a yellow, covered bowl on the table. "J. T., can I get you something?"

"Coffee, please."

I poured a mug for both of us, took my place at the table, and rattled open a granola bar. Stale, but still food. Kind of.

"Alright, now you called and told me the two of you were in Lipstick and Lace, and the alarm was going off. Is that correct?" J. T. looked pointedly at me.

I tried to chew faster and swallow a mouthful of stale granola bar.

Darlene pulled a leg into her chair and shook her head, sending her long, silver earrings dancing, and answered in my place. "Not quite. I came down because the security company called and told me my alarm was going off. I was at home when they called. Before I went into my shop, I noticed Dawna was here, so I knocked on the window and asked her to go in with me. After what happened to Warren, I was scared to go into the boutique by myself." She batted her long lashes as if she was looking for sympathy.

"Okay. And you said you were here to get Steve's home address? Even though I made it clear you weren't supposed to be in the building." J. T. looked at me.

"Yes, but when I talked to Bill this morning, he told me Steve's car had been parked out back Friday morning when the guys were in having coffee. It kept nagging at me because Steve didn't get to work until after ten, right after I found Warren's body. Anyway, I wanted to talk to Steve about it face-to-face rather than on the phone, so I stopped in to get his address out of the filing cabinet. Honestly, I didn't even think about the fact I wasn't supposed to be in here. I'm sorry." I tried to give the police chief the most innocent expression I could muster.

J. T. clenched his jaw, his facial muscles flexing under the pressure. "I'm going to need to get Steve's address from you when we're finished here. Now, tell me what happened when the two of you went inside Lipstick and Lace?"

Darlene jumped back in, telling him how we'd noticed the door to the hallway was open a crack and how it had to be closed for the alarm to be set. She'd set it Friday when she left, and it hadn't gone off until ten this morning. "Which means someone opened the door this morning." She jabbed a finger toward the hallway to make her point.

"Is there any chance it wasn't closed tight, and the wind may have pushed it open? Maybe there's a window open somewhere?"

I shook my head, pursing my lips. "No, none of the windows in the building open. Sometimes when we open the warehouse door, it creates a suction that pops the hallway door open, but I didn't open the back door, and nobody else has keys right now. Except for the one I gave you." Another thought occurred to me. "Well, wait a minute. Did you or one of the other officers open the back door after you found Steve's body?"

He shook his head. "Nope, we sure didn't. Besides, we weren't here until almost eleven. The call about the suspicious activity came into the station at ten forty-five. According to Darlene's timeline, her alarm went off quite a while before we arrived. However, there was another key. Officer Bowman found one on the floor of Steve's car. He must've gotten a second key made, and I'm guessing it was Steve who opened the door today."

I nodded. "It would've been easy enough for him to get a key made. We make them right here in the store." I frowned. "Funny he didn't mention the second one when I asked for his keys yesterday."

Why had Steve been acting so sneaky? What had he been up to?

J. T. focused his razor-sharp gaze on Darlene. "You said the alarm went off about ten, but you didn't arrive at the store until noon. Did it take that long for the security company to contact you?"

"No, of course not. They call immediately when it gets tripped. I know for a fact because I've accidentally triggered it myself a time or two by not getting the door shut tight enough. They call so fast I can't even get the code punched in to turn the alarm off before the phone rings. I came as fast as I could today, but I still had to shower and put my face on. I don't care how much of an emergency it is, I'm not going anywhere without my hair and makeup done." She looked at J. T. like he'd lost his mind, and ran manicured fingernails through her thick black hair.

I stared at the woman, my eyes wide and not a stitch of makeup on my face. Sure, usually I dabbed on some eye shadow and mascara, and a hint of lipstick made me feel pulled together, but I hadn't thought twice about running out the door without it this morning when Kim had called. "Seriously? Anything could've happened while you were painting your face. What in the world were you thinking? Why didn't you at least call the police and have them check it out?" *Or had Darlene called the police station? Was she the anonymous caller?*

Darlene blinked her eyes like a barn owl and let out a small huff. "Because if it's a false alarm, I can get a fairly hefty fine, so I figured I'd just check it out myself." She shrugged her shoulders. "It's not a big deal."

"Isn't it? Had you called right away, we might have caught the person who killed Steve, Miss Lovelace, or even saved his life. Now it's too late. I should fine you for *that*." J. T. didn't mince his words. An edge of anger in his voice cut like a knife. He rubbed both hands over his face and grunted.

Darlene studied her fingernails, not saying a word.

The police chief stared at her for a full minute before he turned his attention back to me. "Do you have contact information for Steve's family? Next-of-kin type of thing? Maybe somebody to call in case of an emergency?" He flipped to a clean page in his notebook.

"Are you done with me? Can I go?" Darlene interrupted. Her voice was small and timid. Tears threatened to well over in her dark eyes.

Better not cry. It'll ruin your makeup. I felt petty as soon as the thought popped into my head.

J. T.'s tone was gruff, and he didn't waste a glance on Darlene. "Yes. Fine. I'll be in touch if I have any other questions." He turned, leveling her with a fierce glare. "And, Miss Lovelace, if your alarm goes off again, call the station straightaway. Got it?"

She nodded, grabbed her purse, and slipped outside. The sound of sniffling trailed away as she left. From the tone of his voice and the questions he'd asked, I didn't think Darlene was on J. T.'s radar as a possible suspect in Steve's murder, and I couldn't think of a single motive the woman would have. Unless she'd killed Warren, and Steve somehow knew about it. I sighed. *Simply because I can't stand her doesn't mean she's a killer, but I'm going to keep my eye on Miss Thing anyway.*

I unlocked the filing cabinet and pulled out the file I'd been looking through earlier. "I don't remember Steve giving me any family information." I licked the tip of my index finger and shuffled through the paperwork. "Nope, I'm not seeing any personal information. Didn't think I'd need it. All I know is he rented a room from a guy on Juniper Lane. It's the small green house back behind the sawmill. I'm not sure of the roommate's name. Steve never talked about his private life."

J. T. jotted the address down and flipped his notebook shut. "All right, I'm going to head over there. Since you were his employer, do you want to ride along? You seem to be pretty wrapped up in this investigation as it is. Might as well go with me so I can keep an eye on you." He raised an eyebrow.

Was he admitting these two murders might be related? Whatever the case, I wasn't about to waste the opportunity to do a bit more digging, police sanctioned this time.

"Yes, I'd like to go. Thank you. Maybe Steve's roommate will know something to shed some light on all this craziness."

So much for lunch. I grabbed another stale granola bar and headed out into the sunshine behind the chief of police.

Chapter Eighteen

The house at 1224 Juniper Lane was a small, ramshackle cottage badly in need of a paint job. The green siding was covered with more mold and moss than paint. A patch of dirt in front of the house looked far more like a junkyard than a lawn. Knee-high weeds, brittle and dry in the late summer heat, tried to hide the piles of rusty debris lying scattered across the yard. Discarded rubber tires were thrown in helter-skelter for good measure. Three vehicles in various stages of disrepair were parked in the gravel driveway. A rusted El Camino, missing its windshield and all four tires, seemed to be a permanent yard ornament. A glimpse of the backyard through a silver chain-link fence showed more of the same. A red and white "Beware of Dog" sign hung crookedly on the fence, one corner having come loose from the zip-tie that once held it in place.

As J. T. and I picked our way to the front door, I spied a claw-foot bathtub in all the rubble. Sanded and repainted, it would be a beautiful addition to someone's home. Clawfoot tubs were back in vogue. Sinking into a deep tub for a long soak with relaxing bath salts, candles glowing, a glass of wine nearby, and a good book in hand, was pure bliss. I'd tromped across muddy fields more than once to save a tub from its sad fate as a green, algae-covered horse trough. *Better let April know there's one here for the picking.*

"Are you coming?" J. T. pulled my attention away from the bathtub.

I trotted to catch up before he knocked on the grimy front door. A menacing bellow from the dog the sign warned us about echoed from inside the house. We both took a big step back, but no one came to answer the door. J. T. waited a minute before hammering again, louder the second time.

From the depths of the house, a man shouted, "Hang on!"

The barking increased as the door was wrenched open. *Holy fright!* I shrank back when a black Labrador the size of a tank pushed his way out of the house with all the grace of a charging buffalo.

"Thor. Get back. Sit."

The beast sniffed my shoes and then, satisfied I wasn't there to rob the place, slapped a wet tongue across my fingers. Tentatively, I patted his enormous head. Thor smiled as only a dog can do and licked me again. His tail whipped the air in a dance of sheer joy. I shook my hand to rid myself of any leftover slobber and wiped the rest of the wet off on the leg of my blue jeans.

Thor's human eyed J. T. and me from behind a screen door. He was dressed in a tank top that'd been white at one time but was now a grungy gray. Dirty jeans streaked with mechanic's grease, and unkempt, sandy hair in desperate need of a shampoo, completed his look.

"What can I do for ya, Officer?" A cigarette clenched between his teeth bobbed up and down as he spoke. He kicked the screen door open and raised a scrawny arm above his head, resting his bent elbow on the doorframe as he squinted at the pair of us standing on his doorstep.

J. T. flashed his badge. "Chief Dallas, Pine Bluff Police. And this lady is Dawna Carpenter." He flicked his thumb my way. "We understand Steve Harrison lives here. Is that correct?"

"Greg Cottrell." The man held out a hand for J. T. to shake.

I offered my hand, but Greg ignored me altogether. *Yep, still invisible.*

Greg took the cigarette from his mouth, letting out a long trail of smoke. "Used to. Steve *used to* live here. He's been renting a room from me for a couple of years, but I kicked him out last week. Couldn't stand the nagging anymore. Would've kept my old lady around if I'd wanted to listen to all the bull. He was always going on about picking up after myself, washing the dishes, and mowing the lawn. Last straw was when I came home from work and the guy'd been cleaning. Threw out a bunch of my stuff. Said we didn't need stacks of newspapers sitting around. That they were a fire hazard. This is *my* house, by God, and I'll keep it how I like it. Threw him out the same day. Good riddance."

He flicked ashes into the yard. I cast a wary eye on the dry weeds. Talk about a fire hazard. Greg took another long drag off his cigarette, blew out the smoke, and looked at me with surprise. *Ah. He can see me now. My invisibility cloak must've fallen off.* I waved the smoke out of my face and coughed.

He shook a finger in my direction. "Oh, Carpenter. You're the broad Steve works for."

"That's right. Do you remember when you saw Steve last?" I wanted to strangle him but chose to smile instead.

"Uh. Let's see. Wednesday afternoon, I think." He paused, looking at the sky and chewing his bottom lip. "Yep, Wednesday. Came by and took most of his stuff. He mentioned you were letting him sleep at the store until he found a place. Like I cared. Why ya asking anyway?"

J. T. explained how Steve had been found dead in his car behind Carpenter's Corner Hardware and how we were trying to get some background information about him so the police could notify his family.

"Well, I'm awful sorry to hear he's dead, but it don't have a thing to do with me. The guy's not my problem anymore." He squinted at us through a screen of cigarette smoke.

J. T. pressed a finger to the bridge of his nose and sighed. "Just doing my job, Mr. Cottrell. Since this was Steve's last known residence, you're my first stop. What can you tell me about his family?"

Greg scratched his head. "Not a thing. The guy was nothing more'n a roommate. I needed someone to help pay the rent after my old lady left and I got sacked at the mill. Laid off, they said. Bunch of junk. Boss was out to get me. Fired, is what I call it. Anyway, at first I tried to get Steve to drink beer with me, play cards, that kind of thing. It was like pulling teeth. I finally gave up. The guy was a real downer. No fun at all."

"From what I understood from Steve, you two have a mutual friend. Someone he knew when he lived in Walla Walla, which is how he heard you had a room for rent. Is that right? Can you tell us who the friend is?" I asked.

"Yeah, my buddy Cliff. Steve worked with him for a while over east, swinging hammers."

"Does this Cliff have a last name?" J. T. asked.

"Myers."

"He still in Walla Walla?"

"Far as I know. Haven't been in touch recently."

"You mentioned Steve took *most* of his things. Do you mind showing us what he left behind?"

Greg shrugged, stepping back and holding the screen door open for us. "Sure, I don't care. The stuff's still in his room."

He whistled for Thor, who was running in circles between the junk piles, trying to nose out all the smells he could in the time he'd been given.

Stale cigarette smoke, sour beer, and wet dog assaulted my nose the minute we stepped into the house. The smells mingled together to create a perfume I imagined was heaven for rodents. A pizza box sat open on the cluttered coffee table; one greasy, coagulated slice of what must once have been pepperoni pizza lay amid the remains of discarded crust. A trail of ants marched across the dirty tan carpet and up the leg of the table, intent on pizza for lunch. The dog sniffed at it but turned away. He thumped onto the floor with a heavy sigh and laid his snout on his crossed front paws. In the dim light, I accidentally kicked an empty beer can, sending it rattling across the floor. I followed J. T. and Greg down a dark hallway, where Greg flung open a scratched and dented wooden door and then flipped a light switch. The light spilled down the hallway and illuminated the filthy carpet.

"Here you go. Nothing much to see." Greg stepped back, allowing us to enter the room.

The bedroom was no bigger than a coat closet. A dusty ceiling fan with a single bare lightbulb circulated the stale air in the room. A twin bed, stripped of any bedding, was pushed against one wall, the mattress stained and sagging in the middle. One green ratty towel hung over the footboard while two shirts and a coat took up space in the minuscule closet. I headed straight for a small stack of books leaning against the wall by the head of the bed. A copy of *Catcher in the Rye* and four Clive Cussler thrillers. *A Short History of Nearly Everything* by Bill Bryson had the Pine Bluff Library label affixed to the spine. Hoping something worthwhile was tucked between the pages, I thumbed through the books and gave each one a good shake. No notes, no love letters—nothing fell out that could point us in the right direction or tell us a thing about who Steve was. Disappointed, I dropped the books back onto the floor with a thud, keeping the Bill Bryson book to return to the library.

"Is this it? Where are the rest of his belongings?" J. T. turned to Greg after searching the coat's pockets and coming up empty.

"Nothing else. He only had a few clothes and them stupid books. Like I said, he took most of it when he left the other day. Guess you should take the rest. It ain't no use to me."

"Wow, I guess he really traveled light." I turned in a slow circle, taking in the tiny room. How could a person get to be forty-two years old and not have a single memento to remind himself of the life he'd lived? My house was stuffed with trinkets, each one holding a memory of a specific person or day. What in the world had Steve so broken that he hadn't held on to a single item from his past?

"Take these." Greg thrust the stack of books at me, interrupting my thoughts and bringing me back into the present.

J. T. pulled the few clothes out of the closet and thanked Greg. The men shook hands once more, and J. T. asked Greg to call him at the station if he thought of anything significant.

"Sure thing. Ya know, there's one thing of Steve's I'd like to hang on to, for old times' sake."

"What's that?" J. T. cocked his head and narrowed his eyes.

"His car. I'd sure like to get my hands on Steve's Chevelle. Where's it at?"

"For old times' sake, huh?" J. T. grunted. "I thought the two of you weren't close. What makes you think you should get Steve's car?"

Greg hemmed and hawed before he came up with a good reason. "He owed me back rent. The Chevelle would about pay it off."

Funny, he hadn't mentioned a thing about back rent until now.

"Do you have any proof Steve was delinquent with his rent?" J. T. asked.

"Well, no."

"Right. Well, get it out of your head right now. It's not going to happen. A homicide occurred inside Steve's vehicle, so it's part of an active investigation. The car will be held at the police garage until the case is closed, and then it will be released to Steve's closest family member. You're out of luck on that front." J. T. swung the clothes over his shoulder and scowled at Greg before he headed out of the small bedroom.

Passing back through the living room, I bent over and patted Thor on the head. The big black dog melted with delight, flopping on his back for a belly rub. I happily obliged before following the police chief out into the bright day.

"What a sweetheart," I whispered to J. T. as we picked our way across the front yard masquerading as a junkyard, and back to the police cruiser.

He gave me a sidelong glance and snorted. "Seems so. Quite the charmer."

Rummaging around in my purse, I pulled out my old, beat-up camera and snapped a couple of pictures of the clawfoot tub lying in Greg's yard.

"For the love of Mike, Dawna. What're you doing now?" J. T. stood with the driver's side door of the cruiser open.

"Taking a picture of this tub for April. Maybe she can talk Greg out of it one of these days. For the right amount of money, of course." I tucked the camera back into my purse and climbed into the car, balancing the stack of books on my lap. "It all looks like a pile of junk, but I think there might be some good antique picking right in his front yard."

J. T. snorted derisively. "I'm surprised the city hasn't been all over him to get it cleaned up. What a mess."

For the few short blocks back to Carpenter's Corner, I kept quiet, mulling over Steve's living arrangements. I couldn't get the picture of him curled up behind the garden hoses in the hardware store's warehouse out of my head. J. T. pulled the car to the curb, and I reached for the door handle, but a thought struck before I got out of the car.

"According to Greg, Steve was sleeping in my store. I suppose it explains the extra key he didn't mention, and the blanket and pillow you found during your search. You know, if he'd only told me, I would've let him stay at the house. Could've even rented him the upstairs apartment." I formulated my thoughts. "Do you think he witnessed Warren's murder? It could explain why he was acting so strangely yesterday. Maybe Steve was killed to keep him quiet?" I shivered at the thought.

"Except you're forgetting one thing. Warren's killer is in custody." J. T. glanced at me, then turned away and muttered something under his breath.

"What was that? Sounded like a bit of foul language, Chief."

J. T. sighed. "Yeah, sorry. I guess I have to agree with you. It's a pretty big coincidence Steve was killed on the same premises where another murder took place yesterday. Speaking of murder, until this is all solved, I don't want you or anyone else going into the building."

"I know. You've said that already a time or five." So it didn't appear like I was gloating, I chose not to say a single word about J. T. finally admitting I might be right. No need to rub it in.

"But you don't seem to listen. I mean it. I'm not messing around, and that order includes Miss Lovelace, as well. It's too dangerous. Bill's in custody, so we darn well know he wasn't the one who shot Steve." J. T. narrowed his eyes at me. "I want to hear you promise you'll stay out of the building."

I made the sign of the cross over my heart. "Absolutely. Cross my heart and hope to die." I chuckled. "Okay, terrible choice of words, but I don't have any intention of going back in there by myself."

J. T. leveled me with a glare. "You say that, but you went in the building today without a second thought."

"I know, but I won't do it again, not after Steve was killed too. I don't have any power over what Darlene will do, though. Nor do I want any."

J. T. huffed. "Let me handle Darlene."

"Gladly. You'll try to get a hold of Cliff Myers next? What happens to Steve's body if he doesn't have any family to claim him?"

"I'll make every attempt to find his next of kin. If no one can be found in a reasonable time frame, they'll label his body as unclaimed. If it goes that far, the state will take over and dispose of the body in the cheapest way available. In Steve's case, the body won't be released until we've done everything we can to find his killer. I hope we'll find his family before that happens."

I rubbed my neck, considering the information, and quickly came to a decision. "Steve will *not* be an unclaimed body. If you can't find his family, I'll claim him and bury him here in Pine Bluff. It's the least I can do." How I'd pay for funeral costs would be a hurdle I'd jump over later.

I finally opened the door and climbed out of the police car. As soon as I closed the passenger door, it occurred to me I'd never told J. T. about my second visit to the Wilders' this morning. Before he could pull away from the curb, I wrenched the door back open.

J. T. looked at me in surprise. "Is there something else?"

"As a matter of fact, there is. In the shock of Steve's death, I forgot to mention Kim and I looked through Bill's work truck. We found his tool belt, but the framing hammer he thought should be there was missing."

J. T. slammed his hand against the steering wheel. "Son of a gun, Dawna. Do you realize you could've compromised everything? The police needed to search his truck, not you. All you proved is the identical hammer Bill admits to owning isn't where he said it should be. Did it even occur to you this isn't a good thing for him?" The police chief's steel-blue eyes pierced right through me.

I met his stare, glare for glare. "It did occur to me, as a matter of fact. What the whole thing does seem to prove is Bill's hammer is missing from his truck. The truck he parked behind my store, unlocked, with the windows open, on Friday morning. Anyone coming through my back lot could've grabbed the hammer and used it to kill Warren."

J. T. pinched the bridge of his nose. At this rate, he was going to soon pinch it right off .

"See. You hesitated. You hadn't considered that scenario, had you?" I couldn't help but crow.

"I hesitated because I'm trying hard not to lose my patience with you," he said through gritted teeth. "I appreciate your theories and your help, but you need to stop investigating. Let my officers and me do our jobs, will you?"

Chapter Nineteen

I threw my purse over the back of a kitchen chair and plopped down at the breakfast table. Putting my elbows on the table, I rested my chin in my hands and let out a huge sigh, fluttering my silver bangs out of my eyes.

"Bob? Are you here?" I sniffed the air for any hint of my late husband. "I need you right now more than ever." With two murders in the same number of days, the world felt like it was spinning out of control, and I was going with it.

The subtle scent of sawdust and coffee filled the kitchen. Either I'd completely lost my mind, or Bob was letting me know he was here and ready to listen to my ramblings.

I told him all about my visit with both Kim and Bill and how I couldn't imagine Bill losing control enough to actually kill Warren. Then I took a deep breath and told him about Steve being shot dead this morning.

"It sure would be easier if ghosts were real and I could talk to Steve. He probably knows who shot him and why." Tears spilled down my cheeks as I talked. "I just feel so helpless."

Grabbing a tissue, I mopped my tears, then launched into a tirade of worries about Carpenter's Corner. "J. T. says with these murders, I need to install a security system. He's absolutely right, but winter's coming, and it's not something I budgeted for. I don't know if the store can absorb the cost. And what if people stop shopping at Carpenter's Corner because of the murders? We've already taken somewhat of a hit with the new big-box home improvement store opening in Greenwood. Maybe it's time to think about shutting it all down."

I loved my hardware store: the way the sunlight played across the old hardwood floors, the smell of wood and varnish, and helping friends and neighbors pick out the right thing for their projects. Until yesterday, I hadn't been ready to let it go.

"Tell me what you think I should do."

A gardening spade I'd left on the bench hit the floor with a clatter.

I laughed and clapped my hands. "Oh my gosh. You're absolutely right. I've always done my best thinking when I'm digging in the dirt. Thanks, honey." I picked up the spade.

"Mom, who're you talking to?" April peeked around the screen door, looking like she wasn't sure she wanted to come any farther into the looney bin I called home.

"Your dad. I told him about my morning and asked him for advice about what to do with the store." Usually I tried to hide my crazy, but what the heck. Might as well tell her the truth.

April cocked her head and raised one eyebrow. "I see. And what did he have to say?"

I held the spade out for her to see. "Dad told me to get my butt out there and weed the garden. A little dirt therapy's good for the soul." I stood and stretched. "Come out with me. Something big happened while you were out junking. Plus, you need to tell me about the treasures you found today. Grab us a couple of glasses of iced tea on your way out, will you?"

Ten minutes later, April settled herself on the grass, crossed her legs lotus style, and watched me attack the weeds between the zucchini plants like a lunatic. On her way out, she'd made a pit stop in the bathroom and changed from jeans into a comfortable pair of old soccer shorts and a loose purple V-neck tank top.

"Alright, spill it, Mom. What's going on?"

Gathering my thoughts, I stared at the churned-up soil for a moment, then sat back on my heels and swiped a wrist across my sweaty face. "There was another murder at the hardware store today. I'm still trying to process it all."

April sprang off the ground like a bottle rocket, her voice loud and the words shooting out like bullets. "What? When? Who? Why didn't you call me right away?"

"Because there wasn't anything you could do. No need to cut your junking short."

"Don't be ridiculous. You should've called me. Now tell me what happened. Who died?"

"Steve. The police found him in the lumberyard, shot dead in his car." I stood, brushed the dirt off the knees of my jeans, and tossed the dirt-covered spade back into the garden beside the rows of carrots.

April handed me the glass of iced tea she'd brought outside for me.

I motioned for her to follow me to the lawn chairs set up around the brick firepit. Once settled, I filled her in on all the details of the day she'd missed, from the time I stopped by the hardware store to get Steve's address, to the alarm going off at Lipstick and Lace, the anonymous call to the Pine Bluff PD, and the visit with Steve's roommate.

"I feel so bad for poor Steve. He didn't deserve this. The only good thing about it is it removes him from my list of suspects. I'd rather have him alive, though." I smiled wryly.

"Unless he was an accomplice to Warren's murder and was killed to keep him quiet." April threw a wrench into my theory.

"Now who's been reading too many mystery novels?"

"Think about it. What else could it be? Steve's murder has to be directly tied to Warren's death. If it isn't, we have a serial killer running loose in Pine Bluff, and that scares the blazes out of me. Holy bananas!" April was talking fast and getting wound up. Her voice got louder and louder, and her hands waved around in the air as she talked.

"I said the same thing to J. T., and one hundred percent agree with you. There's no way this is a coincidence. We don't have random murders in Pine Bluff."

"You're not going back in the store until whoever's responsible for these murders is arrested. Do you hear me, Mom? It's not safe." April pointed a sharp finger directly at my nose.

I grabbed her demanding finger and held on. "Settle down. I appreciate your concern, but I already promised our mighty police chief the same thing. You don't have to worry about it." I let go of April's finger and took a gulp of my iced tea. "Maybe I'll never go into the store again. This might be the catalyst that changes everything. It might be the time to sell out and retire. I don't know what I'm going to do."

April's mouth snapped shut as she stared at me. "You love the hardware store. I didn't know you were thinking about closing Carpenter's Corner."

"I wasn't. Not until yesterday anyway. But what if people are too leery to shop there after two murders on the property? It could really hurt the business. Then there's the cost of a security system, which I'll definitely be getting if I decide to stay open. Plus, with Steve gone, I'm back to not having any help in the store. I lucked out finding him with his construction background. Probably won't get so lucky the next time around." I clasped my hands in my lap and jiggled my legs, a nervous tic I'd displayed my entire life.

April frowned. "What about the money you got from Bill when he bought out Dad's side of the business? Is that gone?"

I chuckled. "Long gone. Dad and Bill had a deal that if one of them died, the other would get the business for ten grand. Being small business owners, your dad and I kept putting off the cost of life insurance, so that money went to pay for your dad's funeral. It barely covered it."

"Mom! You told us kids your plan covered it." April gaped at me.

I shrugged. "I lied. Well, not really. My plan did cover it, it just wasn't an insurance plan."

April stared at the sky and muttered something I couldn't make out. "Is this the stuff you were chatting to Dad about when I came into the house?"

"Yeah. I know you think I'm nuts, but it makes me feel better to talk to him. Sometimes I swear I feel his presence, like he's still here."

Here we go. Guess I added more fuel to the Mom's-off-her-rocker fire. April would most likely go running to her sister and brother and they'd have me institutionalized before the day was over.

April sighed. "I don't think you're crazy, though I was beginning to wonder when I first came back to town and found you making comments about talking to Dad all the time. Maybe your nutso is rubbing off on me, but I swear I've seen him out of the corner of my eye a couple of times too. When I turn around to look, nothing's there. I think Dad might be hanging around to make sure you're okay, you know?"

I stared at my daughter, grateful for her understanding nature. I reached over and squeezed her hand. "Like my guardian angel?"

"Yeah."

"I hope so, April, I really do."

The two of us sat in companionable silence for a few minutes, sipping our tea.

I stood and stretched. "What do you say we walk over to Hungry Bear and get burgers and fries? I never got around to eating lunch today, and I'm starving. We can bring it home and watch a sappy movie. I'm really in the mood to not think, and I've been craving barbecue French fries."

"Sounds fabulous. Ooh, I'm going to get a peanut-butter milkshake too. Yum." She licked her lips in anticipation. "Hey, the farmer's market should still be open for another hour. Do you mind if we stop there first? I've been wanting to get a jar of pear butter from Goose Hill Farm."

"Sure, I love their condiments. Have you tried their garlic or jalapeño jellies? They're to die for." My stomach rumbled for the hundredth time today.

"Let's drive then. It'd take too long to walk, since we're going to the park." April grabbed her keys off the counter. "I'll drive."

Colorful tent tops in whites, reds, and yellows lined the sidewalk at the park. The sight reminded me of a circus, exciting and fun. A few of the vendors were sold out and tearing their booths down for the day, but plenty of other tables were still heavy with summer produce and flowers. Baskets full of tomatoes, cucumbers, green beans, and potatoes in shades of brown and purple sat waiting for customers to take them home. The scent of sweet, summery peaches filled the air. I followed my nose to a stack and walked away with half a flat filled with luscious peaches and juicy purple blackberries. My mouth watered at the thought of the delicious cobbler I planned to make from them.

April grabbed my sleeve to hurry me along. We trotted to Goose Hill Farm's booth at the end of the row. Not only did they sell scads of yummy jams and jellies, but they also had mouthwatering baked goods sweetened with pear juice from their orchards. April snatched a jar of the pear butter she'd come for, then added a jar of vanilla apple butter to her basket.

"I'm getting you a jar of the garlic jelly you like so much." She added the jelly to her basket, then stacked two fried hand pies on her pile—one cherry and one apple. "These are going to be delicious for dessert."

"You won't hear me arguing." Though I'd have to do my best to ignore Bob's voice in my head, harassing me about my eating habits.

Loaded down with all kinds of goodies, we finally headed back to the car. April laughed when I veered off to purchase a bouquet of dahlias in every hue under the sun.

"How in the world are we going to carry another thing?"

"Don't worry. I've got it all under control."

I asked the woman who sold me the flowers to lay them on the top of my overflowing arms. "See? I told you I've got this."

I gripped a large bag of kettle corn by the tips of the only two fingers not otherwise occupied. Okay. So maybe my fingers were cramping, but every bit of pain was worth it.

"Looks like we'd better be done." April laughed and slipped the bag of popcorn out of my cramping fingers. "Good thing we decided to drive over instead of walking."

With our mission accomplished, we loaded our treasures into the back seat of April's car. Live music flowed out of the band-stand and caused my foot to tap. I glanced over to see what was going on. Marti was teaching a square dance lesson to a group of people spinning and laughing with the music. Today Marti wore a mid-calf-length red dress with a scalloped skirt and lace trim, a white petticoat peeking out from underneath the skirt. The bod-ice of the dress was done in a floral print with a high neckline, and white lace encircled Marti's throat. She stood on the band-stand, calling out moves to the dancers below her. "Allemande left, do-si-do, now swing your partner and take it on home."

I grabbed April and do-si-doed her around the car.

"You know, we should take lessons from Marti one of these days. It'd be a hoot. I haven't square-danced in years. What do you think?" I grinned at my daughter.

"Sure. I'd be up for it. It looks like a lot of fun, and it'd be great exercise. But right now, I'm ready for the burger you prom-ised me." She slid into the driver's seat of her VW Beetle and started the engine. "You coming?"

The Hungry Bear Drive-In was a local icon. It was a tiny place with a drive-up window on both sides and room for only one picnic table and two benches out front. My aunt and uncle opened the Hungry Bear back in 1957, a few years before I was born. Uncle Estel and Aunt Flossie owned and operated the drive-in for twenty years before selling it to another Pine Bluff family in the '70s. After the deal closed, my aunt and uncle moved to the southern Oregon coast to spend their golden years at the beach.

Over the years, the new owners developed a special barbecue-flavored seasoning salt for the fries. You couldn't claim to be a true Pine Bluffian if you didn't crave barbecue fries from time to time. I laughed every time I saw the horrified look out-of-towners got when someone mentioned they needed to try them. People couldn't even fathom what in the world barbecue French fries would taste like. It was a secret I was more than happy to keep to myself.

The Hungry Bear was only two blocks away from my house. When the kids were little, I'd give them each a dollar once a week during the summer to treat themselves to soft-serve ice-cream cones. Now, I was the one walking over several times a week for fries and the world-famous—well, Pine Bluff–famous anyway—Sawmill Burger—a half-pound burger loaded with bacon, cheddar cheese, lettuce, tomato, onion, and pickles, and dripping with their homemade barbecue sauce. The burger was so big I usually got at least two meals out of it. Sometimes three, depending on my appetite. Going for a burger was easier than figuring out what to cook for myself all the time. And it tasted a whole lot better than the crazy concoctions I usually ended up throwing together.

By the time we got back home with our burgers, my fries were almost gone. I'd been so hungry I'd shoveled them down on the short ride home. Dang it. I should've gotten a large order.

I nestled into the big leather armchair in the living room while April sprawled across the oatmeal-colored couch. It took all of thirty seconds before we started to argue about which cheesy movie to watch. My choice, *The Lakehouse*, finally won out. I settled in to watch Sandra Bullock and Keanu Reeves fall in love. The best part was, it didn't have a single thing to do with anyone getting murdered. Bonus.

"Tomorrow I'll regroup and figure out who had a reason to kill Warren and Steve," I said, wiping burger juice off my chin.

Chapter Twenty

After the closing credits of the movie rolled, I took myself to bed and lay there, glaring at the ceiling. My mind refused to shut off and let me sleep. I tossed and turned, trying to find the most comfortable position. For the thousandth time, I flipped my pillow over and punched it into submission, but the sandman remained elusive. I turned on the ceiling fan. Turned it off again. Thank goodness there was a remote control for the thing; otherwise, I would've been up and down a gazillion times.

"This is ridiculous." I threw the sheet off and got out of bed. Might as well get up, make some tea, and read for a while.

I padded barefoot to the kitchen, tiptoeing past April's room so as not to wake her. There was no need to turn on the kitchen light since I always left the light above the kitchen sink on at night. It provided plenty of illumination to make a cup of tea. I managed to be fairly quiet while rummaging through the cupboards for a box of lemongrass and spearmint herbal tea, but then dropped a spoon in the sink with a clatter loud enough to wake the dead. I threw a guilty look over my shoulder, hoping April was in a deep enough sleep that it didn't bother her. I jumped a mile high and screamed like a banshee when I caught sight of a dark figure standing in the shadows beyond the dining room entrance.

"Blast it, April. Don't sneak up on a person like that. You scared my socks off." I pressed a shaking hand to my racing heart, then laughed in relief that my intruder was only my daughter. "Did I wake you? I was trying to be quiet."

April stepped into the kitchen, rubbing her eyes. "No. I couldn't sleep anyway, but you were nowhere near quiet. I keep wondering what else I can dig up about Warren, so when I heard you banging around in here . . ."

"I wasn't banging."

"Yes, you were. Anyway, I decided to join you. Is there enough tea water for me to have a cup?" She shook the kettle and, deciding there was plenty, poured hot water into a mug before opening the lid on the smiling pig cookie jar and peering in. "Oreos. Perfect." She grabbed a handful of the black-and-white treats and settled at the dining room table, with her laptop open.

I huffed. So much for getting in some middle-of-the-night reading. "Since neither of us can sleep, I might as well hang out with you." I pulled out a chair and sat, grabbing one of April's cookies and licking the creamy center before munching on the chocolate wafers.

For the second time in less than twenty-four hours, April typed Warren's name into her search bar and hit "Enter." Sipping tea and munching cookies, she scrolled past the gossip blog we'd read this morning. I tried to pay attention, but April scrolled so fast I thought I was going blind.

"I don't know how you're even seeing anything. Slow down."
She shot me a dirty look.

"Wait. What was that? Go back up." Somehow, in the race down the internet hole, an article had caught my eye.

April stopped and scrolled back up the screen.

"There." I pointed it out.

The headline screamed *"Prominent Local Land Developer Accused of Fraud."* Highlighted in yellow were the names Warren Highcastle and Highcastle Development. April clicked on the article and read every word out loud. The reporter claimed Warren had grossly inflated the sales figures of a condominium development in Denver in order to get people to buy in. His accusers said he'd shown them documents stating seventy-five percent of the high-end units had been sold before they purchased their own. Warren claimed the units were in high demand and had pushed buyers into contracts well over the initial asking price. After closing and moving in, the five plaintiffs found more than half of the units were empty. Unsold. They claimed they'd all been victims of a scam. Warren denied any wrongdoing. The investigation was ongoing.

April finished reading the article. "Holy cow. I had a feeling the guy was a crook. This proves my gut instinct was right."

"Never ignore your gut." I shook my head. "I don't know how people who do things like that can sleep at night."

April clicked back to her search and continued to scroll. More articles with similar stories caught our attention. Highcastle Development accused of real estate fraud in Santa Monica, California, where he'd allegedly filed two separate insurance claims on a fire in a theater he was restoring. Highcastle Development accused of fraud in San Pedro, Texas, after allegedly defrauding six investors out of several million dollars. They claimed Warren convinced them to invest heavily in a new beachfront luxury hotel. In return, they were to receive large shares in the property. Three years later and those shares had yet to materialize.

All told, we found ten articles with Warren at the center of ten different real estate fraud cases. The properties were scattered all around the United States. He'd managed to wiggle out of three of the lawsuits, but seven of them were still pending.

"And this isn't even digging deeply," April said. "I wonder how many more cases are out there?"

"Unbelievable. What in the world is wrong with some people?" I grabbed the last Oreo off the table and absentmindedly shoved it into my mouth, instantly regretting it. My stomach was a little queasy from all the sugar. *I need to counteract the sweet with some protein.*

April's eyes stayed glued to the computer screen, looking for more articles. When the third page of results yielded nothing new, I patted her shoulder.

"Come on, girlie. That's enough. We both better try to get at least a little sleep."

April shook herself out of her trance and glanced at the time on the bottom corner of the screen. "Yikes. It's almost three." She closed the laptop and stretched.

"Yep, and I'm headed to bed. I suggest you do the same." I yawned, though I was feeling far from sleepy. With any luck, I could still get a chapter or two in.

Chapter
Twenty-One

Dove-gray early morning light filtered through the blinds and sheer curtains. I'd finished the entire book before I reached over to turn off my bedside lamp. Leaning back against the pillows, I closed my eyes, hoping to get a few winks in before the day got going. In my foggy brain, Lilac jumped onto the bed with me, pouncing on my toes before the little cat curled into a ball and settled down to sleep. In the little part of my brain that was still awake, I knew she really wasn't there.

I'd just drifted off when Bob came to visit me in my dreams. He settled on the bed beside me, though he didn't make even the slightest indention on the mattress. Lilac roused herself, stretched, and climbed into his lap for a cuddle.

"Hey, honey. It's so good to have you home," I mumbled sleepily. I reached over to take his hand, finding only air under my grasping fingers.

Bob simply smiled and stroked the cat while I drifted into a deeper sleep. Someone's car alarm blared down the street, and my eyes flew open. I searched the room for Bob and Lilac before realizing their presence had only been a sweet dream.

Now that I was wide awake, no way was sleep going to reclaim me. With a resigned sigh, I threw off the covers and got out of bed. Outside my open window, birds chirped, and a soft breeze played sweet, tinkling music on the wind chimes hanging in the old maple tree. Sunday mornings were normally my favorite time of the week. I loved the peace and quiet that settled over the whole town. With two murders hanging over our heads, and next to no sleep to speak of, today felt different. The tension in the air was palpable.

I pulled on a pair of old ratty jeans and slipped my feet into gardening clogs before tiptoeing through the house and slipping outside. Once again, I needed some garden therapy. The morning smelled of fresh grass damp with dew, the sweet citrus of the bee balm warming under the sun, and a neighbor's first pot of coffee brewing. *Delicious.* Retrieving the spade from between the carrot tops where I'd thrown it yesterday, I sank to my knees in the dirt. Something about digging in the dirt and letting the soil sift through my fingers always grounded me and helped clear my mind.

Evonne had given me a flyer the other day for a workshop called "Earthing" the local yoga studio was putting on. It had something to do with being barefoot outside while doing yoga. It claimed electrons from the earth traveled up through your bare feet, getting you in sync with the earth and giving you a jolt of energy. I'd brushed it off as poppycock, but maybe there was something to it. If I had time, maybe I'd check out the yoga studio next week to see what it was all about. It couldn't hurt to get more information.

A pile of weeds filled the wheelbarrow by the time April emerged from her slumber. Her feet were bare, and she had a cup of coffee cuddled between her hands.

She yawned and rubbed her eyes. "How long have you been awake?"

Uh . . . since yesterday. "A couple of hours. I woke up feeling out of sorts, so came out here. Good thing too. The weeds were doing their darndest to take over my garden. Turn my back for a day or two, and they explode. There's no rest for the wicked."

"There's a simple solution. Stop turning your back."

I tossed a clod of dirt at my smart-aleck daughter. She reached for a handful of dirt, so in order to distract her, I pointed at the tall bushes crowding one corner of the garden. "Hey, take a look at those tomatoes. Can you believe that's only three plants? Two heirlooms and one cherry tomato. They're loaded this year and some are starting to ripen. I'm going to have to get out the canner pretty soon."

My ploy worked. April dropped her fistful of dirt and went to check out the tomato plants instead.

"Mmm. They look great." She reached between the deep green leaves of one plant. "There're a couple of ripe ones here. How does an omelet with fresh tomato sound for breakfast?" She held out a ripe, red tomato like a prize.

"Heaven. Pinch off some of the fresh basil to go in it too." My mouth watered at the thought of breakfast and coffee.

April had gotten her mad kitchen skills from her dad. Like him, she loved to cook, and I was grateful she did. It'd been more than nice having her in the house the last couple of days.

"Is there any coffee left?" I finished weeding a row of onions and pulled my gardening gloves off.

April already had a handful of basil and was headed back into the house with her garden treasures. "Sure is," she called over her shoulder.

Over omelets and toast, we volleyed our individual theories back and forth about the two murders. April's laptop sat on the table, where she'd left it when we'd gone to bed in the wee hours of the morning. She flipped it around to take another look at the pending Highcastle Development lawsuits.

"Not sure if these cases have anything to do with Warren getting himself killed or not, but between the fraud and his belief he was God's gift to women, it sure isn't painting a nice picture of the guy, is it?" April brushed toast crumbs off the table and into her hand.

"To put it mildly. All this real estate fraud reminds me I want to talk to Kristi today, but I need a reason to stop by." I tapped my forefinger on my chin, thinking. "There's a bumper crop of zucchini in the garden. I could pick a bunch and take them to the neighbors. Probably need to drop a few by the Fisher house, don't you think?"

"You've got a devious little mind." April gave me a side-eye. "But I guess it's a better idea than any I've got. Since it's Sunday, you might even catch her at home. Do you want me to tag along?"

I took my plate to the sink and rinsed it off. "Sure. It'd be fun to have you go with me. I'll get the zucchini picked. We can clean the kitchen later." I glanced at the teal teapot-shaped clock above the sink. "It's nine now. Do you think it's too early for a Sunday visit?"

"Nah. By the time you get the squash picked and we drop off a few on the way, it'll be closer to ten before we get to their house. You know you'll run into a ton of people to chat with on the way."

"True story." I let the screen door bang behind me as I headed back to the garden.

Chapter Twenty-Two

The kid's old red Radio Flyer wagon was buried under layers of woodchips and grime. I pulled it out of the woodshed and hosed off the dirt and spiderwebs before loading it with freshly picked zucchini. Getting rid of the excess squash wasn't always an easy task. Most people who planted a garden ended up with more than they could use by late August. There was a standing joke around town that to give away zucchini, you had to leave it on your neighbor's porch when they weren't home or sneak it onto their doorstep in the middle of the night. That way, they wouldn't know where it came from and couldn't bring it back.

One day last year I'd come home from work and found a huge zucchini dressed like a baby sitting on my front porch. It had googly eyes glued on it and a smile made from red felt, and it wore a pink dress with a matching bonnet. The stupid thing made me laugh until I cried. And I'd nearly wet my pants. Evonne had finally come clean and admitted to being the culprit. I started giggling again thinking about it.

The Fisher family lived on Cedar Street, one road over from my house and then down about six blocks. Kristi's husband, Travis, was a local fishing guide, and their house sat on the bank of the Elk River. April and I started out, leaving the first zucchini offering on my neighbor Smitty's porch. Smitty didn't sleep well at night. She'd told me her best sleep came in the early morning hours, so she rarely got out of bed before mid-morning. It made her the perfect candidate to receive a rogue squash.

"Smitty's probably the only one who'll appreciate this." I place two medium-sized squash on her doorstep. "She'll most likely be over in the next few days with a loaf of warm zucchini bread."

"Aha. Another devious plan of yours." April chuckled, then grabbed a squash out of the wagon and dashed across the street, her red Converse tennis shoes slapping the pavement.

I choked back laughter as my daughter raced around, leaving squash on all of our neighbor's porches. I didn't want to laugh too loud and have someone notice us.

"This is fun. A couple of zucchini bandits on the prowl." I took the next squash and gently lowered it over a white picket fence, leaning it against the gate, where it wouldn't be missed.

We crossed over Main Street and headed down Cedar. Rocking M Coffee Stop was getting busy with people coming out for Sunday morning breakfast and coffee.

"You better not leave one of those on my porch, Dawna Carpenter," Judy Hassin, a member of the Women's Service Club, yelled good-naturedly when she spotted my little red wagon full of squash.

"You never know what might happen when you're not home."
I grinned, raising my shoulders and hands in an exaggerated
shrug.

April had been right, of course, about running across people
to chat with. It'd be rude to not say hello when we passed homes
where my friends and neighbors were working in their yards or
sitting on their porches enjoying their morning coffee. There
were a ton of hellos and how-are-yous and a lot of "Oh my gosh,
I heard about Steve" to get through before we finally made it to
the block where the Fishers lived.

It was a few minutes after ten when the Fisher's two-story, white
Craftsman house came into view. April opened the gate on the
white picket fence, and I pulled the wagon through, stopping at
the front porch steps. I didn't make it all the way up the steps before
the screen door opened, and Kristi poked her blond head outside.

"Good morning. What's up?" A baggy, cream-colored knit
cardigan slipped off her slender shoulders, revealing a white
T-shirt over blue-and-white-striped cotton shorts.

"Good morning. I hope we aren't interrupting your breakfast. April and I were out dropping off zucchini to friends and
wondered if you needed any. My garden's exploding this year. I
can't use it all myself." I gestured to the wagon behind me.

As I'd hoped, Kristi held the door wide open and invited us
in. "You're not interrupting at all. We were done with breakfast
an hour ago. Travis has a group out fishing this morning, and the
boys are watching cartoons. I was about to take my coffee out to
the backyard. Why don't you two join me?"

April raised her eyebrows and held out a zucchini in each
hand.

"Sure," Kristi said. "I didn't get a garden planted this year, so I'd love a couple. Thanks."

April handed over the squash, grabbing two more out of the wagon on her way into the house. She left them on the kitchen counter as Kristi led the way into the backyard.

The Fishers had a great view of the river from their large backyard. When I commented on it, Kristi explained that instead of the standard cedar privacy fence, they'd opted for a chain link, so the kids were corralled, but the view was still intact. A tall, red-leafed maple tree threw shade over a corner of the house and onto the redwood picnic table sitting on the slate patio. A large wooden swing set in the far corner of the yard looked like a kid's paradise, with a fort, slides, and a climbing wall.

"Lucky kids." April nodded to the play structure. "I'm tempted to have a go at it myself."

Kristi smiled. "Sometimes I do." She invited us to have a seat at the picnic table. "Can I get either of you something to drink? Coffee or something a bit colder? I have lemonade or water."

"I'd love a glass of water. It's already toasty today." I fanned my face with my hands. Plus, the glass would give me something to do with my hands while I prodded our hostess for information.

April nodded. "I'll take water too, if you don't mind. Thank you. We didn't stop by so you'd have to wait on us, though."

"Oh, it's no bother. It's nice to have company." Kristi disappeared into the house, emerging moments later with two glasses of ice water, each with a slice of lemon floating on top. She shrugged her sweater off and placed it on the wooden bench before taking a seat. "Definitely don't need a sweater out here. Travis likes the air conditioner set so low it feels like perpetual winter inside the house. I prefer it a bit warmer." She laughed softly.

"After our morning walk, I thought it felt good in your house, but I bet it'd get cold pretty quickly," I replied.

Kristi nodded and took a sip of her steaming coffee. "I heard about Steve's death. So sad. He seemed like a nice man, always ready to help. It must be a shock for you."

"Yeah, I can't seem to wrap my head around these murders. It's all pretty horrible. I wish I'd made more of an effort to get to know Steve better. He was always close-mouthed when it came to talking about himself. It was hard to get him to open up, so I stopped trying." I pushed my glasses up. "Hopefully, the police will figure out who killed him, sooner than later. Two murders in two days is absolutely insane." I fidgeted with my water glass, trying to decide how to ask Kristi what I wanted to know. *Jump in and do it.* "Since you're the real estate agent Warren was working with, can you tell me what happens now? Is the contract negated because of his death?"

Kristi shook her head. "Not necessarily. I've never had something like this happen before, but legally the contract could remain valid as long as whoever holds Warren's power of attorney moves forward with it. Once the transaction is complete, the property would become part of the estate of the deceased buyer."

"Really?" Her information surprised me. "How interesting. Do you think that'll happen with the Emery Theater?"

"I seriously doubt it. Warren was getting a commercial property loan. I think it will be pretty difficult to convince his lender to fund the loan. The contract is contingent on financing, so if the lender pulls the loan, the contract's dead. There are still a few outstanding documents he needed to provide to the bank, and honestly, after the things I found out recently about the man's integrity, I don't have any desire to chase those documents down, even for his estate."

"What do you mean? I don't want to be nosy, but Warren died in my store, so it all feels a bit personal to me. And to be perfectly honest, I heard yelling coming from Elk River Realty when I was on my way to work Friday morning. April and I stopped in later the same afternoon, and Marti mentioned Warren had been yelling at you about signing some documents." *Okay, so I do want to be nosy.* Another little white lie to add to my growing list of transgressions.

April jumped in with questions of her own. "Was he trying to get you to do something underhanded? Your Aunt Marti made it sound like the guy was a real snake in the grass."

Kristi sighed, worry shadowing her big brown eyes. She gulped the rest of her coffee and stared, unblinking, out at the river. After a minute had passed, she drew her focus back to April and me. "What wasn't he trying to get me to do is more the question. Initially, when Warren first contacted me, he offered me a large bonus if I could track down the owners of the Emery and get them to sell him the property. A finder's fee, if you will. It's not illegal, but it doesn't happen often. I'd get the finder's fee after we closed on the property, along with my normal commission. It was a big deal for me, and I was excited. We're coming into fall, and Travis's river guiding business is seasonal. He doesn't have any clients in the winter, you know?"

"I sure do." I thought about my own struggles with business in the wintertime.

"Anyway, it took some digging, but I finally tracked down the woman who owns the Emery Theater. She's a many great-granddaughter relative of Richard Steinman. He was the man who had the opera house built all those years ago. Do you know much about him?"

I nodded. "Quite a bit, actually. He was a big player in the early history of Pine Bluff. I didn't realize a descendant of his still owned the building, though."

"Yep. Her name is Dolores Adams. She lives in Paradise Valley, Arizona. She hasn't been to Pine Bluff for many years and is more than ready to sell. Nobody in the family is interested in the building or its upkeep anymore."

"So, after you spoke with her, you let Warren know she wanted to sell, and he made an offer on the building?"

"Basically, yes. As soon as I let him know, he came to Pine Bluff to tour the building and made a solid offer the same day. Everything was going along smoothly until a few days ago, when it got a little bumpy." Kristi paused and sighed. "I probably shouldn't be talking about this, but Warren's dead now, so I guess it doesn't matter anymore."

Oh, don't stop now. Kristi was barely getting to the good stuff. I reached across the table and patted her arm, hoping to keep her talking. "It's good to talk about things troubling you. You'll feel better once you get it all out. What happened a few days ago?"

"Warren called Thursday and said he needed me to create a second contract the seller wouldn't see. He wanted it to show a purchase price twenty percent higher than the original contract stated."

"Seems suspicious. What in the world was he going to use it for?"

"With a higher purchase price, the bank would give him a larger loan on the building. He wanted a full second set of settlement papers drawn up, and told me he had another contact willing to forge the seller's signature on the paperwork. He was confident I could find an escrow officer who'd agree to provide the new documents he wanted. I told him no way was I going to be involved in his scheme. Not only is it against the law, but it could cost me my real estate license. Maybe even jail time." Kristi stood and began pacing the patio. "Can you believe it? I have young children, for crying out loud. Becoming involved in fraud could ruin my entire life."

April shook her head. "Unbelievable. It's hard to imagine he'd ask you to do something so dishonest."

"Right?" Kristi's face flushed red, a combination of the hot coffee and anger. "I couldn't believe it either."

"What'd Warren do when you told him you wouldn't do it?" I asked.

Kristi sat back down at the picnic table. "He hung up on me. I didn't hear from him again until I got to the office on Friday morning, and he was there waiting for me. Aunt Marti was already at work and had the front door propped open to let the fresh air in. I guess it's why you could hear us yelling. Warren wanted to discuss things." She made air quotes when she said the word *discuss*. "It turned into a shouting match pretty quickly. I tried not to lose my temper, but when I told him I wasn't going to change my mind, he called me a few choice names and then fired me. Warren said he was going to bring in a real estate agent who'd do what needed to be done, and then he said he'd never had any intention of paying me the finder's fee in the first place. Called me a gullible, empty-headed idiot." She swiped at her eyes with the back of a finger. "I hate how I cry when I'm mad." She dipped her head to hide the tears.

"I get it. I've always done the same thing. In fact, the only time I cry is when I'm mad or scared." I tried to empathize with Kristi. "I know this is hard for you to talk about when it's so fresh, but do you know what time it was when Warren left your office Friday morning?"

"Yeah, he finished by saying he was going to report me to the board of realtors for misleading him about the condition of the property, then he left. It was about a quarter after eight. Still early."

"Had he been misled about the condition of the property?"

"No, of course not. The guy was a jerk. He wanted his own way and was mad I wasn't making it easy for him."

"I know, Kristi." I shook my head and then nodded at April. It was time to fill Kristi in on what a genuine piece of garbage Warren had been.

April understood my nod and took over. "I've been doing some research on Warren. Did you know he's been brought up on real estate fraud charges no less than ten times?"

Kristi sat straighter and blinked slowly. "What? Are you sure?"

"Yep. With a quick internet search, I found quite a few articles from various newspapers across the country, spelling it all out. It looks like about seven of them are still active investigations. My guess is if those lawsuits go to trial, it'll effectively close

Highcastle Development for good. *Jerk* is too mild of a word for who that man was."

"From the consensus around town, *jerk* seems to have been his one personality trait. Well, everyone except Darlene, who thought he was the cat's meow." I rolled my eyes. "Speaking of Darlene, she mentioned you were in Lipstick and Lace Friday morning. Must've been right after your argument with Warren."

Of course, since Darlene's shop wasn't open until eight thirty, Kristi couldn't have been in there before the fight.

Kristi nodded. "Yeah, I went in for mascara. I have a hard time finding makeup gentle enough it doesn't give me an allergy attack. Darlene carries a brand with more natural ingredients than most of them have. It's the only mascara I've been able to find that doesn't make my eyes red and itchy after a few minutes."

"I have a problem with allergy eyes too. What brand is it?" April asked.

"It's called Pure Eyes. Comes in a silver tube. They make eyeshadow as well. You'll love it. It's so nice to be able to wear eye makeup again." Kristi suddenly turned to me. "Why are you asking all these questions? I already told Chief Dallas most of this."

Trying to act casual, I shrugged my shoulders and picked at a fingernail I'd broken during my early morning gardening session. "No reason. I'm trying to piece things together. Warren's murder feels personal to me since he was killed in my hardware store. You didn't happen to see him in the boutique when you were there, did you?"

"No, and it's a darn good thing I didn't. I was still fuming. After I purchased my mascara, I went for a long drive to clear my head."

Or to establish an alibi?

"You went on a drive by yourself? When did you get back?"

Kristi studied me over the rim of her coffee cup, her eyes narrowed and suspicious. "You know, Dawna, I'm starting to feel like you're interrogating me. Let me be perfectly clear. I had nothing to do with Warren's death." She stood and turned to go into the house. "See yourself out the side gate. Oh, and thanks for the zucchini," she added in a sarcastic tone. Kristi marched into her house and slammed the sliding door behind her.

Well, that conversation had gone downhill fast. I puffed out a breath and sighed regretfully. "Yikes. I guess I wasn't tactful enough. Now I feel like a heel. To top it off, I honestly don't think she had anything to do with the murders. What are your thoughts?"

April shook her head. "Not for a second. Kristi's a genuinely nice person. She's always been super sweet. I'll have to make amends with her later. Let's get out of here."

We slipped out the side yard as directed and circled around to the front of the house to grab the Radio Flyer wagon.

"Looks like we still have a bunch of squash to get rid of." I frowned.

We were halfway up the block when we met Marti on her way to her niece's house. We exchanged hellos, and April and I kept going. At the corner, I turned and looked back at the Fisher house. Marti stood in the yard, her arms crossed and her jaw set as she watched us walk away.

April and I walked the next block in silence, both lost in our own thoughts. April kicked a small rock in the road. It skittered up the empty street, and she followed it, giving the rock another swift kick.

She caught up to the rock and picked it up, worrying it between her fingers. "There's something I've been wondering about."

"What's that?"

"Why do you suppose Warren picked Pine Bluff for his next project? And how did he know about the Emery Theater in the first place? He approached Kristi and asked her to contact the owner, which means the theater was already on his radar. How? It's not like our little town's a booming tourist destination."

I scratched my head and frowned. "That, my dear, is an excellent question."

We managed to unload all but three of the zucchinis before circling back around to my house.

"Good job, Mom. You should be proud of yourself for finding all those empty doorsteps to leave your unwanted squash on."

"Sure, until they figure out it was me and bring them all back." I chuckled and followed my daughter into the kitchen, purposely letting the screen door slam behind me. Such a satisfying sound. It reminded me of hot summer days when the three kids were in and out of the house a thousand times in one afternoon.

"Holy cow, Mom. Do you know how many times you've yelled at me for slamming the screen door? This makes the second time you've let it bang today." April's hands were on her hips, and her foot tapped as she channeled her inner me.

I reached over and pushed the door back open, letting it go to bang closed one more time. "Yep, but it's my house, and I do what I want. And now I want to take a cool shower since I didn't take one this morning. Maybe I'll figure out what our next move should be. I do my best thinking in the shower."

Of course, with no sleep to speak of, my brain didn't function any better in the shower than it had been functioning out of the shower. Afterward, I put on a cotton robe, toweled off my hair, and padded into my bedroom for a change of clothes, but the bed looked way too good to my exhausted body. I fell across the mattress, thinking I'd lie down for a few minutes.

Chapter Twenty-Three

F our hours later, I awoke feeling groggy and out of sorts. Late afternoon shadows from the tree outside my window played across the walls of my bedroom. I lay there, thinking about the murders, but had no more of a game plan than I'd had before falling asleep. I heaved myself off the bed and ditched the cotton robe for a moss-green T-shirt with the Grand Canyon National Park logo on the front and a lightweight pair of creamy linen shorts.

"April," I called out, "are you still here?"

"Yep. I'm in the sunroom reading," came the quick reply.

April sat in her dad's old leather armchair with a paperback copy of *The Night Circus* open in her lap.

"Hey, sorry I fell—"

April held up a finger, effectively cutting me off with the reader's universal signal. It means give me a minute. I need to finish this paragraph. Or page. Or chapter. I zipped my lips and waited until April fumbled for the bookmark she'd tucked under her leg.

Once she wedged the bookmark into her book, she looked at me. "What's up?"

"Nothing. I wanted to say sorry to have fallen asleep on you. I thought I'd lay down for a few minutes, but it looks like the entire afternoon got away from me instead."

April shrugged. "No worries. Neither one of us got much sleep last night. It was nice to chill out and get some reading done. This is a brilliant book, by the way. You should read it sometime."

I laughed. April had read *The Night Circus* so many times the cover was perilously in danger of pulling completely away from the spine. Over the years, she'd told me every single detail about the book, so I felt like I'd read it myself a time or two.

I plopped onto the couch. "Did you want to do something this evening?"

"No, I think I'm going to reorganize my studio a bit and decide what piece of furniture I want to work on next."

"Sounds like a plan, but you're going to stay here again tonight, right?"

April rose from the chair and stretched. "Yeah. I'll be back." She grabbed her purse and car keys off the coffee table and headed for the door. "Oh, Mom. A couple notifications came in on your phone while you were napping. I think somebody was texting you. See you later."

My phone was on the dining room table where I'd left it when I'd gone to take my shower. I thumbed it awake and clicked into my text messages. There were two, both from Evonne.

Hey lady. Up for a Sunday afternoon slice of pie?

An hour later. *Dawna?*

It'd been an hour and a half since Evonne's last text, but since I'm always ready for pie, I shot off a belated response.

Am I too late for pie?

Never. Come on over.

I didn't waste another minute.

Five minutes later, I pulled up in front of the Ford's craftsman bungalow. How Evonne managed to keep her house looking like a cool oasis in this late summer heat was beyond me. A green expanse of lawn edged with beds of cascading red, purple, and pink petunias, white Shasta daisies, and black-eyed Susans led the way to the wide front porch. The house was painted sea green with garnet-red trim and creamy accents.

Evonne and I'd been best friends since fourth grade, so her house felt as comfortable to me as my own. In all the years they'd lived here, I'd never once knocked on the door. Instead, I let myself in through the Mission-style door and shouted hello to announce my presence.

"In the kitchen," Evonne answered back.

Acting as if I lived there, I tossed my purse on the couch on my way through the house to the kitchen. As it always did in the summertime, Evonne's sunny kitchen smelled like lemonade. I'd never quite figured out how she achieved that delicious and cool smell, but I'd always loved it.

The large, homey kitchen with the corn silk–colored cabinets was one of my favorite places on earth. I took a seat on one of the bar-height padded chairs at the kitchen island while Evonne puttered around her kitchen, taking blue-and-white hand-painted stoneware dessert plates and matching coffee cups out of a bubble glass-fronted cupboard. When the coffeepot stopped dripping, I jumped back up to pour us each a mug while she plated slices of pie. Grabbing a carton of half-and-half out of the refrigerator, I gave each mug a splash and carried them back to the island.

"Oh, my soul." The cool and creamy lemon icebox pie melted in my mouth. "Heavenly."

"Thanks. I know it's one of your favorites."

"It is, especially this time of year. So good." I savored another bite of the luscious pie. "So, what's up? Was there something you wanted to talk about?"

"No," Evonne answered. "Do I need a reason to share a piece of pie with my best friend?"

"Of course not. I thought maybe you'd heard something about the murders you wanted to share with me."

She hadn't, but it didn't stop the two of us from launching into a whole tirade about our theories and how we thought the murders of Warren and Steve had to be connected. Individually, we each went off on separate tangents, accusing various townspeople of murder but ultimately circling back around to the same suspect list I'd been agonizing over. When I mentioned Darlene being at the top of my list, Evonne blew a raspberry with her lips and dismissed my theory.

"No way the woman would take the chance of getting blood on her hands. Cross her off your list."

I shook my head. "Nope. Not until I can prove beyond a shadow of a doubt she didn't do it."

"And exactly how do you propose to do that?"

"I don't know. Nothing I've tried so far has come to fruition." I blew out a breath and pushed my empty plate away. "You know, I'd really like to get inside the theater and have a look around."

"What for?" Evonne narrowed her eyes at me over the rim of her coffee cup.

I shrugged. "To poke around. Maybe there's something in there that could give me a clue, or at least point me in the right direction. I'm not sure what the something might be, but I have a feeling the answer is tied to the Emery Theater." I huffed and crossed my arms on the island. "Too bad there's not a way to get inside."

Evonne cocked her head and shot me a Mona Lisa smile. "Who says there's not?" She winked.

I whipped my head around and stared at her. "Spill it. What do you know?"

"It's possible I might have the keys to the building."

"What? How did I not know this?"

"Apparently you haven't been paying attention. Remember a few years ago, when we were having work done at City Hall, so we moved my office to the Emery for a couple of months?"

"Yeah." I raised my eyebrows and pushed my glasses up. "Go on."

"Well, I still have the keys. Obviously."

"No, it's not obvious."

"You remember I'm Pine Bluff's city manager, right? I hold the keys, or at least a copy of the keys, to every building the city owns or has a rental agreement for."

"It makes sense, but it hadn't occurred to me. So, the city still has a rental agreement with the owner of the Emery?"

"We do, in case we need to use it again. We pay a minimal yearly rent to Mrs. Adams and, in turn, keep an eye on the building for her. It's how I knew she'd be willing to sell and why

I proposed the idea of the fundraisers to the Women's Service Club to help fund the purchase of the building in the future."

"Interesting. I heard a different story from Kristi." I paused for a moment. "Can I borrow the key?"

"Not so fast, little lady. You're not going in there without me. And Kristi wanted that finder's fee."

I eyeballed my best friend, then held out a hand to shake. "You've got yourself a deal. The two of us go. When can we leave?"

Evonne shook my hand. "Is now too soon?"

*   *   *

An ornate green metal awning with "The Emery Theater" painted in faded gold lettering across the facade sheltered the front door of the theater from inclement weather. Even though it was bright daylight on a Sunday evening and my best friend held the key, I kept looking over my shoulder, feeling like we were breaking and entering. Evonne jiggled the key in the lock and, with a flourish, swung one side of the glass front doors wide open. She ushered me inside and relocked the door behind us.

I ran my hand along the iron railing lining the four steps leading to the old concession stand. I barely touched it, but the railing was loose and fell to the floor with enough of a clatter to wake the dead. Evonne and I both jumped and shrieked. We looked at each other and burst out laughing. We were a couple of sorry Nancy Drews if a falling railing was enough to send us packing.

"Remember junior prom night?" Evonne asked. "Wasn't that a hoot?"

"Do I ever. I'm still terrified." I shuddered, staring at the faded and chipped brown-and-white checkerboard tile covering the floor in front of the glass-cased concession stand.

When we were in high school, the theater had still been in operation, showing movies only on the weekends. For our junior prom, our class had raised enough money to rent the theater. After the dance, we'd all trooped from the high school gymnasium to the theater for a double feature that'd lasted until nearly four in the morning and traumatized some of us so badly our entire student body was sleep-deprived for weeks.

"I don't remember who the adults were who approved those movies, but they failed big time." Evonne laughed and wiped tears out of her eyes.

"Yeah, we sure pulled one over on them, didn't we?" My tone was more than a little sarcastic.

Either the parents who'd been in charge all those years ago hadn't known much about recent movie releases, or they simply hadn't cared what their own kids watched. The first movie was a raunchy comedy called *The Pom Pom Girls*. It was rated R and showed way more skin and passion than I'd ever seen on the screen before, or anywhere else for that matter. The second movie, also rated R, scared the holy living tarnation out of me—as well as a good number of my classmates.

"Sure, *Carrie* was set during a prom, but what in the world were they thinking? I slept with the light on for six months after watching those movies." Evonne leaned against the concession counter while we reminisced.

We were chuckling over our teenage trauma when the salty scent of fresh buttered popcorn wafted by. A quick glance at Evonne told me she didn't seem to have noticed anything unusual. Must've been my love of movie theater popcorn and wishful thinking. I clapped my hands together once, ready to explore the Emery.

"Where should we start? Do you want to check out the space my office was in?" Evonne pointed to a door to the left of the front entrance leading to empty office spaces upstairs.

When the opera house had been built, Steinman had allocated offices for the theater manager and himself on the second story of the building. After the original City Hall burned, they moved the city offices into the theater until a new building could be built. And when they remodeled City Hall a few years ago, the city employees had moved in once again. Apparently, it'd been a long-standing arrangement between Pine Bluff city management and the owner of the Emery Theater.

"No, I think I want to check out the auditorium and stage first." I headed through the doorway to the seating area and down the ramp toward the stage.

It felt like a hundred years since I'd been inside the Emery Theater, but I was pleasantly surprised at the state of the main room. I paused and looked around, taking in the pressed-tin ceiling and ornate plaster tiles lining the front of the balcony. Evonne had found the light switches and turned on the dim lights lining the auditorium walls. She scooted down the aisle and trotted to my side.

"By the way, what're we looking for exactly?"

I shrugged. "I have no idea. When we see it, I hope we'll know."

"Well, that was helpful."

"You're welcome."

With nothing catching my attention on the main floor, we veered to the left and ascended the few wooden steps to the stage. A heavy blue velvet curtain still hung as a backdrop, as if a production had recently ended. The stage itself was empty—nothing but a dusty hardwood floor, but the smell of popcorn was stronger than ever.

"Do you smell the popcorn?" I whispered to Evonne in case there was someone else inside the theater with us.

She frowned, sniffed the air, and shook her head. "I don't smell a thing."

Huh. How is that possible? The smell was so strong to me I could almost taste the buttery popcorn. I pulled back the curtain and peered into the dark depths of the backstage area.

"I can go back and see if I can figure out which light switch is for backstage."

"Nah. I've got it covered." I dug around in my purse until I found two small flashlights.

Evonne laughed. "Of course you do, Mary Poppins."

"Hey, a girl's got to be prepared for anything." I turned my flashlight on and stepped behind the curtain, with Evonne right on my heels.

The backstage area was fairly clutter-free. Metal shelving lined the back wall, with dusty cardboard boxes and crates filling the shelves. A tall metal ladder, some lumber, and other various items leaned against the walls, and a set of beige lockers took up one corner of the room. A "No Smoking" sign hung over the red metal exit doors.

A shadow crossed in front of my flashlight beam, causing my heart to leap into my throat. I shrieked and swung my light from right to left, looking for whatever had caused the moving shadow.

"What? What's the matter?" Evonne grabbed my arm, her fingernails digging into my skin.

I shrugged. "Apparently nothing. I thought I saw something move, but there's nothing here. I'm just a scaredy-cat."

We laughed before turning and heading back up the main aisle and out into the lobby. Back in better lighting, I switched off my flashlight and looked around. A picture of the original owner of the Emery Theater still hung on the wall next to the concession stand. It was one of those disconcerting photographs where the subject's gaze seems to track you as you move around the room. Richard Steinman stared straight into my eyes from the old black-and-white photograph; he was wearing a top hat and a fancy suit of the era, with a cane tucked in the crook of his arm. His lips rose in a slight smile below his iconic walrus mustache.

"He looks like he was a nice man. You can still see the twinkle of amusement in his eyes, but"—I shivered and turned to look at Evonne—"don't you get the feeling he's watching us?"

Evonne shook her head in confusion. "No. His gaze is clearly off to the left."

I frowned at her. "What're you talking about? He's staring straight ahead."

Turning back to the picture, I gasped. Mr. Steinman's eyes, the eyes that had been watching my every move, were now staring directly at a door to the left of the stage. Was he trying to tell us something? Was I closer to crazy than I'd thought?

Chapter
Twenty-Four

Pointing to the closed door in the corner of the lobby, I asked Evonne, "Where does this lead?" I tried the handle, but it was locked. "We need to get in here. Do you have a key to this door?"

Bless Evonne's heart—the whites of her eyes shone like a spooked horse, but she nodded and inserted the key to the door into the lock without another question. "This is the door to the basement," was all she said as she swung it open.

A set of steep stairs descended into a musty, dark pit. I turned my small flashlight back on and pointed it downward, where it illuminated only two steps in front of me. Pushing the niggle of worry aside, I headed down the stairs, with Evonne following. When we reached the basement, it was a little lighter thanks to a series of three transom windows high on the wall at ground level. Loose stones and bricks lay scattered among mildewing pieces of fallen sheetrock on the dirt floor of the basement. A ten-foot-long rusty stovepipe rested on the debris, and pieces of discolored insulation hung from the open ceiling.

Evonne and I carefully picked our way across the rubble. It all looked as if it'd been discarded years ago. Nothing set off any red flags in my brain, so I headed to the open doorway of a second room, with Evonne right on my heels.

This room was smaller than the main part of the basement. Pipes ran across the walls, electrical wires crisscrossed the ceiling, and yellowed fiberglass insulation hung between wooden ceiling joists. Everything was ancient and decrepit except the two bright blue plastic tubs pushed up against the wall. One tub held tools, while the other one was full of what looked to be cans of paint. The tub of tools sat on the floor under a network of rusty pipes attached to the wall with metal clamps. I played my flashlight beam over the tools. The light glinted off the shiny blade of a hacksaw. I picked out an orange-headed tube cutter, a pair of pliers, and a plumber's torch that all looked fairly new. The second tub held a few cans of paint and a gallon or two of vinegar. I kneeled and rummaged through the contents. There was a can of copper paint and a can of iron paint, along with a couple paintbrushes and a sponge. What I thought had been two gallons of vinegar turned out to be an iron activator and a blue patina activator.

"Huh," Evonne grunted. "The tools make sense if someone was needing to work on the plumbing, but the rest is sure a strange combination."

"Agreed." I swiped my finger across the top of the can of copper paint. "No dust. These were left here recently."

I straightened and pushed my glasses up the bridge of my nose, concentrating on the tangle of pipes crisscrossing the wall. Realization about the purpose of the products in the second tub slowly dawned on me. I'd used those same products to add a vintage patina to a metal tailgate. My clients had commissioned me to build them a bench to sit beside their pond. They'd wanted the back of the bench made from the tailgate of the Ford pickup they'd gone on their first date in, but they'd wanted it to match the rustic feel of their farm, so I'd distressed it and added a beautiful rusty patina, using copper and iron paint, then oxidating it with the same type of paint activators in the tub of products. When I'd finished, the tailgate looked like it come from a truck decades older than it was. My clients had been delighted with it.

"Highcastle was up to something here, but I'm just not sure what. Something fraudulent would be my guess. I think he hired someone to cut the pipes, for some reason, and then distress the fresh cuts to make it look as if the pipes had burst some time ago."

And I'd bet my last dollar it was Roy Dejean and that nervous man I'd seen him with at the grocery store.

"What? How do you know?" Evonne asked.

"I don't. It just an educated guess from knowing what you can do with these products and knowing what a shyster Warren was. I'm sure he was trying to get Mrs. Adams to lower the purchase price." I tapped my index finger on my chin. "If that's the case, though, I wonder why they didn't follow through?"

"You really think he would've done that? It's hard to imagine people being so underhanded." Evonne rubbed at her arms as if she had a chill. "It's cold down here. Have you seen enough?"

I snapped a few pictures with my phone, though the light was bad. When I thumbed back through, they showed only a grainy black screen with a weird ball of light in the corner. Oh well, it'd been worth a try. I shrugged and slipped my phone back in my pocket. Evonne and I headed back to the main level of the theater. As soon as we topped the stairs, I glanced over at the photograph of Richard Steinman. Once again, he was staring straight into my eyes, and this time, I would've sworn I saw him wink.

Evonne shivered. "Brr. I'm still cold. Let's go."

We stepped out into the August evening, and Evonne locked the door to the Emery Theater behind us. Without saying a word to each other, we climbed back into my Jeep. I drove to Evonne's house, and we settled in the backyard, each with our own bottle of red wine, before we launched into a lengthy discussion about murder and mayhem in our peaceful little town.

Chapter
Twenty-Five

When I woke much later than normal on Monday morning, I had an idea of what I needed to do next. While I lay there trying to figure out a game plan, I kept drifting in and out of sleep. At some point, my imagination conjured up the cat again. Lilac jumped onto the bed beside me. She looked so real and solid. I reached out and tried to stroke her silky white fur, but my hand passed right through the little cat. It must have been a strange sensation, because she shrank back and hissed. She glared at me out of her lavender eyes, jumped off the bed, and disappeared through the wall with a flounce of her fluffy tail.

"Fine. Be a brat. See if I care," I hollered after her, even though I knew she was just a figment of my sleepy brain.

My bedroom door flew open, and I was suddenly wide awake.

April eyeballed me warily. "Are you talking to me, crazy woman?"

Shoot. I'd forgotten she was here. Oh well. "Yeah, I called you a brat for ignoring me."

"I wasn't even in the same room. Settle down." She flopped onto my bed, where my imaginary cat had been seconds before. "What'd you want?"

I laughed. "Nothing, really. Thinking out loud, is all."

"And?"

"I think it's time to talk to Roy again. He's another person we know who was in Lipstick and Lace Friday morning. Then there's the weird scene I witnessed in the grocery store the same afternoon. Time to find out what he knows, if anything."

Not wanting to get Evonne in any trouble for taking me inside the theater, I hadn't filled April in on our discovery or the fact that I thought Roy was most likely involved in whatever shenanigans had been planned for the ancient old plumbing.

"Agreed. I wonder if he'll be working today. This time, I'd like to decide what we're going to say to him ahead of time, instead of winging it. Not having a plan didn't go so well with Kristi."

I rubbed my hands over my face. "Indeed. It'd be nice not to make a big mess out of this one. I don't want *everyone* in town mad at me."

"How about I kick you if you're getting too intense?"

"Good plan." I laughed and then kicked my daughter off my bed. "But first things first. I need about a gallon of coffee and a big bowl of oatmeal with raisins."

After breakfast, I grabbed my phone to call the grocery store and inquire about Roy's schedule. Already this morning I'd missed a few calls from the same unknown number that had called my phone on Friday a few times. *Huh. It must not be too important, or they would've left a message.* I shrugged it off and dialed the number for Mill Street Market. Roy wouldn't be at work until after lunch, so April and I spent the morning puttering around the house.

It was nice not to have to be anywhere. I gave the kitchen and bathroom a thorough cleaning and ran the vacuum. Cleaning was almost as therapeutic for me as gardening was. Without concentrating on any one particular thing, I let my mind wander and was surprised how often a solution to a problem came while I wasn't even thinking about the issue. Today was no exception. It was suddenly clear to me that I shouldn't beat around the bush when I visited with Roy, but instead be honest about why I wanted to talk to him.

When I shut off the vacuum, my cell phone was ringing. A quick glance told me it was the same unknown caller I kept missing. This time I answered, curious to find out if my car warranty had expired.

"Hello? Dawna Carpenter speaking."

"Mrs. Carpenter, this is Frank Stockwell of Elkins National Bank in Greenwood. How are you today?"

"Fine," I replied tentatively.

Frank cleared his throat. "We've been trying to reach you in regard to your loan that is in serious default with us. Is now a good time?"

No, now is not a good time. "I'm sorry, Mr. Stockwell, but your bank has its wires crossed somehow. I've never had a loan with Elkins National Bank."

"I see." He cleared his throat again. "You are the wife of the deceased Robert Clay Carpenter, are you not?"

"Yes, but—"

"And you are the owner of Carpenter's Corner Hardware and Building Supply, correct?"

"Yes, but—"

"I see here you signed for a certified letter from Elkins National Bank on Friday."

This time I raised my voice. "I did, yes. But there's been some confusion. Yes, the letter was addressed to me, but I'm telling you, there's been a mistake. It's not my loan. You need to figure this out on your end and stop harassing me. I've had enough."

I hung up the phone and went in search of April.

I found her sitting at her dad's desk in his office, a shoebox full of old family photos opened in front of her. She glanced up when I came in, and held out a picture. "Is this Aunt Alta?"

The black-and-white photo was of a cheerful woman in a floral-print dress with a corsage pinned to her lapel. She had chin-length wavy hair, round glasses, and looked like she could be a twin sister of Aunt Bea from *The Andy Griffith Show*. I smiled. "Yes, that's Aunt Alta. I took this picture on Mother's Day the year before she passed. Do you remember her?" I handed the picture back to April.

"Not really. I have a vague image of her in my head, but I don't know if it's an actual memory or an impression from you and Dad talking about her so often when we were young." She frowned and shook her head. "How long did she live with us?"

"About two years. You were only three when she died, so I don't imagine you remember much about her. I still miss her."

Alta Francis was Bob's great-aunt. After her husband died, we'd moved her into the upstairs apartment in our house. The apartment was a one-bedroom with a small kitchen, a bathroom, and a living room. Alta had her own space but was always welcome to join us for meals. She'd been a huge help with our three small children and was always a sheer delight to have around. It had devastated the entire family when she'd passed away after a brief bout of pneumonia. Even though she'd been gone for over thirty years, and our kids had taken over the apartment when they were teenagers, we all still thought of it as Aunt Alta's apartment.

"I think we should frame this one." April set the picture aside. "Were you looking for me for a reason? Are you ready to go have a chat with Roy?"

I brought my thoughts back to the present. "Yes, and yes. I've decided to come right out and tell Roy we're conducting our own investigation, and not beat around the bush. I'm going to mention how I can't even reopen Carpenter's Corner until the killer, or killers, are caught, so I'm asking around to see what I can find out. I'm going to straight-up tell him I heard he was working for Warren and ask him what they hired him to do. Don't you think it's the best approach?"

April threw her hands in the air. "Wait. What are you talking about? Who hired him to do some work for Warren? Where'd you hear that?"

Shoot. Now I'd stuck my foot in my mouth. I'd forgotten April wasn't privy to Evonne's and my little excursion last night. "Uh. Somebody mentioned it. I don't remember who, but I thought I told you."

My pile of lies kept getting bigger and bigger. The pile would topple over and crush me soon if I wasn't careful.

"No, you did not." April frowned at me. "But yes, I think it's a good idea to be up front about it when we talk to Roy. You keep saying *you*, but I'm planning on going too, you know."

"Sorry. Yes, *we*."

"On the other hand, what if Roy's the killer? It might be dangerous to tell him we've been poking around."

I shrugged and leaned against the doorframe. "Yeah, I suppose it could be, but this is Pine Bluff. I'm sure everybody knows about the two murders by now and also knows we've been asking questions. News travels fast in this little burg."

"Now that's a true story. There's nothing like the Pine Bluff rumor mill." April chuckled. "Yeah, let's tell him why we're asking. Are you almost ready to head out?"

"Yep. Let me put on my face first. Give me fifteen minutes."

* * *

April pulled her VW Beetle into one of the empty parking spots in front of Mill Street Market, and we climbed out of the car. The grocery store was quiet inside this afternoon. Only a handful of people pushed shopping carts down the narrow aisles.

"I should start doing my shopping on Monday afternoons. You can actually get to the shelves," I said.

"I don't know, Mom. Not enough people for you to chat with. How're you going to get all the good gossip?"

I smacked my daughter on the arm. Smart-aleck kid.

Smitty, my neighbor, stood in the cookie aisle, muttering to herself. I pointed her out to April. "I'm going to see if Smitty needs any help."

"Ah, see. I spoke too soon. There's always someone for you to chat with." April shook her head good-naturedly.

"Hello, Smitty. How're you doing?" I smiled at my next-door neighbor and tenant.

The elderly woman wore her trademark plaid pants. Today's red-and-green plaid gave her the nostalgic glow of a Christmas tree. I was short by most standards, but the top of Smitty's head only reached as high as my shoulder. She was standing on her tiptoes, trying to peer at the cookie packages on the top shelf.

"Oh, Dawna. Thank goodness. I didn't know what I was going to do." A wobble shook Smitty's voice.

"Can I help?"

"Oh, yes. They've moved my cookies." She pointed to a red bag of peanut-shaped wafers on the top shelf.

"That does create a problem, doesn't it?"

"Yes, indeed." Smitty blinked her rheumy eyes behind tortoiseshell glasses wider than her face. A piece of masking tape on the nosepiece held the frame together.

I stood on tiptoe and stretched as far as I could. With a small hop, I was able to knock a package of the cookies down with the tip of my finger, catching it before it smashed to the floor. "Here you go." I handed the package to Smitty.

"Bless your heart." The tiny woman hugged the cookies to her chest as if they were a long-lost niece before she placed them gently in her cart and tottered off without a backward glance.

I grinned and made a mental note to check on her later and see if she needed a ride to the optometrist's office.

As luck would have it, when April and I came around the corner into the produce section, Roy was stacking red apples onto a display table. His face lit up when he saw me. I nudged down the guilt rising in my belly.

"Oh, hey there. Are you ladies needing another watermelon already?"

I laughed. "Nope, there's still plenty of the first one left. It was excellent, by the way. The first bite was to die for."

"Good to hear." Roy winked and continued to stack apples in a pyramid. "Something else I can help you with today?"

"As a matter of fact, there is. April and I were hoping we could talk to you for a few minutes. Do you have time to chat?" Feeling a bit nervous, I pushed my glasses farther up my nose and brushed a strand of hair out of my eyes.

Roy cocked his head, then wiped his hands on his green apron and took a quick survey of the produce section. Not a customer in sight. "It looks like a good time for a break to me. Meet me out back?"

Mill Street Market employees parked their vehicles behind the grocery store in a gravel lot. A weathered picnic table sat under a trio of tall pine trees on the far side of the lot, where the store staff took their breaks when the weather cooperated. April and I went out the front door and walked around the building. Roy was wiping off the picnic table with a blue hand towel.

"Sorry for the mess. Some people don't seem to know how to pick up after themselves." He moved a rusty tin coffee can full of cigarette butts over by the trunk of one of the pine trees. "We don't need to smell those nasty things while we talk."

Roy wedged his lanky legs under the table and gestured for April and me to take a seat. He rubbed his hands together and smiled like he anticipated a pleasant chat. I hated to disappoint him.

"Now, what can I do for you? Are you going to try to talk me into teaching those produce classes you mentioned the other day?" He smiled again, shifting his gaze between April and me, and then back to me again.

"Not yet, but I haven't given up on the idea." I returned the smile before settling my face into a more serious expression. "No, we're hoping to talk to you about your relationship with Warren Highcastle."

Roy visibly flinched at the mention of the dead man's name, but didn't say a word.

Aha. He did know him.

"I'm sure you've heard Warren was killed in the bathroom my store shares with Lipstick and Lace."

"Well, of course I have. From what I understand, Highcastle's head met the business end of Bill Wilder's hammer. Pretty crazy to think you and Bill were in here buying watermelons that same afternoon. He sure wasn't acting like he'd recently killed someone. It's hard to believe."

"Agreed. It's hard to believe because Bill didn't do it. It's one of the main reasons April and I are trying to sort this out. Bill's not a murderer. I'd bet my life on it." The words came out harsher than I'd intended. "Sorry. I'm a little wound up. Yesterday the man who worked for me was shot and killed in the parking lot behind Carpenter's Corner. It's been a lot to take in."

Roy nodded. "I heard, and I'm sorry for it. Never got to know Steve, but it's a shame."

"Indeed it is. I can't help thinking both these men's deaths have to be connected somehow. There hasn't been a murder in Pine Bluff in . . . well, ever, that I know of. Now we've had two in two days' time, and both happened at my hardware store. Not a coincidence. The police are doing all they can to find out who's behind the killings, but April and I are doing a bit of poking around of our own." I paused to take a breath. "We're trying to talk to anyone who had any connection to either Warren or Steve. Do you mind helping us out?"

"It's terrible, and I feel for you and the victim's families, but I don't understand what any of this has to do with me." He rubbed his hands together several times, as if warming them before a fire.

"Maybe nothing, but your name has come up a couple of times." April placed both elbows on the table, leaning her chin on propped-up fists. She fixed her gaze on Roy's face as she waited for his reply.

"Oh? From who?" His narrowed gaze darted back and forth between us.

"For starters, your name was on a list of people who'd been in Lipstick and Lace Friday morning."

"Sure. I was in there. Is that a crime? I was looking for jewelry for my mom. Friday was her eighty-first birthday. I didn't find anything I thought she would like, though. Mom likes simple things, and Darlene's jewelry is too flashy for her."

"How's your mom doing?" I asked. "Nola's always been one of my favorite people."

"She's doing great. Living in the assisted living home on the hill. Pioneer Ridge. After her stroke, she couldn't live alone anymore but didn't want to move in with my family and me. She said she didn't want to be a burden. It's been a good move for her. She loves playing bingo and enjoys having the other residents around for company. There's always someone to talk to, you know? Mom doesn't seem to get lonely living there. The residents who're well enough and can afford it are going on a leaf-peeping tour to New England in October. Mom's really looking forward to the trip."

"I bet she is. She's always been a social butterfly. I'm kind of jealous of her trip. New England in the fall is on my bucket list. I can't even imagine how spectacular it must be. Once this mess is behind us, I'll make sure and visit her."

"She'd be tickled to death." Roy smiled.

April jumped in to steer the conversation back to the murders. "While you were in Lipstick and Lace the other day, did you happen to see Warren come in?"

"Actually, I did. He came into the store as I was leaving." Roy crossed his arms over his chest. "The guy seemed to be in a big hurry. Knocked right into me and didn't even bother to acknowledge it."

"What time did you leave? Do you remember?" I asked.

He rubbed his chin. "Must've been right about nine. I had the ten-to-seven shift Friday. I left Lipstick and Lace, then went to see Mom for a few minutes before heading to work." Roy glanced at his watch. "Anything else? I've got a couple of minutes left then I better get back inside."

"Yes, I'll try to be quick." I shoved my glasses back into place. "I understand Warren hired you to do some work at the Emery Theater. What kind of work did he have you doing?" I was curious to see how he would react to my questions.

Roy jerked back again, similarly to the first time I'd mentioned him working for Warren. "Who in the world did you hear that from?"

I shook my head. "Sorry. I can't tell you who told me." *Since it was just a solid guess on my part.* "It's true, then?"

"Maybe." He stood and adjusted the yellow pencil behind his ear. "Jack said the job needed to be done sometime this weekend, but Highcastle was dead by then. Honestly, I was going to back out anyway. Nobody needs money that badly."

"What was he wanting you to do, if you don't mind my asking? Did it have something to do with the plumbing?"

Roy stared at me for a minute without blinking, then lowered his gaze to his feet. "Well, it seems like you already know, and it's not something I'm willing to talk to you about if you don't. Now, if you'll excuse me, I've gotta get back to work." Roy walked away but turned back before he entered the store. "Sorry I wasn't much help to you. Good luck with your quest."

"Wait. I know you need to go, but one more thing first, if you don't mind." I held up my index finger.

Roy raised his eyebrows with a look of annoyance on his face. "Yeah?"

"When I was in the grocery store Friday afternoon, right after you helped Bill and me with our watermelons, I witnessed a man getting in your face and heard him ask if you'd done something yet. He mentioned the two of you might be in trouble. Who was he? Does he have something to do with Warren?"

"Well, yeah. That was Jack." Roy's tone was matter-of-fact. He rubbed a hand over his close-cropped hair. "It's been a pleasure, ladies. I hope you get to the bottom of this, but I assure you, I didn't have a thing to do with either of those murders." He saluted us before pulling a white access card out of his apron pocket, swiping it through a black card reader, and disappearing through the back doorway of the store, without another glance.

April slapped her hands onto the top of the weathered picnic table. "Who's Jack? And where do we find him?"

Chapter Twenty-Six

"What now?" April plopped into the lawn chair next to where I sat under the shade of the big elm tree in my front yard.

"I don't have a clue. Literally." I lifted my hair off the back of my hot neck, fanning myself with my free hand. Releasing my hair, I kicked off my shoes, pulled off my socks, and ran my feet through the thick, cool green grass. "Roy sure acted surprised when I asked him about working for Warren. Did you notice his reaction when we first mentioned Warren's name? He's hiding something—I'm sure of it."

"But do you think Roy's the killer? That's the most important part."

"No, not really." I rubbed my forehead, mentally going over the events of the last few days and everything we'd learned. "Right now, I think we need to figure out who exactly Jack is and where we can find him. He's got to be the guy I saw with Roy the other day. My guess is Jack worked for Warren and hired Roy to do something less than upstanding."

"None of which is surprising, knowing what we do about all those fraud cases Warren had pending." April studied my face. "You look like the heat's getting to you, Mom. You're all red in the face. We should probably go inside and get the air-conditioning turned on."

"In a minute. Right now, the shade and breeze feel good, and I don't want to move."

The afternoon temperature had crept up past one hundred degrees, though a steady but light breeze rustled the leaves and cooled my hot skin. A symphony of chants, clapping, yells of encouragement, the sharp tweet of a coach's whistle, and the metallic clang of a blocking sled drifted down from the high school, less than a block away. The Timbers football team was practicing for their first game of the season. Between the sounds of football and the breeze, it felt like fall was right around the corner.

"I'm going to get you a glass of water, at least." April stood and bounded up the big stone steps leading to the rarely used front door of the house.

The kitchen had always been the heart of our home, and family and friends used the kitchen door as the main entrance. If someone rang the bell on the front door, we knew the visitor wasn't anyone close to us.

As April opened the metal screen door, a piece of white paper fluttered to the ground from where it'd been sandwiched between the screen door and the frame.

"What've you got there?" I asked.

April unfolded the sheet of paper and read the note. Her face blanched white as she read. Instead of answering my question, my daughter stood deadly still, rooted to the spot, as if stuck in concrete, her green eyes wide.

I held out my hand, wiggling my fingers for the paper. "What is it?" I asked again, louder this time.

April reluctantly handed over the note.

"Holy fright!" I dropped the note and jumped to my feet, staring at the thing like it was a coiled snake.

"Looks like someone doesn't like us poking around," April whispered.

The note was typed in all caps. The message was simple yet clear.

STOP ASKING QUESTIONS OR YOU'LL BE SORRY. THAT GOES FOR YOUR NOSY DAUGHTER TOO.

"We need to take this to the police station, Mom. Now."

I turned in a slow circle, surveying my neighborhood. Was the person who left this note watching to see how we would react? Despite the heat of the afternoon, a chill raced up my spine, and I shivered.

* * *

The police station felt stuffy inside. A couple of cheap box fans turned to full blast pushed the stale air around. Chief Dallas sat straight as a rigid light pole as he read the threatening note for the thousandth time. He'd deposited it into a clear plastic evidence bag in the hopes the forensics lab could lift incriminating fingerprints from the paper.

"This note is straight out of a B-rated movie, but you two need to take it seriously." J. T.'s eyebrows squashed together in a ferocious scowl. "Whoever did this is probably trying to scare you off, but we have to treat it as a genuine threat." He pointed a scolding finger at me. "And I'm telling you, back off. Leave this matter to the police. I assure you, we're investigating both Warren and Steve's murders and have it all under control. You two need to stop snooping around."

I titled my head, eyeballing J. T. over the rim of my glasses. "I can't say this note didn't rattle me a bit. April too. But you've got to understand I'm already smack dab in the middle of this investigation. One of my best friends is sitting behind bars for Warren's murder, and I know he didn't do it. Then my employee was killed, and both murders took place on my property. Now, if my questions and poking around help bring the killer out of hiding, then great." I smacked my hands against my thighs for emphasis.

"Mom's right," April chimed in. "We'll be extremely careful, I promise. I will not let anything happen to my mom, but there are some things we need to follow up on."

Good. We're on the same page. I threw her a grateful look.

J. T. shook his head. "No. Now, if you'd like to join the police academy, we'll talk once you graduate. In the meantime, you need to stay out of my investigation. I told you: we've got it under control."

"Do you really, though?" April stared daggers through the police chief. "You don't have much manpower here in Pine Bluff, and excuse me if I'm wrong, but I don't see how one extra patrol sent over from Greenwood is much help."

J. T. dipped his head in acknowledgment. He remained silent, studying the faded tile floor under his feet.

"Since you're on top of things, you must know Warren hired Roy Dejean to do some work in the Emery Theater before his purchase was even finalized, right? There's something shady about it, if you ask me." Which he hadn't. I lifted my chin in defiance while simultaneously feeling a jab of guilt for throwing Roy under the bus.

"Can't say I did. And how did you come upon this information?" The police chief shifted in his office chair and leaned back to open his desk drawer. He pulled out an ink pen and a yellow legal pad and jotted down some notes.

"Um. Uh . . ." *I can't tell you how I found out. Think fast, Dawna.*

"Didn't you say someone mentioned it to you?" April wrinkled her nose and poked me in the arm with one finger.

"Uh, yeah." I mumbled something incoherent. "But Roy said so himself, and maybe Kristi mentioned it when we stopped by her house." She hadn't, but I was babbling and couldn't rein myself in.

J. T. scrubbed a hand over his face. "You even went and questioned Kristi? Find out anything new there?"

April crossed her tan legs and sat back with a wry smile. "No, but I'm one hundred percent sure Kristi had nothing to do with either of these murders. We managed to make her mad, though. It wasn't our intention, but it happened. I'm going to make cupcakes to try to make amends with her over my mom's bad behavior."

I huffed. "I don't think I was that pushy."

April leveled a glare at me.

With his eyes closed and hands steepled in front of his face as if in prayer, J. T. remained silent. His desk phone rang, but he ignored it. After what seemed like an eternity, he opened his eyes. "Okay. I'm going against my better judgment here. The two of you have my permission to keep your eyes and ears open, but nothing else. You need to report back to me every single, tiny thing you see, hear, or smell. You get my drift? Either my officers or I will check on you on a regular basis and patrol the streets near your house. You can expect to hear from us a lot. Do you understand?" He let his words sink in. "And I want a cupcake. Or two. Lemon."

"You got it, Chief." I jumped to my feet, all of my five feet three inches at military attention.

"Oh, are you the one baking cupcakes, Mom? Way to agree so fast to me slaving away in the kitchen in this heat." April laughed.

"Hey, whatever works."

"At ease, soldiers. And sit back down, please. You still have some questions to answer." J. T. grilled us about our conversations with both Kristi and Roy. "Jack, huh? If he worked for Highcastle, and I'm guessing he did, I doubt he was a local boy. There should be something in Highcastle Development's business records to indicate who he is. I'll find him." He scribbled more notes on the legal pad. "Now, you mentioned you think you saw him at Mill Street Market the other day, Dawna. Can you describe Jack to me?"

"Sure. He's fairly tall. I'd guess about six feet. He had on jeans, a T-shirt, and a baseball cap with dark, curly hair sticking out from under the cap. He's got his arm in a sling and a full plaster cast from his shoulder to his wrist. I honestly didn't get a good look at his face. Not enough to give you a decent description. He'd be hard to miss with the cast. I'm positive I've never seen him in Pine Bluff before, though. Not incredibly helpful, I know."

"Any little thing helps." J. T. sighed and looked me in the eye. "From here on out, I'll be taking over the questioning of any suspects, including Roy. It sounds like the two of you probably wouldn't get any more out of him anyway, but you're done questioning people—got it? If you hear anything else, you come directly to me. Both of you." He stared at me for a beat before shifting his gaze to April. "Got it, April?"

"We get it. Sheesh." She rolled her eyes and chuckled. "Are we free to go yet, Chief?"

"Not yet." J. T. leaned back. The chair squeaked, and he rested a booted ankle across his other lanky leg. "I've been looking into Steve's background, trying to find any family members."

"Oh?" I scooted to the edge of my chair. "Have you found anyone yet?"

"No, but I was able to track down the guy he used to work for in Walla Walla. Cliff Myers. The one who connected Steve to his roommate, Greg."

"Great. What'd Cliff have to say? Did he know anything about Steve's family?"

"Unfortunately, not much. According to Myers, Steve was a nice guy who'd had some sort of tragedy happen in his life. He wasn't sure what, but he mentioned Steve moved around a lot. He didn't stay anywhere for more than a few years, but Steve wasn't in any trouble with the law or anything, as far as Myers knew. He didn't think Steve was running from anything specific, other than his own demons." J. T. paused, a look of reflection on his face. "I don't think a person can get too far away from the monsters in his own head."

"Have you been able to find out what the tragedy was? I wonder what happened to him. Whenever I asked him about family, he said he didn't have any. I never pressed."

"Myers seemed to think whatever happened had been in Northern California somewhere. He was fairly certain Steve had lived down that way for quite a few years. Even though he knows more about Steve than anyone else I've talked to so far, his information was still vague. I've got Sam using her research skills to try to find records on him from that area." J. T. stood and stretched, indicating the conversation was over. He took a wheat-colored, straw cowboy hat off the top of a tall metal filing cabinet and deposited it on his head. "I'll let you know if and when we find out more. Now, if you'll excuse me, it seems I have a produce clerk to interview. I'll walk you ladies out."

He held the door open for us as we left the police station. April and I were half a block away when J. T. called out, "Hey, hold on a minute." He jogged to where we stood, his cowboy boots clomping on the concrete sidewalk. "Stay away from the Fisher house. Don't be so quick to write Kristi off as innocent. There're a few holes in her story." He tipped his hat to us and sauntered away.

Chapter
Twenty-Seven

I dug through my purse to find the ringing phone that'd fallen to the bottom. Ugh. It was time to clean the darn thing out again. *Ah. There it is.* "Hi, Evonne. What's up?" With my free hand, I swung the heavy purse onto a hook by the kitchen door, then leaned back against the counter to chat.

"Sure. What time?" I looked at my wristwatch. *How in the world has it gotten to be four already?* "Yep. I agree. See you there."

I ended the call, then reached into the cupboard for a glass and filled it with infused cucumber water from a pitcher in the refrigerator.

"See her where?" April filled another glass with cucumber water. "What's going on?"

"Wouldn't you like to know? Join the Women's Service Club, and I'll tell you all about it."

I'd been trying to get April to join the organization ever since she'd taken over the decorating and furniture restoration side of my business, but so far, she'd refused.

"Whatever, Mom. I'm not ready to wear polyester pants and go to a meddling women's meeting." My daughter rolled her eyes and tapped her wrist like she was checking a watch. "At least not for another . . . oh, let's see . . . twenty years."

I threw my hands in the air and looked down at the pink-and-white-striped T-shirt, cotton shorts, and leather sandals I wore. "Do you see polyester pants here? Don't think so, missy."

"No, but your meddling is showing. Better get it tucked back in."

The two of us cracked up like a pair of cackling hens.

"Anyway, Evonne called an emergency meeting tonight. Without a feasible buyer for the Emery, we need to regroup and double our efforts to save the theater for Pine Bluff."

"See? I knew I wouldn't have to join your stuffy old ladies club to get the scoop. You can't keep from talking about it." April grinned. "But seriously, it's a good idea. What time's your meeting?"

"Seven. Why? Are you coming with me?"

"Nope, not going with you. Will you stop, please?"

I laughed. "Never."

"I think I'm going to head to the workshop and finish the dresser I've been working on. Maybe I'll work until your meeting is over. It should give me a few hours to paint."

Workshop was an overreaching word for the storage unit where April refinished and stored the pieces of furniture that were the heart of her business, Carriage House Designs.

"Do you think it's wise to be there alone right now? You could stay here and bake those cupcakes you promised J. T."

"It's too hot to bake. I'll do it tomorrow morning while it's still cool. I'll be as safe at my workshop as I'd be here by myself.

Don't worry. I'll text J. T. to let him know where I'm at, okay? You need to do the same thing when you leave the house, and then text me when you're heading back home from your meeting. Plus, drive your Jeep. No walking tonight."

"Deal, bossy cow."

April and I pinky swore. There was no going back on our deal now. With a pinky swear, it was completely unbreakable.

"The meeting isn't for several more hours, though. I have some time to kill. Think I'll turn on the air-conditioning unit in the sunroom and read for a bit after I start a load of laundry. It's too hot to work in the garden right now."

"Sounds perfect. And don't say *kill*." April glowered at me in jest before she turned to head outside.

I grabbed the dish towel hanging on the stove door handle and snapped my daughter on the rear end before she made it outside.

"Oh, lady, you're going to be mighty sorry you did that." April let the screen door bang behind her for good measure. "Lock the door," she called over her shoulder.

I obliged and locked the door behind her, afraid she was already planning her revenge for the towel-snapping incident.

Alone in the house, I wandered through the rooms, gathering any stray laundry needing to be done—a dishrag and towels from the kitchen, a lone cloth napkin left behind on the dining room table, and hand towels from the bathroom. I dumped them all into the washer along with my dirty gardening jeans and a handful of T-shirts, not bothering to sort by color or fabric. My mother would've been mortified to see how I did my laundry these days. Thank goodness she wasn't still hanging around to keep an eye on my housekeeping skills.

"Now I need caffeine," I told the empty house. It didn't matter that it was already four thirty, and a cup of coffee this late in the day would probably keep me awake all night. I'd deal with that problem then. I filled a tall water glass with ice and added an inch of creamer then filled it to the rim with coffee from a glass pitcher I kept in the refrigerator. Each morning during the hot months, I dumped in the leftover coffee from my morning pot. By the time I wanted an iced coffee in the afternoon, it was already chilled. My version of the cold brew all the coffee shops were serving the last few summers, only a gazillion times cheaper.

I carried my coffee into the sunroom and settled into my reading chair, with the fan from the air-conditioning blowing straight on me. Glancing around my familiar room, I imagined Bob lounging in his old armchair with Lilac curled on his lap.

"Hello, sweetheart. I'm so glad to see you," I said out loud.

I told Bob about Evonne and my exploration of the Emery Theater and how I could've sworn that old picture of Richard Steinman led me to the discovery of the tools and paint supplies in the basement. "I'm not sure how something like that could even be possible, but I'm not writing it off. Stranger things have happened, right?"

My cell phone rang, and Bob and Lilac both faded away.

Chapter
Twenty-Eight

"Hey, Dawna. I'm calling to check on you, like I said I'd be doing." J. T.'s deep baritone boomed through the line. "Are you Carpenter women safe and sound? Behaving yourselves?"

"Yep, all's good here. I'm lounging under the air conditioner before I head out for a Women's Service Club meeting. You saved me from having to call and let you know where I'm going. I assume April texted to let you know she's at her workshop? She darn well better have."

"Uh, no. She did not."

"The little stinker. She even pinky swore she'd shoot you a text."

J. T. grunted. "I'm headed to my truck right now to go check on her. It'll take me two minutes to get to her workshop."

I let out a sigh of relief. "Thank you, J. T. I appreciate everything you do. Hey, I meant to ask earlier: Have you had any luck getting a hold of Warren's wife yet?"

"Finally, yes. The phone call I ignored while you and April were in my office this afternoon was Mrs. Highcastle. Audrey."

I took the last sip of my coffee. "How'd she take the news?"

J. T. didn't answer right away, his voice rough when he did. "I hated making that call. As you can probably guess, she was shocked and upset. Didn't take it well in the beginning. To her credit, she pulled herself together and called me back less than half an hour after I gave her the news."

"Why did she call back? Did she have an idea of who might've done it?"

"No. I'd asked her to call back. I wanted to talk with her more after she'd had a chance to process the fact that her husband was dead."

"Sure. Makes sense. Was she able to shed any light on anything?"

"Somewhat. My biggest question for her was why Highcastle Development had chosen Pine Bluff for their next project."

"Exactly," I interrupted. "April and I've been wondering the same thing. Why here? Did she have an answer for you?"

"She did. Audrey let me know in no uncertain terms the Highcastles run in affluent circles. I've had Sam researching the family, so we already knew they were wealthy. Warren was a self-made millionaire, but Audrey was born with a silver spoon in her mouth. Her family, the Drapers, are from old Texas oil money."

"Oh, really? No wonder Warren divorced his first wife for her. Colleen was a wannabe actress when they met. From what we found online, she came from an average middle-class family."

"Could be. Anyway, when I questioned the latest Mrs. High-castle about why Warren had chosen Pine Bluff, she said a year or so ago they were at some sort of fancy gala event. It was a fundraiser for a museum or some such thing. At dinner, Warren was talking about the project he was working on at the time. Later, a woman who'd been seated at their table mentioned her family had built one of the first opera houses in the Pacific Northwest. She said she still owned it, but it'd been sitting empty for years."

"Dolores Adams," I said.

"Yep. Warren asked Mrs. Adams where the theater was located, and the rest is history. Audrey said Warren was sure he could get the building for a steal, restore it, and sell it for a fortune. That's how he made his living."

I snorted. "Yeah, and how he defrauded people out of millions of dollars in the process."

"Oh, you know about the fraud charges?"

Even though the police chief couldn't see me, I tapped my temple. "You'd be surprised at the things I know."

"It certainly appears that way." J. T. laughed. "From what I'm finding out, Warren wasn't a nice person. So far, the only one I've found who seemed to have liked the man is his wife. And I wonder how much she really knows about his work ethics."

From the gossip blog April and I had read, Audrey and Warren were dating when he was still married to his first wife. The Highcastles were prominent figures in Denver society, so I couldn't imagine Audrey had been unaware Warren was married. They were part of the same prestigious circle, after all. If a woman didn't have any qualms about dating a married man, would she care how he'd come by his millions? As long as he kept her in diamonds and vacation homes, I bet Audrey hadn't given a rat's behind how he'd made those millions. Maybe the woman even helped him plot and plan how he'd defraud the next sucker who came along.

"Anyway, I'm at the storage units now. To ease your mind, I can see April, and she's fine. Has her music turned up so loud she doesn't even know I'm here."

"Good night! Anyone could sneak up on her. Give the girl a piece of your mind, will you?"

"I intend to. I'm sure you'll hear all about it later." He chuckled and ended the call.

Chapter
Twenty-Nine

At ten to seven, Evonne and I met on the steps of the refurbished Italianate house that was home to the Pine Bluff Community Library. For a library, it was small, but the perfect size for a town with a population lingering a hair under twelve hundred souls.

The building had started life as the town's first hospital but had shut its doors as travel became easier for people to get to the larger hospital in nearby Greenwood. Next, a local family purchased the two-story building and turned it into a beautiful home, resplendent with stained glass windows and white wooden columns across the wide front porch. It had remained in the same family for over a hundred years, until the young people all moved away and the last of the older generation found final resting spots under tall pine trees in the Pine Bluff Cemetery. After years of neglect, the town had purchased the home and converted it into the welcoming library it was today.

Every librarian who'd ever spent one minute alone in the building had a story to tell about catching a glimpse in their peripheral vision every now and again of a woman in a long white gown who was rumored to have died on the upper floor from tuberculosis in the early 1900s. They all said she wasn't a scary presence, but instead felt wistful and a little sad. In every telling, they said she liked to flick the lights to let them know she was still there. I glanced at the upstairs window. I'd always wanted to get a peek at her so I'd have my own story to tell. *Nope. Nothing. Darn.*

We headed inside and straight up the stairs, where the kids' section sat alongside the nonfiction section. Two long tables in nonfiction provided a perfect place for our meetings, where most of the other members were already seated around the tables, chatting away.

Laura Barker slid a plastic container into the middle of the table, along with a stack of paper napkins. "I made brownies today. Please eat them. I only wanted one but had to make an entire batch. Heaven knows Vern and I don't need to eat them all."

"You don't have to tell me twice." I didn't hesitate to reach for a brownie.

Evonne banged a wooden gavel on the table and called the meeting to order. "Thank you for all coming tonight on such short notice. Because this is a special meeting, we're going to dispense with reading the minutes from the last meeting and with reading the treasurer's report. We'll pick those back up at the next regularly scheduled meeting on the first Thursday of September."

"Do I still need to take minutes for this meeting?" Helen Snow, the club secretary, had a red spiral notebook and an ink pen ready on the table in front of her.

"Yes, please." Evonne nodded at her then cleared her throat. "I've called this emergency meeting so we can discuss the Emery Theater. While it's a tragedy the potential buyer has died, it means the opera house is available once again. Or will be shortly. Do we all agree we need to redouble our efforts to try to save this piece of Pine Bluff history for our town?"

All around the table, the women nodded and murmured their agreement. Someone moved to resurrect our "Save the Emery Theater" campaign. I seconded the motion, and it passed unanimously with a show of hands.

Evonne glanced around the table until her gaze fell on the bottle-blond Marti Campbell. "Marti, would you be able to tell us if the real estate contract on the building is dissolved yet?"

"No, not yet. It's only been a couple of days, and most of that was a weekend. Kristi had me reach out to Mr. Highcastle's estate attorney to get a feel for what they're thinking about doing with the contract. There's a possibility the estate could continue to pursue the purchase, though highly unlikely. Anyway, I left a message but haven't heard back from the attorney yet. I'll keep trying and let you know what I find out. It may take some time for the property to be clear and ready for sale once again. I'll email the group when I get an answer." Marti jotted a note as a reminder to herself. The silver bangle bracelets around her wrist clinked out a tune as she wrote, and her long silver earrings danced in the light.

The sparkling earrings reminded me. "Oh, did you find your missing earring?"

Marti rolled her eyes and pulled back her hair to show me the earrings. "Sure looks like it, doesn't it?" Her tone was condescending and ugly.

The only problem was the pair of earrings she wore tonight didn't exactly match the ones she'd worn Friday. They were close, but not quite right. I clearly remembered admiring the other earring. It had a turquoise stud with a dangling silver concho. The pair she wore tonight had fishhook ear wires instead of studs. The silver concho hung from a smaller concho, and the turquoise stone was centered in the middle of the larger concho. I was certain it wasn't the same pair. Why would she lie about something so silly?

"Thank you for the update and information, Marti. Even though it may take a while, we can still plan some activities to jump-start our campaign." Evonne opened the discussion for more fundraising ideas, effectively drawing my attention away from Marti.

"The cookbook fundraiser had barely gotten off the ground before Warren placed his offer on the Emery." I wiped brownie crumbs off my fingers with a napkin. "Do we know what we made from the few cookbooks we've sold so far?"

Judy Hassin, the group's treasurer, shuffled a pile of papers on the table in front of her. She studied them for a minute before looking up with a grimace. "Well, ladies, after the cost of printing and shipping, we've made a whopping total of sixty-two dollars and forty-seven cents with our cookbooks. Any amount helps, but we're certainly not going to be purchasing the Emery Theater with less than seventy dollars." She shook her head, setting her wild red curls bouncing.

"I don't want to sound critical," Marti said, "but to be honest, I never liked the cookbook idea. It's been done to death. Every town has done it. I, for one, won't be trying to sell any of them. Not my cup of tea." She glared at me across the table. "Not everything Dawna suggests we do is a winning idea. She's not all-knowing, like you all seem to believe."

Silence fell over the group. We all stared at one another as if nobody was quite sure how to respond.

Well, okay then. Apparently, with my little visit to Kristi, I'd made me an enemy out of Marti. Sheesh.

Trying to smooth things over and take the high road, I spoke up. "It's fine if you don't like them, Marti, but the fact is, we voted on the cookbook fundraiser, and it passed with a majority vote. You don't have to participate. Nobody will hold it against you if you don't. We'll be holding other fundraisers, and hopefully they'll be something that suits you. Maybe you have some ideas you'd like to share with the group?"

"Oh, you know I'm not normally one to complain . . ."

Yeah, right.

". . . but I thought you all should know how I felt about it," Marti said.

"Okay, then. Moving on. We do still have stacks of cookbooks and *almost* everybody loves them." Laura looked pointedly at Marti with her remark. "It's time to set our booth back up at the Saturday market before the season ends. There are only two weekends left. I'll take this coming Saturday. I have three full boxes of cookbooks piled up in my guest room. It'd be nice to have the space back again. My husband's starting to complain."

I raised my hand and volunteered to take the booth for the last Saturday of the season. The weather should start cooling down a bit by then, I hoped.

Evonne called for more ideas. An ice-cream social, bingo, bunco, and a yard sale were all discussed, with the pros and cons of each idea heavily debated and volleyed about. We didn't settle on a thing. Sometimes the problem with a roomful of strong-willed women is it becomes a tug-of-war. We all think our own idea holds the most merit, so we end up not making any progress.

I yawned and glanced at my watch under the table. *Come on. Let's wrap this up.* I grabbed another brownie and stuffed it into my mouth.

Judy stood and clapped her hands amid the chaos. When everyone looked her way, she spoke. "You know, these are all great ideas, but not one of them is going to bring in the kind of funds we need. Yes, they'll all help, but we need to think bigger. I propose we start by asking the town officials and business owners for donations. We're trying to save the Emery for the town, after all, right? Let's get the town involved. I'll start it off by donating one thousand dollars." She reached under the table and dug out a small green purse. After wrestling out her checkbook, Judy wrote the check, ripped it out of the book with a flourish, slapped it onto the table, and gave it a good pat. "There. This seed money should start the campaign off on the right foot. Money attracts money, right?" She winked at the rest of us.

Immediately, people began pulling checkbooks out of their purses. I reached for my own and wrote a personal check for two hundred and fifty dollars.

"I can't do anything close to what Judy did, but here's my donation of one hundred dollars." Laura grinned when she handed her check to Judy. "What a great feeling."

Allie Gibbons raised her hand.

Evonne nodded at her. "Go ahead, Allie."

"I'm sorry, but I have a quick question. If we're not able to buy the theater in the long run, what happens to the money we're donating? Will I get it back? I need to know so I can tell Jeff. We rarely spend large amounts of money without clearing it with each other first."

Allie taught kindergarten at Betty Gram Elementary School in Pine Bluff. At twenty-six, she was the youngest active member of the Women's Service Club. Small and slender, Allie always came across as if she were apologizing whenever she spoke during meetings.

"No need to be sorry. It's a legitimate question," Evonne answered. "Because we're a nonprofit, most donations go into our general fund. It means we use them as we need them when various expenses arise. If you'd like your donation to go strictly to the purchase of the Emery, then you'd simply give us a letter stating your donation is restricted to this particular project. That way, we can only use your funds for the cost of purchasing or maintaining the Emery Theater. And if we aren't able to purchase it, the funds will be returned to you. Does that help?"

Allie nodded. "Yes, thank you."

"This is a long-term project. If you need to talk to Jeff first, by all means do so. You can donate anytime, okay?" Evonne paused before addressing the entire group. "With these larger donations coming in, we probably should think about opening a separate account for the Emery. Then the funds wouldn't be mingling with our day-to-day operating funds, and we will have a clearer picture of what we actually have available for this project. Maybe even a short-term investment account? What do you all think?"

Here we go again. I tried my best to keep my face from show-ing my impatience. It wasn't an easy task.

The group launched into discussions about the pros and cons of investment accounts. More questions were raised than answered. Judy volunteered to research various options and promised to arrive at our next meeting prepared to present her findings. She mentioned she'd also see if she could get the invest-ment advisor from the local bank to attend and help answer questions.

After we all handed our donation checks over, Judy quickly tallied them. "Ladies, with only the seven of us here tonight, we've already collected twenty-five hundred dollars. Think how much more we'll raise when we get the community as excited about this project as we are."

Evonne beamed. "This is great. Thank you for the idea, Judy, and for starting it off with your generous donation. Since I spend my days at City Hall, I'll spread the word with the other city employees. Do we have any volunteers to start hitting up the local business owners?" She pointed at the spunky, redheaded, retired elementary school teacher. "Judy, my vote would be for you to head up the donations team."

"I'd be happy to." Judy accepted the position with grace.

A few other members agreed to work alongside her to canvas Pine Bluff business owners.

With that settled, Evonne adjourned the meeting. I scraped my chair back and wiped brownie crumbs off the table into a napkin.

"It looks like Mother Nature might be gearing up for a wild night," I said to Evonne as we stepped outside.

"Sure does. I bet we're in for another thunder and lightning storm. I hope it doesn't start any new fires. There's been smoke in the air for the last couple of days." Evonne took a quick look at her watch. "Better get home and batten down the hatches."

The sun had been setting when we'd arrived for the meeting, and now, at nine, it was darker than usual for this time in late August. Thick clouds blocked any sign of stars in the sky. The wind was beginning to howl, and the air felt charged with a crackling energy. The group of women separated, some to their cars and others disappearing down the street as they walked home through the dark night.

I jumped into my Jeep, put the hammer down, and headed for home.

Chapter Thirty

Five minutes later, I tripped and stubbed my toe on the concrete steps outside my kitchen door. Lightning flashed overhead and thunder rumbled in the distance. My prediction was coming true. It was going to be a wild night.

"Dang it." I hopped on one foot with my bleeding toe gripped in my fist. I cussed the sandals on my feet, the concrete steps, and myself for forgetting to leave the porch light on. It'd still been daylight when I left the house, so it hadn't even crossed my mind to turn a light on. Now the entire house was pitch-black, and the screen door flapped in the wind as I fumbled for the doorknob. Once inside, I flipped on the kitchen light.

Normally, I don't spook easily, but tonight a knot of unease sat heavy in the pit of my stomach, and the hair on the back of my neck stood at attention. I shivered and brushed it off. *That stupid threatening note has me on edge.* Or maybe I could chalk it up to the two brownies I'd shoveled down my hatch tonight. Too much sugar made me jittery. The dancing shadows on the walls, from tree branches buffeted by the wind, weren't helping the situation. Another streak of lightning lit the sky, with a booming crash of thunder immediately behind it.

I jumped. "Holy fright. The storm's a little too close for comfort."

Over the wind and deluge of rain cascading down the windows, I nearly missed the jazzy notes of my cell phone's ringtone. "Hello?"

"Sorry I'm late, Mom. I meant to get home at the same time you did, but I lost track of time. I still have to clean up my mess, but I should be there in about half an hour. Keep the doors locked until I get there, okay? I'll let myself in with my key."

"Sounds good." I didn't mention I'd forgotten and left the door unlocked when I left for my meeting. "You should probably hurry, though. This storm's getting pretty intense. The lights are already flickering."

April assured me she'd be quick, and home in a flash. We ended the call. I turned the lock on the kitchen door and pulled the blinds on the window before stumbling to the front door to lock it as well. I pulled the curtains closed against the dark, then hobbled to the bathroom and fished out an old, dusty bottle of hydrogen peroxide from under the bathroom sink. I rummaged through every drawer in the cabinet before finally finding a box of Band-Aids stuffed all the way to the back of the bottom drawer. With a wet washcloth, I cleaned the blood off my stubbed and scraped toes. *Son of a biscuit eater.* The hydrogen peroxide stung so badly, tears sprang to my eyes. I hissed out a breath and applied the purple bandage with bright orange pumpkins dancing across it.

Another gust of wind rattled the windows. The lights flickered twice, and then the house went black. "Good night!" I'd hoped to have time to dig out a couple of flashlights before the power went out. No such luck.

I fumbled my way down the dark hallway until I came to the floor-to-ceiling built-in bookshelves lining the dining room wall. Fumbling around blindly on the shelves, I searched for a flashlight. Finally, my groping fingers closed over a small metal flashlight. I pushed the rubber button, hoping for the best. A feeble light glowed from the end of the stick.

"Fantastic." The only thing between total blackness and me was a flashlight with a beam so weak I couldn't even see my feet. *Nice. Note to self: Bring home a decent flashlight or two from the hardware store.*

With the weak light in hand, I rummaged through the drawers on the built-in cabinets until I found a box of wooden matches. I lit the white pillar candle in the centerpiece on the dining room table. It didn't throw much light, but it was better than nothing. If the power was still out when April got home, I would make her go to the basement with me to find the camp lanterns.

"Bob? Are you here?" It had quickly become my standard greeting when I got home. "I could really use some company right about now." I sighed and reached for a deck of cards sitting on the table. It was too dark to read, but I needed something to occupy my mind. "A rousing game of solitaire might do the trick."

I'd started playing solitaire as a teenager, and it was still one of my favorite ways to pass the time. April had tried to show me how to play it on the computer, but I was old-school enough to prefer the feel of the cards in my hands instead of clicking away on a keyboard. I felt the same way about books. E-readers didn't even tempt me. They were another reason for people to spend their lives with their faces buried in a screen.

I laid the cards out and was halfway through the draw pile, doing my best to ignore the thunder rumbling overhead, when the screen door banged against the side of the house like a gunshot. I screamed and jumped. The playing cards in my hands went flying, scattering over the table and the floor in a perfect game of fifty-two-card pickup.

"You okay?" April came through the doorway, yellow light spilling out from the heavy silver flashlight she carried. She was soaked to the bone.

I pointed out the cards lying helter-skelter all over the room. "April Mae, look what you made me do. You almost gave me a heart attack." I laughed to cover the jolt of fear. "Apparently, I was so wrapped up in my game I forgot you were coming home. And to be honest, this storm has me a little uneasy tonight."

"Sorry about banging the door. The wind tore it out of my hands. It's crazy out there." April set the flashlight on the counter and grabbed a clean dish towel from a kitchen drawer. She dried off her face before rubbing the towel through her short red hair. "It's really coming down. I'm soaked to the skin from walking from my car to the house. Sprinting to the house, actually."

"I imagine. I can barely hear you over the pounding rain."

April tossed the towel onto the kitchen counter and strolled into the dining room, where I was busy picking up my cards. "Is the candle the only light you've got, Mom? You'll ruin your eyes." She chuckled. "Grandma used to tell me that all the time when she thought it was too dark for me to be reading."

"Or sitting too close to the TV."

"Yep. That one too."

"I didn't look very hard, but this is the only flashlight I could find, and its batteries are low, of course." I tried to turn the flashlight back on. "Well, not low. Dead."

"There's a flashlight on your phone, Mom. Don't tell me you've never noticed it."

Okay. I won't tell you.

April snatched my cell phone off the table and flipped on the flashlight app, then held it out for me to see.

"Well, will you look at that?" I shoved my glasses up the bridge of my nose to peer closer at the screen. "I'll be darned. Good to know." I turned my attention from the phone to my daughter. "So, I hear you had a visitor at your workshop this afternoon."

"Yeah. Thanks for siccing the police on me, Mom." Even though her voice was sarcastic, her smile reached her eyes.

"Hey, you can't blame me. You're the one who pinky swore you'd text him, young lady."

"I know, I know. When I got there, I started working and forgot. Believe me, J. T. let me know I was in a lot of trouble. Apparently, he stood there watching me for a while before I noticed him. Said he could've bonked me over the head, and I wouldn't have known what hit me. He wasn't wrong."

"That makes me feel so much better." I shook my head. *Good grief.*

"You'll be happy to hear I told him I'll take someone with me when I work from now on until they catch the murderer."

"Good. I'm glad you're not being stubborn about this."

"No, I get it." April sighed. "On another note, J. T. picked out a table and chair set he wants in my workshop today, so I have another custom order to do."

"Great. Which table?"

"It's a fairly small, round dining table with a chunky pedestal base. Oak. I picked it up at the yard sale over on Douglas Street earlier in the summer. You were with me."

"Yep, I remember the one. Nice." I shot April a sidelong, flirty glance and batted my eyelashes at her.

"Come on, Mom. Don't read anything into it. J. T. needs a table and chairs, and I happen to specialize in furniture restoration. There's nothing more to it. I guess Chandler will be back home for Thanksgiving, and she's already making jokes about eating on the couch with their plates on their laps. He thought it'd be fun to surprise her with an honest-to-goodness kitchen table."

"It'll be nice for the two of them. Chandler's such a sweet girl, and I know he misses her a lot. Hard to believe she's already twelve years old. It's a shame her mother moved her so far away when she and J. T. divorced."

"It is, but at least Chandler comes to stay quite a bit. I bet she's beautiful now. I think she was three the last time I saw her. She had a mop of curly, dark hair and those piercing blue eyes. She was stunning, even then."

"She's still a beautiful little girl."

"Anyway, J. T. wants me to go to the ranch in a few days to see the space where the table will go. I'll show him some sample colors and pictures of a few of the other tables I've done so he can decide exactly what he wants."

I kept my head lowered and smiled. One thing I was certain about was that J. T. was every bit as interested in April as she was in him. I'd seen his eyes light up when she walked into the room. Now with the two of them spending time together over furniture restoration, maybe they'd finally figure it out. I could only hope.

April ran her hands through her wet hair. "I'm going to go put my pajamas on."

"Wait a minute, please. How about going down in the basement with me first so we can get the propane lanterns?"

"Ew. I hate going into the dungeon. So many spiders." April grimaced, then shivered.

"Oh, come on. I know right where they are. It'll only take us a minute. Don't be a big baby."

"Fine. Let's get it over with," April replied through gritted teeth. "Then I can get out of these wet clothes."

"For such a tough girl, you sure can be a wimp sometimes."

April swatted at me as the two of us headed downstairs. Her flashlight beam led the way.

"Wait a minute. Who are you calling a wimp? You didn't get them by yourself, I noticed. Instead, you waited for me to get home and protect you."

I giggled. "Not true. I was caught up in my card game, is all."

"Right." She wasn't buying it.

Access to the basement stairway was through a doorway in the corner of the kitchen. Another door at the base of the stairs led into the basement. When we reached the bottom of the staircase, April wedged a wooden block under the door to keep it propped open while we fetched the camp lanterns. As soon as she swung the door open, the mustiness of old dirt and decay crawled out of the basement and smacked us square in the face. I stepped around April to peer into the dark and damp cave. She slammed into me from behind, pitching me face-first into a sticky spiderweb.

"Ew." I howled, pinwheeling my arms around my head. "Get it off. Gross." The more I tried to fling the spiderweb off me, the more it clung like sticky cotton candy.

April directed the beam of light straight at me. It hit me square in the eyes.

"Great. Now I'm blind on top of it."

She reached over and pulled the biggest part of the web off my head. "The good news is I don't see a spider. He probably abandoned this web a long time ago."

I shook myself one last time and tried to pull myself together. "Yeah, sure he did. Let's get the stupid lanterns and get the heck out of here. My skin's crawling with the thought of the spiders I'm sure are all over me. Makes me want to go outside and stand in the rain to wash them all off."

Back when the kids still lived at home, the washer and dryer had been in the basement. In those days, I'd kept the shelves in the cellar filled with canned fruit and vegetables from my garden. The basement had been full of commotion; the washer and dryer in constant use, food taken from the pantry and shuffled upstairs daily, and sports equipment rotated off the shelves with the changing seasons. Once the kids had all moved out, we turned an extra room into an upstairs laundry room, and I didn't need the extra food, so I didn't do much canning anymore. These days, I rarely had a reason to wander into the basement. The unswept concrete floor under my feet was a testament to my neglect.

"It's creepy down here." April shivered.

The thick walls of the basement muted the sound of the storm. It felt eerie, with a stillness at odds with the wind, rain, and thunder still booming overhead.

"I'll concede it's a little spooky, especially with the power out, though that's probably a good thing, so we can't see the monsters hiding in the corners."

The flashlight threw creepy shadows, making even the smallest things appear to be huge against the dirt and brick walls of the basement.

"The lanterns should be on these shelves somewhere." I stopped in front of a tall metal rack of shelving loaded down with all kinds of camping gear. There were sleeping bags, tents, cast iron frying pans, and a couple of old cots. Everything a person would need for a week under the stars. Personally, I preferred my comfy bed.

"Here it is." April pulled a rusty, green metal lantern off the shelf. "Do you have any cans of propane?"

"Yep, there's a couple on the floor right here." I nudged the bottles of propane with my foot. "There should be one more lantern too. Keep looking."

The basement door swung shut with a crash and sent my pulse racing.

April shrieked right in my ear. "What in the holy heck? You saw me push the wedge under the door to hold it."

A muffled bang from the kitchen screen door flying against the side of the house followed the slamming of the basement door. It crashed back and forth in a steady rhythm.

"Apparently, I didn't get the screen door closed tight enough either. The wind must've grabbed it again."

"Sounds like it's about to be ripped off the hinges. Hurry! Grab the other lantern and let's get out of here." I had a green, two-burner propane stove propped on my hip, the handle of a blue-speckled enamel coffeepot clutched in a fist, and the two bottles of propane clasped to my chest.

"Are you planning on cooking something?" April eyed me warily. "You have a hard enough time with the regular stove, let alone a camp stove."

"Hey. Behave yourself. I wasn't planning on cooking, but I'm anticipating morning coffee, and since I'm not about to come back down here in the dark again, I'm dragging it all upstairs now. Hopefully the power will be back on by morning, and it'll all be for nothing."

"Do you even know how to make coffee with that thing?"

I shot my daughter the stink-eye. "I'm not worthless turtle droppings, you know. Your dad was always excited when the lights went out so he could break out his camp coffeepot. He swore it was the best coffee in the world when it was made outside. Said it tasted like campfires and sunrise."

"Yeah, I know all about Dad. My question is whether *you* know how to use it, not if Dad did."

"Yes, I certainly do, Miss Smarty Pants." *I think. How hard can it be?*

"Good, because I absolutely don't." April bumped me with a hip check, then opened the basement door and let me go through first.

Once we made it up the stairway and back into the kitchen, April kicked the stairwell door closed then leaned back on it. She took a deep, gulping breath, as if to fill her lungs with clean air.

"We made it out alive. All the monsters and spiders are locked in the dungeon where they belong."

"Except they're getting in up here. The kitchen door is wide open." I hurried to deposit my armful of camp supplies on the kitchen counter. Once my hands were free, I scrambled to pull the screen door closed against the howling wind and pushed the kitchen door shut.

April added her own armful of camping supplies to the pile on the counter. The light from her flashlight glinted off a puddle of water the size of a small lake on the kitchen floor.

"Geez, did I not get the door shut like I thought when I came home? Look at all this water. Pretty sure I wasn't that wet."

Rain was coming down by the bucketful outside, beating against the windows while the wind howled, lightning flashed, and thunder boomed every few minutes.

"Not a big deal. It's only water. Dang. This is the longest-lasting storm we've had all summer." I checked the window over the sink, to make sure it was closed and latched.

April opened a kitchen drawer and grabbed a handful of clean dish towels. She tossed them on the floor and then bent to mop up the puddle of water. "Weird. Mud too. Was I muddy when I came in?"

My shoulders rose to my ears, and I stood stock-still. Something, or someone, moved in the deep shadows of the dining room. I squinted, trying to see into the dark corners. The crashing of the storm drowned out any sound coming from inside the dining room. A chill raced up my spine.

"Mom, what's wrong?" April looked at me from where she still squatted on the floor, mopping up the puddle of water.

Without taking my eyes off the corner of the room where I'd detected movement, I quietly told her to stand up slowly. Without asking why, April stood, still clutching a dripping kitchen towel. She peered into the dining room with me. The only light was the flickering candle I'd left burning on the table.

"What is it?" April asked.

I shook my head and whispered, "Not sure. I swear something moved. I think someone's in here."

I grabbed the closest thing at hand—a metal pancake spatula—out of the utensil crock next to the stove. Brandishing it like a sword, I motioned for April to follow me as I tiptoed into the dining room.

"Shouldn't we call J. T.?" April whispered.

"No time. Come on."

I peeked around the doorframe leading into the dining room. The flickering candlelight felt menacing now instead of cozy and comforting. My heart raced and my mouth was as dry as sawdust. My gaze darted back and forth around the room, searching for any sign of movement coming from either the hallway or the living room. There it was again. A slight shift in the darkness. My body stiffened.

"Did you see it?" I hissed to April. "Something moved in the hallway."

I took a step forward. A figure lurched out of the dark shadows and into the flickering candlelight.

Chapter
Thirty-One

"Marti. What in the world are you doing here? You scared the daylights out of us." Lowering the dangerous and intimidating pancake spatula, I strode into the room with a hand over my pounding heart. "April and I were in the basement getting lanterns, so I didn't hear you knock. Good night! You're covered in mud. Let me grab a towel for you." I moved toward the hallway, headed for the bathroom and a stack of dry towels.

Marti threw back the hood on her navy-blue rain jacket, splattering drops of water on the bookcase behind her. I gasped at the sight of her. Marti's blond hair stood on end, wild and charged with the energy of the storm raging outside. Mascara dripped down her face, forming tracks of tears like she was a sad circus clown. A crazy clown who was probably a little violent when it came right down to it. Marti narrowed her eyes, training her angry gaze on my face.

"No, you don't. Stay right where you are." She pulled a small black handgun out of her jacket pocket and pointed it straight at April and me.

What in the name of Zeus is happening? I glanced at my daughter. Her face had gone a ghostly white.

Marti waved the gun and raised her voice. "You've always been a nosy busybody, Dawna Carpenter. And you've raised your daughter to behave in the same meddling way. Couldn't mind your own business, could you?"

I cocked my head, feigning confusion. "I don't know what you mean, Marti."

"You most certainly do. Drop the stupid act."

"No, I honestly don't. I'm sorry, but you're going to have to explain it to me." I hoped playing dumb could buy us a little time and get Marti talking. And heaven knows, Marti liked to hear herself talk.

"Nobody in this town cared one iota about that narcissistic jerk Highcastle getting himself killed. But no, you two couldn't leave it alone. You had to go and accuse my sweet niece of killing the man. Kristi, who wouldn't harm a fly. Who do you think you are, slandering her name and ruining her reputation?"

Marti's eyes glinted with the fury of a wolf moving in for the kill.

I raised my pancake turner back up in defense. "Marti, please calm down. Tell me what you're going on about. Neither April nor I accused Kristi of anything. Yes, we visited with her yesterday morning, but we were trying to piece a timeline together of everything that happened Friday morning. We never, ever thought Kristi killed the man."

I looked at April, who nodded her agreement. In an effort to slow my racing heart and keep my voice from shaking, I took a deep breath. *I hope Marti can't hear my traitorous knees knocking together.*

"Marti, Warren was murdered inside my building, and Steve not only worked for me, but he was killed on my property too. Try to remember, both murders are personal for me. They *are* my business. Now, please lower the gun and let's discuss this like civilized people."

My mind spun. How was it possible I'd overlooked one significant suspect? Had Marti, the sixty-eight-year-old queen of the dance hall, killed Warren? But why?

Keep her talking, Dawna. Keep her talking. "Why are you doing this? I don't understand."

With Marti's focus on my face, I slowly reached over and grabbed April's sleeve, tugging it until April edged her way behind me. Behind my back, I tapped the cell phone in my back pocket, hoping my daughter would understand what I was trying to tell her. April nodded subtly, and I hoped my message had gotten across. I tuned back into what Marti was saying.

"I know you're not the brightest tool in the box . . ."

The sharpest tool in the shed, genius.

". . . but you know exactly what I'm talking about. The darn police chief was at Kristi's house this evening, asking her all kinds of questions. He knew all about the finder's fee Highcastle was supposed to pay her, and even about the extra contract he'd tried to get her to write up." Marti cocked her head. "The funny thing is, not many people knew about either of those things. I did. Kristi did, of course. And then, the two of you knew about it. You ran your big mouth to the cops, pointing your stubby little fingers at my niece. No, we won't be discussing anything except who I'm going to kill first."

"If Kristi didn't do anything wrong, why would those things matter? We assumed she'd already told J. T. about them."

Marti's knuckles were white as she waved the pistol between April and me. Candlelight glinted off the barrel of the gun. An unhinged smile lifted one corner of the crazed woman's mouth. She ignored my question altogether. "Bet you didn't know I'm a crack shot, did you? I used to hunt deer and elk with my daddy. He taught me young. I was the oldest and there weren't any boys in our family. I've always had a pistol to protect myself, living alone and all. Turns out I'm still as good a shot as ever. Don't you worry none. It'll be quick. You most likely won't feel a thing. Too bad I can't blast you both at once. I don't want to see you suffer."

April slid out from behind me. "Miss Campbell, I sense you don't really want to do this. How is killing us going to help anything anyway?"

Marti blew her bangs out of her face with an exasperated look. "You don't get it, do you? You're the only ones who know what happened. I don't have a choice. I have to get rid of you."

"But we don't know. We haven't solved the murders." April's voice sounded innocent and young.

"So you say. Even if it's true, it's only a matter of time before you uncover the truth, poking around like you've been doing."

April shook her head. "You're not going to get away with killing us, you know. The police will figure out what you did."

Marti threw her head back and laughed. "Sure I am. Your little bodies will be fried to a crisp when I'm done with you. Everyone in town is going to be so sad the two of you died in a tragic house fire. See, your house is going to be struck by lightning tonight. At least, that's what they'll all think, with this crazy storm and all." She grinned. "The worst part for me will be losing this beautiful house. Another piece of Pine Bluff history gone up in smoke. Oh well, nothing to be done for it. I'll be home, tucked into my cozy bed by the time the sirens go off. In the morning, I'll be as shocked as everyone else to hear about the tragic deaths of the Carpenter women."

"Marti, please. Think about Kristi. I told Mom earlier how Kristi's one of the nicest people I've ever known, and that's the truth. I'm positive she didn't have a thing to do with the murders. Chief Dallas will figure it out sooner or later, and everything will be fine. He didn't arrest her, did he?"

Marti shook her head. "No, of course he didn't arrest her. She's innocent. But she's terribly upset. So am I."

I jumped back into the conversation. "It's not Kristi you're worried about right now, is it, Marti? You're the one who killed Warren, aren't you?"

Marti's hands trembled, causing the barrel of the gun to shake. Fear flashed across her pale features. "Okay, yes. You might as well know. I killed the jerk. He deserved it. Can you blame me?"

"Why did you do it? Because he was trying to pull a fast one on your niece?"

Did this mean she'd killed Steve too? It must've been Marti who'd left the threatening note on my door.

"Nobody should be talked to the way he talked to Kristi. I'm not about to stand by and let someone treat my baby girl the way he did. Highcastle was verbally abusive and cheated her out of money that was rightfully hers. My girl works her tail off for every dime she makes."

J. T. had been right to suspect Kristi. He'd only had one thing wrong. It wasn't her story that'd been full of holes. It was her aunt's. All the pieces were finally snapping into place in my mind, like a jigsaw puzzle coming together.

Marti continued with her rant, her cigarette-husky voice rising in crescendo. "I will not let some smart-alecky, highfalutin' city man walk in and jerk the rug out from under her. He threatened to close her business if she didn't go along with his scam. The man was a criminal. You would've done the same for April."

I shook my head in denial. "No, I doubt it. Tell me what happened that day. You must've snuck into Lipstick and Lace to kill Warren, but how did you know he would be there?"

As I talked, I held eye contact with Marti but scanned the room in my head. Was there anything on the table I could use for a weapon? The vase of sunflowers probably wouldn't be any more effective in a gunfight than the pancake spatula had turned out to be.

"I wasn't planning on killing him, you know. After Kristi left for her drive, I tracked Highcastle down. He was going to honor his deal with her, whether he liked it or not. I saw him going into the boutique, and since I didn't want to talk to anyone else, I went around to the back of Carpenter's Corner. I know you usually keep your warehouse door unlocked during business hours."

"Which is where you got your hands on Bill's hammer." It wasn't a question.

Marti nodded. "I was getting nervous about confronting Highcastle. You know I'm not one to pick a fight. Bill's truck was parked back there with the windows open, waiting for me. I reached in and grabbed a hammer lying on the seat. Just in case, you know? To protect myself." Her tone was desperate, imploring us to understand why she'd done what she had.

I nodded, hoping Marti would think I was compassionate to her plight, and keep talking. *Far from it, crazy lady.*

"I slipped in through your warehouse. Snuck into the hallway between your store and Lipstick and Lace without anyone seeing me. Luck was on my side. I opened the door a crack to peek into Darlene's shop. Highcastle stood at the counter, and I was finally able to catch his eye. I motioned for him but was surprised when he actually acknowledged me and walked my way."

"What happened next?" I pressed a hand to my chest to calm my racing heart for the third time this evening. At this rate, I'd be joining Bob in the afterlife sooner than I'd planned.

"I told him I was going to the police if he didn't pay Kristi what he owed her. Told him I'd recorded their conversation when he was in our office."

"Had you?"

"Nope, but he didn't know it. Anyway, my plan wasn't working. Highcastle told me he was calling the real estate board as soon as he went back to his vehicle. He poked me in the chest and said Elk River Realty would belong to him before he was through. When he turned to leave, I lost my temper. I've always had a bit of a problem with my temper, you know." She shrugged, as if it was a minor personality flaw. Not a big deal at all.

"Sure, I see why you'd be angry. So, that's when you hit him with the hammer?" Nervous sweat was beading on my forehead and trickling down my face. I wanted to wipe it away but decided I shouldn't make any sudden moves.

"Yes. Highcastle turned his back on me, and the next thing I knew, I'd raised the hammer and clobbered him on the head. It surprised both of us. He fell like an oak tree, and I high-tailed it out of there. Luckily, you were busy with customers, so nobody saw me coming or going. At least, I didn't think anyone had."

Holy fright. "What I still don't understand, Marti, is why you killed Steve. Was he somehow involved in Warren's scheme?" Might as well make her think I already knew she'd committed the second murder. It'd be harder to deny this way.

Mari grunted. "That idiot simply got in my way. I went back Saturday morning to find my earring. You remember the one? You pointed it out to me Friday that I was missing an earring when you came nosing around the realty office, and then had to bring it up again at the meeting tonight. You can't let anything go. I searched everywhere. The office. Home. My car. Couldn't find the darn thing anywhere. I figured the only other place I could've lost it was in your stupid bathroom at the hardware store."

I tilted my head, trying to get all the facts straight in my spinning mind. "Both stores were locked tight. You wouldn't have been able to get in and look for the earring."

"Wrong." Marti shifted her stance, letting the barrel of the gun dip slightly. "Your backdoor was as useful as it'd been on Friday. It was propped open, so I walked right in. I was smart enough to bring my gun with me the second time."

"The door was propped open?" I sounded like a parrot, mimicking Marti's words back at her, but I hoped it would keep her talking.

"Yep. Steve's car was parked there, so I figured he must be inside. It was dark in the warehouse, so I slipped behind the racks and snuck to the bathroom. Still didn't find the darn earring, but I figure it's a good thing. I must've lost it somewhere else."

A flash of lightning lit the room, and a boom of thunder made all three of us jump out of our skins. Marti adjusted her grip on the pistol, recentering the barrel on April and me.

"You didn't see Steve while you were looking for the earring?"

"Nope. Made it all the way back out the door, but then it clicked closed behind me. I turned around to find Steve standing there staring at me. Scared the almighty dickens out of me."

"I bet. Did he say anything to you?"

"I'm guessing he noticed me go in and was waiting for me when I came back out. He asked what I needed, so I stuck with the truth. Told him I'd been looking for an earring I thought I'd lost the other day. Steve told me the store was a crime scene, and I needed to check with the police. Maybe they'd found it."

"Which you weren't going to do, of course," April added.

Marti sneered. "No way. So, then Steve got in his car, and I started to walk away. I wasn't worried about that little worm. Never thought the guy was overly smart and didn't figure he'd think much more about it." She paused, chewing her bottom lip. "But then he said something to make me rethink my decision."

I held my breath. "What? What did Steve say?"

"He said, 'I saw you the other morning, you know. I know it was you.' They were the last words he ever spoke." Marti's voice was high and singsongy as she relayed Steve's last words.

This woman's cheese has slid off her cracker. "So you killed him."

"He left me no choice. I turned back and shot him where he sat. What else was I supposed to do?" Her nostrils flared, and she gripped the gun tighter, challenging us to contradict her.

Before I had a chance to answer, a gust of wind hit the house, pushing the kitchen door open again. The wind swept in along with the strong, nutty aroma of coffee tangled with the woodsy scent of sawdust. *Was Bob showing up to help us out?* Even though I knew it wasn't logical to think my dearly departed husband was really here with April and me, I felt calmer than I had a moment before. A bolt of lightning ripped through the sky, illuminating the room and Marti's crazed expression for a split second.

I moaned with the thought of Steve facing down his killer. He must've been so frightened. "Poor Steve. He didn't deserve to be killed."

How dare the woman take an innocent life! How dare Marti destroy the peace and tranquility we all loved about Pine Bluff! Without thinking, I took a step toward her.

"Poor Steve?" Marti screamed. She narrowed her aim back on me, causing me to take a step back to where I'd been. "He was going to turn me in. I will not spend the rest of my life in prison because some little twerp spied on me. You're going to join your poor Steve in about two seconds."

A clap of thunder like a sonic boom shook the house, causing Marti to jerk and squeeze the trigger. The gunshot tore across the room, hurtling straight through the gap between April and me. The bullet lodged in the hardwood floor behind us, sending up a spray of splinters and leaving behind the smell of gunpowder.

Hammers and Homicide

I glanced at my daughter while still trying to keep one eye trained on the lunatic with the gun. Panic and dread coursed through my blood and crawled up my spine. How were we going to get out of this? I listened for sirens, hoping April had understood to call J. T. when I'd nudged her as she stood behind me earlier. I didn't hear anyone coming to rescue us. What if the cell towers were down because of the storm?

Marti's face was red with rage. From above her head, an orb of light bounced around, illuminating a heavy book on the highest shelf. Another boom of thunder shook the house. I held my breath as I watched the heavy book shift slowly forward until it protruded a hair over the edge of the shelf. With another flash of lightning and crash of thunder, the book fell, landing with a crack on top of the maniacal woman's head. She grunted under the impact and dropped the gun, which clattered across the hardwood floor as she crumpled to the floor with a hollow thud.

Glancing up, the dancing orb of light was nowhere to be seen. I raced across the room and scooped up the gun, clicking on the safety lever and setting the pistol carefully on the bookcase. Kneeling beside Marti, I checked for a pulse. "She's alive. Out cold, but alive."

April stood rooted in place, staring at the shelf the heavy tome had fallen from. "Holy cow, did you see that? What in the world was that flickering light?" She swallowed hard.

I stood and threw my arms around my daughter, then kissed her cheek in an uncharacteristic show of affection. "I don't know. Maybe the candle was reflecting off a mirror or something. Whatever it was, I'm just glad you and I are still alive."

"Mom, that was a light orb. I think it was Dad." April flashed a cheesy grin. "I mean, can't you smell the coffee and sawdust? It smells exactly like him!"

"Now, which one of us has taken a step or two into crazy town?" I squeezed her shoulders one last time before moving back to stand over Marti and make sure the woman was really down for the count. I didn't want to take any more chances.

Chapter
Thirty-Two

The screen door slammed against the house for the gazil-
lionth time in twenty-four hours. This time, Police Chief
Dallas exploded through the doorway, gun drawn. The two
officers who'd been investigating the murders flanked him with
flashlights, lighting the scene. J. T. slid to a screeching halt in the
dining room doorway when he saw me standing above Marti,
who was sprawled face down on the floor.

Marti's eyes flickered open, and a moan escaped from
between her dry lips. J. T. reacted instantly, training his gun
on the prone woman as she raised a hand to her head. With the
weight of the book that hit her, I imagined her head must be
throbbing pretty badly.

"What in the world is going on here? And why does it smell
like sawdust?" J. T. kept his eyes fixed on Marti as he assessed
the situation.

"She killed both Warren and Steve. And thought April and
I had it all figured out, so she was going to take care of us too."
I chose not to address the smell of sawdust right now. Or ever.

Some things are a little harder to explain and better left unsaid. Not to mention the fact I couldn't quite understand it myself.

Officers Bowman and Everett moved in, pulling Marti to her feet and cuffing her hands behind her back. J. T. holstered his gun once they had the killer contained.

April had understood what I wanted her to do and had pulled up J. T.'s phone number and hit "Dial" while I'd kept Marti's attention laser-focused on me. April said she'd slipped her phone back in her pocket, hoping the call had connected and J. T. could hear well enough to realize we needed help. J. T. said he hadn't been able to make out a single word; he only heard rustling and muffled voices. He'd figured the call might've been an accident, but with the threatening note, he wasn't taking any chances. When the call came in, he was at home on Simmons Ridge. He'd jumped into his truck and broken a speed limit or two as he barreled down the country roads toward town. He told us he'd called the station and told Officers Pete and Sam to meet him at my house.

"I was afraid Marti would notice the light when I turned my phone on and shoot us right then, but I figured I needed to try anyway." April leaned against the wall, looking like she needed it to hold her upright. "I feel like a wet noodle right now. Limp and boneless now that the adrenaline rush has passed. I think I'm going to need a good session of meditation tomorrow."

"You're okay now." J. T. placed a gentle hand on each of April's shoulders, studying her from top to bottom. "The phone call was a good move, April. Quick thinking."

Her gaze flicked to me. "Mom gets the credit. It was her idea." She smiled at J. T.

Don't read anything into it, my foot. I covered my mouth with my hand to hide my smile from the two of them.

"It was also a stupid move. Could've gotten you both killed," J. T. said.

April rolled her eyes and pushed the police chief's hands off her shoulders. She shoved away from the wall and stomped into the kitchen.

Oh, good night. That girl and her temper. "April, what are you doing?"

"Getting a lantern set up so we'll have more light in here," she yelled. She stomped back into the dining room with the lantern and a bottle of propane. She screwed the propane onto the lantern, then struck a match and held it to the mantle. The room filled with yellow light and the soft hissing of the camp lantern.

"Good job. Those lanterns haven't been used for so long I wasn't sure they'd still work."

Officer Samantha Everett stood guard over Marti, who was sitting on one of my dining room chairs. The woman sat slumped forward; her chin lowered to her chest. She rocked back and forth like a car stuck in deep mud. The movement sent the ladder-back wooden chair bouncing and vibrating against the floor.

April and I told the police everything Marti had told us while she'd held us at gunpoint. How she'd confessed to both murders, and how she'd taken Bill's framing hammer from his work truck and used it to kill Warren, leaving Bill to take the blame.

When we'd finished telling the story, J. T. stared at the top shelf where the book that knocked Marti out had fallen from. "Any idea what caused the book to fall? Nothing else seems out of place."

I slid a sideways glance to April and shook my head with the most imperceptible movement I could muster. Now wasn't the time to bring up weird balls of light. "Gosh, I don't know. There were a couple of enormous claps of thunder about the same time. They shook the entire house. You know how these old houses are. Things are always shifting and settling, even when there's not a storm raging overhead. I think the thunder must've shaken the house enough that the book came loose and tumbled off the shelf."

"Must be. Strange coincidence, though." J. T. squinted at me like he didn't quite buy my story. "Darn good timing. Seems that clap of thunder saved your lives."

"I guess so." To change the subject, I bounded across the room and grabbed Marti's pistol off the bookshelf. "Here's the gun she shot Steve with."

I gingerly handed it over to the police chief and then immediately wanted to wash my hands. Touching the gun Steve was murdered with gave me the heebie-jeebies. Forget washing my hands. A full-blown shower to wash all the terrible energy of the day down the drain was more like it. Maybe a good long soak in the bathtub with a tub full of vanilla-scented bubbles would do the trick.

J. T. stood with arms crossed, staring at the murderess. "Not in a hundred years, Miss Campbell, would I ever have thought you were the killer."

Marti looked at him with tears in her eyes. "I was only trying to protect my family." Her face crumpled as if the realization of what she'd done was finally setting in. "Don't tell Kristi. Please. Don't tell her what I've done."

"You know that's not an option. Of course, we have to tell her. It'll be all over town by morning. You, of all people, know how fast gossip travels in Pine Bluff."

I grunted. Wasn't that a fact. Of course, without Marti to fuel the flames, the news might slow down a bit.

When Marti began to sob, I almost felt sorry for her. I understood the need to protect your family, but resorting to murder was taking it a step too far. Or a million steps too far. Had Marti been a bit unhinged before all of this happened? She must've been in order for Warren's yelling at and firing Kristi to throw her so far over the edge of sanity. Was it temporary insanity? Nah. Marti had known exactly what she was doing. She'd planned tonight's attack on April and me. Not only had she planned to kill us, but she'd also planned to burn my beautiful house down to make our murders look like an accident. The woman was a monster.

"What's going to happen to me?" Marti's eyes were sunken and hollow with fear.

"Right now, you're going to be booked into the Pine Bluff jail. Long term, a judge and jury will decide your fate."

J. T. wrangled the killer out of my house and into the summer storm.

"I'm sorry, Dawna," Marti called over her shoulder. "I wouldn't have killed you. You know that, don't you? You'll put in a good word for me?"

I snorted. *I don't think so, lady.*

Chapter
Thirty-Three

Tuesday dawned bright and sunny. The scent of rain from last night's deluge lingered in the air. The storm had knocked tree branches down all over the neighborhood. Pine needles and cedar branches littered my yard and porch. Garbage cans lay upside down or sideways on lawns several houses from where they'd started out. Not being able to sleep well, I'd come outside at the crack of dawn and retrieved my wayward garbage can before putting a few neighbors' cans back where they belonged. I'd swept off my front porch before raking the yard. By the time I was done, I'd filled the wheelbarrow three times over with branches and pine needles. It all got dumped into the compost pile behind my gardening shed.

Next, I eyeballed my garden. More weeds pushed their way out of the dirt between the veggies, but they were going to have to wait until after coffee. Since I'd dragged all the camp equipment upstairs last night, I decided to use the percolator. I set the camp stove up on the picnic table and went inside to fill the blue speckleware coffeepot with water. After adding coffee grounds to the metal basket, I took it back outside, setting the pot on the camp stove burner to heat. Getting the insides of the pot put together was easier than I thought it would be, and I was ridiculously proud of myself for figuring it out. Who says you can't teach old dogs new tricks?

Once the coffee finished perking, I poured myself a cup. My neighbor, Smitty, had come outside and was doing calisthenics in her front yard. Today, she wore a pair of yellow-and-green plaid polyester pants and a blue sweatshirt despite the warm morning.

"Good morning, Smitty. I'm glad to see you weathered the storm well."

"It was quite wild." Smitty's voice was thin and shaky with age. "I had the strangest dreams, though. It must have been because of the wind."

"Do you want to tell me about it?"

I got the biggest kick out of talking to Smitty. She told the most unusual stories and always had something either wise or completely crazy to share.

"Well . . . I'm not sure if I should. I don't want to frighten you."

I cocked my head. "Now, why would your dream frighten me?"

"Because you were in it." Smitty's eyes went wide behind her tortoiseshell glasses. "Someone was trying to kill you."

Sounds about right. I snorted. "I promise I'll be okay. What was this dream all about?"

Smitty told me about her dream that was eerily similar to real life. The wind, the rain, the thunder and lightning, and the banging screen door all played a part. In Smitty's version, a burglar broke into my house and held me at gunpoint.

261

"You're quite perceptive, my friend." I explained what had happened while Smitty was dreaming.

When Smitty insisted she hadn't known a thing about Warren and Steve's murders, I backtracked and filled her in on everything.

"Oh my. That must be where my plaid pants have gotten off to then." Smitty shook her head.

I tried not to choke on the laugh threatening to burst out of my throat. "Your plaid pants?"

"Why yes, my plaid pants. Is something wrong with your hearing?"

"No, I heard you, but I'm uncertain what you mean. Have your plaid pants gone missing?" I tried to keep my gaze from drifting to the colorful plaid pants Smitty was wearing.

"Yes. Someone has stolen my red plaid pants. I'm sure it must have been the awful woman who murdered those two innocent young men." Smitty turned to toddle off to her cottage. "Pardon me, Dawna, but I must make a phone call to the police."

"I understand. Good luck."

Once Smitty had disappeared behind the door of her cottage, I let out a long belly laugh.

"Hellloo," a cheery voice sang out from the street as a car door slammed. I turned to find Kim trotting up the walk, a bouquet of sunflowers gripped in her hand. Kim nearly knocked me over as she threw her arms around me in a gigantic hug.

"Bill's back home." Kim wiped a tear from her cheek. "Thank you so much, my friend, for everything. I had complete faith you'd get to the bottom of this mess and get him back home. We can't thank you and April enough."

I shook my head. "We didn't get to the bottom of a single thing. All we managed to do was flush out the killer."

"And almost get yourselves killed in the process, from what I hear."

I grimaced and wrinkled my nose. "It was pretty awful."

Kim held a hand to her forehead to shield her eyes from the bright sun. "Marti Campbell, huh? I've always thought she had a screw loose upstairs."

"Really? Why?" Kim's assessment shocked me.

She shrugged. "Not sure. Maybe the bizarre attachment to her niece. Didn't you ever feel like something was off with her? Once, Kristi told me she turns off all the lights and hides in her garage sometimes when she knows her aunt's going to stop by in order to get a day off from her. She was embarrassed after she told me and made me promise to never repeat it. Which I just did. Oops."

"Wow." I shook my head. "But no, I didn't suspect Marti at all. She wasn't even on my radar. If she hadn't thought I'd figured it out, she wouldn't have shown up here last night and would probably have gotten away with it. Good thing paranoia got the best of her."

"Well, I don't care what you say, Bill and I are forever grateful for your help." She hugged me again, kissing my cheek with a loud smack. "Now, where's that feisty daughter of yours?"

"Hey, Kim." April stepped onto the front porch, still wearing the cotton T-shirt and shorts she'd slept in. When Kim lurched forward, April held up a finger to stop her. "I'm not a hugger."

Kim laughed and grabbed April in a big bear hug despite her protests. April's feet dangled off the ground.

"You are now, little sister." Kim grinned and set April back on her feet, then settled onto the wide concrete steps. She put an elbow on one knee and propped her chin on her fist. "Now, talk to me, girls. What exactly happened last night?"

"I need coffee before we get into all that again," April said.

I pointed to the pot I'd brewed on the camp stove. "There's plenty, but you'll have to grab a couple of mugs from the kitchen."

April disappeared into the house, emerging a few seconds later with mugs. She poured two cups and handed a steaming mug to Kim. "Sorry about the delay. Carry on."

I sighed. "I don't have the energy to go over it one more time." I set the bouquet of sunflowers on the ground and brushed my silver bangs out of my eyes. "Sounds like you already heard the important parts. I'm more than ready for everything to get back to normal. After I decide if I'm going to keep the store open anyway."

Kim's mouth dropped open. "Why wouldn't you? Carpenter's Corner Hardware is a staple in Pine Bluff. An icon. You're not closing the store." She shook her finger at me to get her point across.

I rubbed my eyes and took a sip of my coffee. "I can't run the store by myself. With Steve gone, I'll have to find someone else. I hate interviewing and hiring. It really stinks to have to choose one person. I always feel bad not giving everyone a job who applies, but obviously I can't. Plus, I need someone with some sort of building and hardware knowledge, which isn't easy to find."

"Mom, I don't think it's too big of a hurdle. Certainly not a reason to close the store. I can help with the interviewing, if you want. I did all the hiring for my office in San Francisco for the last handful of years. Not to toot my horn, but I'm a pro when it comes to hiring staff."

"If I decide to keep it open, I'll take you up on your offer." I nodded my thanks. "There's more, though."

"What?"

"The cost of a security system, which is nonnegotiable after this past week. Also, with the murders, are people going to still want to shop in Carpenter's Corner? What if it feels too weird now, and my regulars stop coming in?"

Kim shook her head. "No, I don't think it'll be weird. The killer's in custody, and everyone knows you had nothing to do with the murders." She paused and stared off into the distance for a minute. "Maybe it's time to think about changing things up somewhat. Give the store a fresh, updated feel. You could add a few new products and paint the walls. It's been years since you've changed anything. Couldn't hurt to freshen it up."

"I'm listening. Like what kind of new products? Do you have something in mind?" A bubble of excitement built in my chest.

"Oh, I don't know . . ." Kim trailed off.

"You can't make a suggestion and then leave me hanging. I'm intrigued now."

"Well, I don't know what specifically, off the top of my head." She motioned between April and me. "You two need to brainstorm and see what you come up with. I'll let you know if I think of anything, deal? But don't close the store until you've hashed over every other option."

I sighed. "You're right. I'm not opening again until next week anyway. April and I both need a break. We're going to drive to

Astoria to visit Becky and the kids for a few days. Spend some time on the beach. Her husband is out on a fishing trip this week."

"Perfect. Grandkid time will do you good. Call me when you get back." Kim brushed off her denim shorts and blew a kiss as she headed to her car.

Chapter
Thirty-Four

April and I sat in silence while we finished our coffees. Thoughts about a new and improved Carpenter's Corner tumbled through my head. What changes could I make? Maybe it was finally time to add the kitchen section I'd talked about for so long.

I envisioned shelves filled with cookware, small appliances, and even spices and tinfoil. Everything needed for a well-stocked kitchen. It'd mean one more group of items Pine Bluff residents could get right in our hometown. More things we wouldn't need to drive to Greenwood for.

While I was daydreaming, J. T. sauntered into the yard, a cardboard to-go box in his hands. He stretched his long, blue jean–clad legs out as he took a seat on the steps next to April.

He handed me the box. "Morning. Instead of calling, I thought I'd stop by with the good news."

"Which is?" April drew her tan legs to her chest and wrapped her arms around them.

Embarrassed to have J. T. catch you in your PJs at ten in the morning, April? I hid a smile behind the palm of my hand.

"With Miss Campbell's confession, Carpenter's Corner is no longer an active crime scene. You're free to open back up for business as soon as you're ready."

I bit my lip and nodded then pushed my glasses up my nose. "Definitely good news. I appreciate you stopping by to let me know. April and I are headed to the coast tomorrow, right after she accepts the position of assistant soccer coach at the high school." I winked at my daughter. "We'll be back next Sunday."

J. T. swiveled his head to look at April. "Congratulations. That's exciting news."

"To be fair, I haven't officially been offered the position yet, but I'll be accepting it if I get an offer." She grinned. "Thank you."

"They'd be crazy to not offer." He turned back my way. "Are you going to check out what's inside the box?"

I'd forgotten all about it, even though it sat in my lap. I opened the lid to reveal a freshly baked peach pie. The flaky crust was golden brown and sprinkled with gleaming sugar. The scent of fragrant, sun-kissed peaches with a hint of cardamom floated out of the box. My mouth watered.

"Yum. You didn't have to do this, but I'm not going to say no. Be right back." I dashed into the house and grabbed a handful of plates and forks. "You're going to stay for a slice, aren't you?"

"You bet." J. T. winked at April. "Got some coffee to wash it down with?"

"Sure. Give me a minute." April jumped up and was gone in a flash.

I suspected her flight was more about taking the opportunity to put on some actual clothes than it was about getting J. T. a cup of coffee.

"Bring me a cup too," I called to her retreating back.

Five minutes later, April rejoined us. She balanced three mugs on a tray and had traded her pajamas for a purple V-neck Foo Fighters T-shirt and a pair of khaki shorts. She'd even added dark gray eyeliner and a light coating of mascara.

"You didn't need to change on my account." J. T. looked April in the eye before dipping his chin. "I thought you looked great in the PJs."

April smacked him on the arm. Her cheeks flamed a dusty rose. "Reel your neck in. Jeez."

"What?" He grinned. "It doesn't make me a bad guy."

She glared daggers at him.

"I should probably shut my mouth now."

"Good call."

He held up an index finger. "One more thing, though, before I shut my trap."

April flung a hand on each hip, her stance wide and defensive. "What?"

I sat quietly in my lawn chair, enjoying the show.

"Didn't you promise me cupcakes?" J. T. squeezed his eyes shut and pulled his neck in like a turtle. It was clear he thought he might get whacked in the next few seconds.

April shook her head with a sigh and didn't say a word.

I couldn't contain my laughter any longer and let it fly. "You did promise him cupcakes. I heard you."

It took a minute, but finally we settled down with plates of pie and mugs of coffee. J. T. filled us in on what had transpired since he'd left with Marti in tow last night. Marti had been booked for murder, and they'd released Bill. Early this morning,

J. T. had sent Officer Sam back to Carpenter's Corner to take a last look. She'd found a silver concho earring wedged under a rack of paintbrushes near the bathroom hallway. It matched the one they'd found an hour later, with a search warrant, at Marti's house.

"Without her confession, we'd have a hard time getting a conviction. It should be a slam dunk now. Plus, we matched the partial footprint found in your warehouse to the boots she was wearing when we took her in last night." J. T. leaned back and rested his elbows on the step behind him.

"I'm glad it's over, though I feel terrible for Kristi. She and her Aunt Marti were so close. Too close, it seems." I sighed.

"It's going to be rough on her," April agreed.

"I feel stupid for thinking Darlene might've been the killer. At least she didn't know I suspected her." I chuckled.

J. T. snorted. "Darlene? Why'd you think she might've done it?"

I shrugged. "Nothing solid. A theory I was kicking around about her finding out Warren was married and knocking him over the head because of it."

"I can't imagine. She might break a nail. It'd be devastating."

I absently brushed crust crumbs off my lap. "Did you find out who the mysterious Jack is?"

"Yep. Roy held nothing back when I went to talk with him yesterday. You must've loosened him up for me."

"Glad I could be of service. So, tell us, who in the heck is Jack?"

"Jack Sherman. Like we suspected, he was on Highcastle's payroll. Sort of his henchman, if you will. Sherman approached

Roy with a one-time, under-the-table job offer. He told Roy the seller was letting Highcastle do some work in the theater before the deal was closed. Highcastle's general contractor and crew weren't in town yet, and with Sherman's broken shoulder, they needed someone local to do the job. Sherman offered him a decent amount of money, so Roy accepted the job without knowing what it entailed. He said it never occurred to him it would be something fraudulent."

"It's unusual to be allowed to work on a building before the sale's final. Was it true they'd really gotten permission to begin work?"

"Not in the slightest. When Roy went inside the Emery with Sherman, he found out they wanted him to open water lines and flood the basement before the final inspection. He was supposed to make it look like the pipes burst from being old and rusty. Then Highcastle would've negotiated a lower purchase price."

Hence the plumbing supplies and iron and copper patina paint Evonne and I had discovered in the basement of the Emery. Glad to know my instincts hadn't been very far off.

"Good night! Real estate fraud at its finest." I shook my head. It boggled my mind to think about the atrocities people would try to get away with.

"Roy backed out of the job when he found out what they wanted him to do. He told Sherman he didn't want any part of it, but Sherman threatened Roy's family if he didn't carry through. Told him once he knew what they'd planned, there was no backing out. He was supposed to get it done over the weekend, but then Warren was killed."

I blew out a breath and slid my glasses back up my nose. "What a hard decision Roy had to make. Keep his family safe or do the job. Luckily, he didn't have to find out if they would have followed through on the threat. What happens now?"

"I've turned Jack Sherman's name over to the FBI for further investigation. The agent said he was already on their radar as part of the ongoing fraud cases against Highcastle Development. Roy may have to testify against him at some point, but it could be several years down the road. Our case will wrap up long before then." J. T. scooped up the last bite of his peach pie, set his empty plate on the step, and leaned forward, resting his elbows on his knees and clasping his hands together. "Speaking of wrapping things up, I received a call this morning from the sheriff's office in Shasta County, California. Sam had reached out to them, trying to find information about Steve."

I focused my attention on the police chief's face. "Okay. What'd they say? Did they have any information about his family?"

"In a sense, yes. About eight years ago, Steve's wife and six-year-old daughter were killed in a car accident. Steve was driving. They were on a winding mountain road when they got caught in a downpour, and Steve veered off the road. The ruling was he was driving too fast for conditions, but the state didn't file charges against him. I imagine Steve had been running from his demons ever since."

An instant tear dripped down my cheek. "So awful. I guess it explains why he kept himself so closed off. It made it easier not to have to talk about his past. I wish I'd known."

"What about parents or siblings?" April asked.

J. T. shook his head. "Nope, there doesn't seem to be anybody left. Steve was an only child. The sheriff indicated his parents were older when they had him, and have been gone for years. He didn't know of any other family in the area."

I pressed my palms against my thighs and rose from the chair. "It's settled then. I'm going to claim his body and pay for the funeral expenses. He'll be buried next to his wife and daughter in California, where he should be. Steve will finally get the peace he deserves."

Chapter
Thirty-Five

Before leaving Pine Bluff, April accepted the assistant girls' soccer coach position. She said the pay wasn't the best, but she loved the game so much she'd have done it for free. While she was at the high school finalizing the details, I moseyed down to my hardware store.

I unlocked the front door and stepped inside. The store felt familiar, like it was back to itself after all the turmoil. Walking fast to the hallway door so I wouldn't lose my nerve, I pulled the door open and glanced around. The cleanup crew I'd hired had done a stellar job. The bathroom and hallway sparkled and smelled like fresh-cut lemons. My shoulders sagged with relief. Thank goodness. I locked up and headed home to pack for our trip.

As planned, we spent a few days with my daughter and grandkids on the Oregon coast before heading to California for Steve's funeral. I hadn't realized how much the stress of the murders took out of me until I got some distance from it. Playing with my grandkids and walking on the beach was exactly what I needed to soothe my bruised soul.

Steve was laid to rest in a pretty country cemetery in Northern California. Only a handful of people attended the funeral: an elderly man who'd been the Harrison family's next-door neighbor; a mother and her teenage daughter, who'd been Steve's little girl's best friend all those years ago; and April and me. I was glad at least a few people remembered the quiet man and came to pay their respects.

When the coffin was lowered into the ground, a shimmering light behind the headstone caught my attention. The sun was in my eyes, but for a second I would've sworn I saw Steve with his arm around the shoulders of a pretty brunette and a small girl skipping by his side. The image lifted a transparent hand in goodbye before disappearing into a mist behind a large black oak tree. I glanced at April.

"Did you see that?"

She shook her head as if confused. "See what?"

"Never mind. Just my active imagination hard at work again." I took her hand. "Come on. Let's go home."

Since the talk on the drive down had been all about Steve's funeral, April and I hashed out possibilities for a new and improved Carpenter's Corner as we went home. We talked about various ideas that could make the store more profitable than it was. Brainstormed ideas to bring in more customers than those looking for a gallon of paint or a box of nails.

April asked me what I thought about carving out a place in the warehouse for her to work on her furniture. "If we can figure it out, I could give up the storage unit. I'd rather pay rent to you."

"I love your idea but have to admit I'm more than a little jealous I didn't think of it myself." I laughed. "We'll rearrange and make the room. No problem."

The more we talked, the more excited I got. With a little time away and a bit of perspective, I'd realized I wasn't anywhere near ready to close the store for good. But Kim had been right—Carpenter's Corner needed an update. I told April about my idea for a kitchen nook. She'd taken a drink from her water bottle while I'd been talking and now snorted water out of her nose.

"What's so funny, young lady?"

"You've got to admit, it's pretty funny that you, of all people, are thinking about putting kitchen products in your store."

I glared daggers at her. "Good night! I'm not that bad of a cook."

"Sure, Mama. Whatever you say." April's green eyes glinted with glee.

Once she got over her hilarity, she admitted a kitchen nook was a great idea.

After a night spent in a cheap hotel halfway home, we pulled up to my house in the late afternoon. April immediately left for her own cottage, to start preparing for her first afternoon of coaching soccer.

I lugged my suitcase inside and deposited it on my bed, then headed right back out to my Jeep. Unpacking could wait for later. My energy level was high, and I was excited to get started on plans for the kitchen nook in my new and improved Carpenter's Corner.

Inside the store, I paced off the main sales floor, measuring only by eyeballing it and jotting down estimated dimensions. I grabbed a piece of graph paper and drew a quick sketch of the store's interior, then started reconfiguring shelving to make room for my kitchen nook. Walking the aisles, for the first time in forever I noticed dusty products that rarely sold anymore but were taking up precious space on the shelves. A clearance sale was in order.

I hauled a flatbed handcart out of the warehouse and started pulling old products off the shelves and piling them onto the cart. By the time I was finished, it was full dark outside, and I'd filled four handcarts with a whole plethora of out-of-date items, including shiny gold faucets, floral wallpaper borders, and boxes of ugly tile in a beigy-gray tone. The stack of wood paneling against the wall would have to go, and I'd even unearthed a mint-green porcelain sink on a back shelf that must've been there since the 1950s. Strange, since Bob and I hadn't opened the store until the early nineties.

Brushing dust off my hands, I pushed my glasses up and leaned against the front counter, grinning. The scent of sawdust and coffee suddenly filled the air, and a soft tingle brushed against my cheek. Bob.

"Hey there, sweetheart," I spoke aloud into the empty store. "Was that your way of giving me your approval on the changes coming to the store?"

I held a hand to my tingling cheek. The next chapter for Carpenter's Corner, and the Carpenter women, was going to be a good one.

Acknowledgments

Who knew one of the hardest parts of getting a book published would be writing the acknowledgment page at the end? There are so many people to thank that I hardly know where to begin, though the natural spot feels like with my family, so here goes.

A ginormous thank you goes out to my patient husband, who not only listened to me rattle on about the people and places I made up in my head, but also helped me brainstorm various ways to kill off those people. Even after all that, he was still enthusiastic about reading multiple versions of *Hammers and Homicide*. To my kids and siblings, who did much the same, thank you all for the unwavering support you've given me on this wild ride.

To my amazing and fastidious first editor, Brittany Sumpter: without you sussing out my awkward sentences and misplaced commas, as well as prodding me to reach deeper into the characters, this book would've gone nowhere. Thank you so much! To my first readers, who waded through countless versions of

Acknowledgments

dribble to help me find the story hidden within—Paula, Beth, and Shilo—you guys rock!

A huge thank-you to my incredible agent, Dawn Dowdle, for her tireless work making sure this story got to see the light of day. I love being a part of the Blue Ridge Literary family, and I know without a shadow of a doubt that I landed in the right place. Thank you for taking me on!

Tara Gavin—editor extraordinaire at Crooked Lane Books—thank you from the bottom of my heart for your insight and for going to bat for this book. Truly, without you we wouldn't be here today. And to the rest of the Crooked Lane team, thank you, thank you, thank you for all of your hard work making this book shine.

Last, but definitely not least, I am forever grateful to my extended family and friends, who cheered me on and preordered my book even before it had a cover. I hope you enjoy your time with Dawna and April in Pine Bluff!